Loving Eva

~

Camellia Hart

Cover design by Camellia Hart ©

Self-published
ISBN 978-0-9976705-2-3

www.CamelliaHart.com

Loving Eva is a work of fiction. Names,
characters, places, and incidents either are the
product of the author's imagination or are used
fictitiously. Any resemblance to actual persons,
living or dead, business establishments, events, or
locales is purely coincidental.

To my fabulous readers...

Chapter 1

At fourteen, she broke her brother's nose.

But he'd asked her to.

Well…he hadn't exactly asked her to injure him. They'd lived far from home, in a boarding school. She should be strong, brave and independent, her brother claimed. He taught her self-defense. Their newest routine, she would throw a punch, and he would duck.

"Hit me, Eva. C'mon hit me."

She didn't. She couldn't. Because how could she? She loved her brother.

"What are you waiting for? C'mon."

She adjusted her stance like he'd taught her. She clenched her hands into fists by the side of her face like he'd taught her. All she had to do now was punch like he'd taught her. But…

"Imagine you're kidnapped, and you are…on a boat."

On a boat…

"You have no one to help you…no mom, no dad, not even me."

Her stomach churned. More than being kidnapped, she feared being on a boat…surrounded by water…confined, enclosed…She wanted to throw up.

"I'm your kidnapper. Hit me. C'mon."

She shut her eyes tight. Heavy tears tumbled down her face.

"Hit me damn it! I'll duck."

Her eyes still closed, heavy tears still rolling, she punched him with all her might…*before* he ducked.

The impact of her fist against the bridge of his nose sparked an agonizing current all the way from her knuckles, over her shoulder, to the middle of her back. She pulled her hand toward her, shaking it, cupping it, from the trembling pain.

Joey covered his face and moaned. Blood gushed from his nostrils down his chin and sprayed all over his white polo.

She'd never punched anyone ever again. One, she couldn't, because the memory of her brother struggling to breathe while she rushed him to the warden for help ingrained in her mind for life. Two, she didn't get kidnapped, nor did she surround herself by water for more than fourteen years.

But today…confined…enclosed…she readied to throw a punch mightier than she'd exercised on her brother.

He asked her to.

Trevor riled her plenty, as he continued to antagonize her uncle with mindless questioning. She'd do anything to wipe out his snarky grin.

Would he bruise like her brother? Would he too bleed?

But Trevor was Clive's best buddy, and she loved Clive. He was also an FBI agent. Would she get into trouble for hitting a federal agent? And why did she question that only now?

She tightened the grip on her fingers intertwined in her lap. Her attempts to suppress her aggression frayed with every passing second Trevor and his partner, Jason, acted out an obviously practiced routine to cause an innocent man to crumble with fright. And that's the point; her uncle, an innocent man, had nothing to confess. So, yes, he did crumble, for the wrong reason. Why did they not see that?

They blamed her uncle for the numerous issues that plagued her company. The informant who'd sent her threatening letters, the informant who seemed intent to destroy every bit of reputation her late father had strived all his life to build, the informant who may, or may not, have killed her father… they blamed her uncle for all of the informant's actions. They suspected he had close relations with the crook. And just when she concluded they'd hollowed their caldron of preposterous accusations, their conversation took another absurd dive when Trevor asked her uncle, "Are you the informant?"

Uncle Dave should have gone with a ridiculously blight *yes*. Instead, his usual jovial expression, now marred by annoyance, grew bleak. He stood behind his desk with his palms planted flat on the table and glowered at Trevor and Jason seated in front of him. "Get out."

Trevor stared at him for a long moment. He then rose from his chair, placed a business card on the mahogany desk in front of him, and slid it toward her uncle. "Call me if you have anything more to share with us."

"I've nothing more to share with *you*." Uncle Dave clenched his jaw.

"Sure you do."

"I've told you everything I know."

"No, you haven't, Mr. Avery." Though unaffected on the surface, Trevor's voice had an underlying simmer of seriousness that made Eva's insides twinge. He suspected her uncle of corporate espionage, but why, what did he know that she didn't?

"How dare you accuse me without proof?"

"Of course, we have proof. We wouldn't be here otherwise, now would we?"

Trevor's jeering heated Eva further. FBI or not, maybe she should reconsider that punch.

Her uncle, a decent man, didn't deserve this sort of mockery. Especially from Trevor, who behaved like a perfect gentleman until today. Somehow, his accusations seemed misplaced. She could never imagine her uncle causing her or her company harm. The FBI definitely had their facts mixed up. They implicated the wrong man.

"Really?" Uncle Dave laughed, sounding confrontational. He eased back from the table and slid his hands into his pant pockets. He lifted his chin. "And what's this proof you have?"

Yes. What proof do you have Trevor?

Trevor's expression remained cold. "You haven't told us about that letter your brother left for you." He cut her a quick look as though to warn *he's hiding things from you, Eva.*

Her heart did a harsh drop. A letter? Her father had left her uncle a letter? Had he left her one too? And why didn't her uncle mention this letter to her? His betrayal sliced her. The whirlwind of emotions that had consumed her during the months after her father's passing rushed back to her mind.

The news of her father's death had come abruptly, unexpected and shocking. A hit and run accident, as the police called it. Had she known the last time she'd spoken to her father their farewell would be everlasting, what could she have done? Could she have stopped him from his routine morning walk that led to his death?

Her uncle blinked. "That's private. How did you even—"

"The more of these secrets we uncover, the less cordial our conversations will get. It's in your best interest to tell us everything you know about this case." Trevor gave the business card he'd placed on the desk two quick taps. "Call us." He leaned toward her uncle. "Call us." He nodded, keeping his voice deathly low.

"Get out." His nostrils flared, his face reddened, he breathed heavy with an amplified wheeze. She'd never seen her uncle this furious.

Trevor slowly retreated, then gave her one last glance and a curt nod goodbye.

"Call us," he said, again, to her uncle and sauntered toward the door. Jason followed. Without saying another word they left the room.

Uncle Dave stared at the door they'd closed behind them. "You don't believe them, do you, Eva?" Though his tone sounded hopeful, uncertainty lingered in his expression.

She remained silent, unsure how to respond after finding he had hidden her father's letter from her.

"Eva…" His mouth fell open.

Of course, her lack of response worsened matters. What was she thinking, not replying to his question? She gulped. "I don't know." *Damn it*! Bad answer.

Her toes curled in her shoes. She gripped the armrests of her chair. Her honesty always got to her. She didn't mean to say those words out loud, but she didn't have another answer either.

"You don't know?" His eyes widened.

"Yes, I don't know." Uncomfortable in her own skin, she sprang from her seat and started to pace across the room. "This is too much for me to handle all at once."

"Too much for you to handle? I'm the one who's being wrongfully accused here, and it's too much for *you* to handle?" He let out a heavy exhale. "How can you ever think that I would harm your father?" He paused. "He was my…my little brother, Eva." His voice trembled.

She too puffed out a heavy breath. She needed to set this straight. Their conversation had veered way off and way too fast. "They have it wrong…they have it all wrong." She did not know if she'd meant to bring her uncle peace or if she had talked out loud for her own sanity.

"Then why did you say you didn't know?" His voice grew louder.

She stopped pacing and faced him. "Because, you didn't tell me about the letter. Why the secrecy? Especially from me?" She too raised her voice.

His face paled. He didn't reply. *Why*?

She swallowed. *Wait*…did she want to know if her father had…did she *really* want to know?

She wanted to know.

"Did he…" her voice broke. Her chest tightened from her rising emotions. She cleared her throat. "Did he leave me a letter?"

"Eva…" Her uncle's expression softened.

She disliked that look. She disliked pity, a self-protective veil people donned whenever a conversation about her late-father emerged. She loathed their sympathy. She loathed feeling exposed.

"Did he or did he not leave me a letter?" Her nerves tightened with every word that left her mouth. She tried hard to keep her voice from wavering. She tried hard to sound a lot stronger than she felt.

"I don't know," he said quietly. "That letter was only to be read if something were to happen to your father."

"What did it say?"

From his desk he picked up a ball with the words *I think I can,* written all over, and started to squeeze.

Do those things work? Should she get one too?

"He wanted you to own the company. He believed if anyone could bring it back to its past glory, it would be you."

"Past glory? S. F. Designs wasn't doing well even before I joined?"

"It wasn't public knowledge." *I think I can, I think I can.* "Nobody knew except your father and I."

"Why?" She shook her head. "All this while, I've been blaming myself, thinking it was my doing, thinking it was my taking over after him that caused this chaos. Why did you let me think that? Why didn't you tell me?"

Her already fueled aggression worsened. She clenched her fists tight, letting her nails dig into her palms. Oddly, the pain helped her keep from wanting to punch her uncle. Would he bruise? Would he bleed? Frankly, she didn't care.

He pressed his lips together. He remained silent.

Then, it dawned on her. "You wanted me to fail." Her stomach knotted as the words left her mouth. She'd hoped dearly he'd correct her interpretation of the situation.

"Yes."

His response shattered her hope. Only one word, but it hit her hard. "Why?" How was it possible that, of all people, her uncle would let her suffer this way? She stared at him, consumed by doubt about the very man she'd trusted unconditionally all her life.

"How else were you supposed to learn, Eva? You're a trained chef! Your father might have believed in your abilities, but I most certainly did not. I needed to see for myself that your old man hadn't gone senile and was setting you up on a pedestal because he loved you." He stared at the stress ball in his palm for a moment, and then set it back onto the table. His tone returned to normal. "And now I know he was right all along. You're the one to mend it all."

Mend it all? *She* would *mend it all*? She had to be asleep. This had to be a nightmare. She pinched herself to ensure, the sting from which confirmed, this was real, all of it.

"How? How can you possibly know that? I've only worked here a few months. I've failed more times than I've succeeded, and not to forget, every step has been a battle."

"Because, you're exactly the spin this company needs. People know me. They know what to expect, and they already know what they don't like," he said grimly. "But you're unpredictable. It brings a new twist to it all, Eva. Don't you see? It builds curiosity. It builds interest."

She related to the part about the *new twist*. Given her expertise, or lack thereof, in this industry, she'd made several decisions based on what she thought right, in that moment. Why? Because, *new twist* was her strong suit.

During the years she'd been a chef, she'd lost count of the number of times she'd started to create a recipe and ended up making something totally different from what she originally had in mind. Her ideas evolved all the time, and that's what made her step away from the norm, find that *new twist*. Of course, she'd end up creating the best recipe of her life, or one that would go directly into the trash.

But working at S. F. Designs couldn't be compared to any recipe creation. Many people's livelihoods were at stake. Though working here didn't come close to her experiences as a chef, the only way she could stay sane was to somehow relate her past familiarities with her present challenges.

So yes, every moment of every day remained unpredictable; she became unpredictable, even to herself. Because here, there was no one recipe of success for her to follow. Every day was an experiment. And she failed every day, although she also fixed her past failures every day.

Uncle Dave held her gaze for a bit longer, then turned to face the window. "He never spoke to me about the informant. He didn't even mention it in his letter. I cannot imagine why Robin hid this from me. I mean…" He turned around, and his gaze darted around the room. "This is huge, Eva. This will burn us. This will destroy us. It already is—"

"Only if we let it." She walked toward his desk, measuring her thoughts with every step. He felt vulnerable, and so did she. Her father's words resonated in her mind; *this company needs a fighter, this company needs you*. But could she be a fighter? Sure, she would be more than willing to stand against all odds, for her father's sake, but there were many times in recent months when she had been close to accepting defeat.

"I don't know yet how we can stop this from tearing us down, but we have to begin somewhere. A-And the FBI is not our enemy." Of course that last part made him look at her like she'd lost her mind, yet she continued, "It's best if we tell them everything we know." More like everything *he* knew, but she didn't want to go there just yet.

And before she did anything else, she had one man to talk to, her father's lawyer, Simon Cade.

***

Eva stormed into Simon Cade's office, not caring that someone already sat with him.

Simon's secretary rushed in after her. "I tried to stop her."

Simon looked up from behind his desk. He stopped whatever he'd been doing and glared at Eva.

"It's OK, Linda."

Eva shot the secretary a *you heard him* look.

Linda narrowed her eyes at Eva and shook her head. She charged out of the room without another word.

Eva brought her glower back to Simon. "Did he leave me a letter?" Her jaw ached when she spoke. She'd clenched her teeth too many times since morning.

"Eva."

She bristled at his tone. It held the same pity her uncle had expressed only moments ago, and now the same pity pierced her ears. And just as she would tell him off, his attention shifted to the man seated in front of him.

The man stared at her, his mouth agape, and she stared right back.

What am I doing? She should control her emotions, at least at her workplace. But, this wasn't *her* workplace. Although in the same building as hers, this was Simon's office. The probability of the man knowing her was high. He would probably

11

gossip about her later to all his friends, co-workers, acquaintances…and yet she continued to scowl at him. His gaze darted between her and Simon. Then, without a word, he sprang from his chair and left the room, closing the door after him.

See…unpredictable.

"Did he or did he not, Simon?"

"Please, take a seat, Eva."

"He did, didn't he?" She tried hard to keep her tone controlled. She fisted her hands tight at her sides.

Simon sagged back into his chair and folded his arms across his chest. "Yes."

"Why am I finding this out only now?"

"I'm not permitted to reveal such details, not until the time is right. You know that."

"This is the first time my father has died, so no, I don't."

He stared at her, his expression blank.

"Is now the right time?"

When he didn't answer her right away, she opened her mouth to protest, but he quickly said, "Yes, it is." Angling forward, he pulled his desk drawer open and brought out a small silver key. He rose from his chair and tugged down the bottom seam of his silk double-breasted vest with both hands, straightening the risen folds. Had he used this time to think how to proceed next? He didn't need to look his best to hand over *a letter*.

"Please, you should really sit down for this," he said again, his tone more caring and less sympathetic. But she remained paralyzed.

Had she not walked into that heated conversation between her uncle and Trevor, she wouldn't have known about the letter her father had left for her uncle. She would have continued to blame herself for the downfall of her company. And who knew when she'd have found out her father had left her a letter? Her thoughts jammed. She rubbed the spot on her forearm she'd pinched earlier. Yes, it was real. All of it.

Simon strolled toward a cabinet standing against the wall next to her. He looked exactly the way he did the first time she'd met him several years ago. His office, too, looked the same.

Simon, an affable, cigar loving, bald man with a penchant for wooden finishes, had worked as her father's lawyer since the time S. F. Designs had setup office in Stanford Tower. Simon's law firm, especially his office, remained imprinted in Eva's memories since the first time she'd visited him with her father. Three of his office walls were covered in cherry wood, and matching beams ran along the ceiling. Rustic hardwood covered the floor. A large shiny wooden desk sat in one corner, behind which stood a high back leather chair in chocolate brown. Bright daylight shone through the window behind the chair, pouring in to awaken his office. Beyond the window was a view of the many piers that extended into the bay curving along the street. How she longed to be out there, by the waterfront, basking in the ocean breeze under the warm sun. How she longed to be anywhere else but here.

From within the cabinet that contained a multitude of grooves filled with kick-knacks, from his collection of signed golf balls, to awards, to a bowl of pinecones, Simon opened an unassuming door and revealed a grey safe with a circular combination lock. He rotated the lock a few times. A light beep opened the door to the safe. He pulled a rectangular box about half way out, inserted the silver key into it and opened the lid, then brought out a white envelope from within.

Eva stared at the envelope he'd held. It was from her father. What did it say?

Simon locked the box and pushed it back into the safe. He closed the door and turned the combination lock dial until it beeped, twice this time. When their eyes met again, he stood still. His gaze drifted down to the envelope in his hand and then back to her. He sighed and handed the envelope over to her.

Evie, her father's handwriting in blue ink on the front of the cover brimmed emotions she tried hard to quell. She swallowed the thick lump that had formed in her throat as she stared at the envelope in her trembling hands.

What was with her and envelopes these days? First, the termination letter from Stanford, then, the threat letter she'd received in St. Barth, and now, the most straining of them all, this note from her father. She inhaled a deep breath to ready herself for whatever she was about to read. She pulled the letter out of the envelope but couldn't bring herself to unfold the paper. She turned to look at Simon who had now returned to his seat.

He rested his elbow on one arm of the chair and chewed on the earpiece of his reading glasses. He studied her from behind his desk.

The seriousness in his expression made her mind falter further. Her legs wobbled. Maybe she should take that seat after all. She stepped, slow and indecisive, toward an empty chair and sat stiff onto the seat. She held in a deep breath, unfolded the letter and read the three words her father had written.

Trust no one

A chill ran through her, raising the hair at her nape. Her breath remained caught. She flipped the letter over, but it was blank. Of the many things her father could have told her, those were all the words he chose to say? What did he mean? *Is this a riddle?* She glared at Simon hoping he might have a clue.

"He's right." He nodded as he removed the earpiece from his mouth and set the glasses onto his desk.

"You've read this?"

"He wanted me to."

"Why?"

"To caution you."

Typical of Simon, to keep his answers clipped. And he did that with his questions too. He'd pose them in a way that despite deep consideration one couldn't possibly know the right answer. Her father had commended Simon for exactly that skill. She might too, had it not been her in the hot seat.

"He trusted no one, not even me at times, and neither should you."

"And yet, you're the only one he spoke to about the informant."

He remained silent. Keeping his face devoid of expression, he gave nothing away.

Was he the only person her father had spoken to about the informant? Was there someone else?

"Was there anything else he wanted me to know?"

Simon's gaze dropped to his glasses on the table. He stared at them for a moment and then looked back up at her. "There's one more envelope, but I cannot hand it over yet."

"Why not? What does that say?"

"I've not been informed of its contents. It's to be read only by you, in due time."

This made no sense. "I already know it exists, why don't you just give it to me now?"

"You know I can't, Eva. I can only turn it over when it's all resolved."

"When what all's resolved?"

Simon pursed his lips. Once again, he refrained from speaking any more than he should.

His methodical silence charred her already broiled up anxiety. She wanted to scream at the top of her lungs. Instead, she went for a heavy sigh.

Had he prepared in advance to have this exact conversation with her? She wouldn't let him succeed in his silence. She needed him to reveal more. "I know you're keeping the FBI posted about the happenings in my company."

He continued to remain quiet. Of course, he knew she knew.

"Did you tell them about this?" She waved the paper in her hand.

"No. Your father didn't want me to."

"But he wanted you to tell them about the letter he left for my uncle. Why?"

"I'm not authorized to say."

"By whom? The FBI?"

"Your father."

"My father's dead," she almost shouted. Her insides did a sharp drop when she realized the harshness of those words that had scurried out of her mouth.

He stilled and so did she.

"It was a dying man's wish, Eva." He sounded bereaved.

What... "Dying man? He knew...? He knew his life was in danger? The FBI told me he was followed, but..." Her breath caught. "Was he being threatened?"

Simon gave her another silent look.

Unbelievable! "Let me guess, you're not authorized to say."

Chapter 2

Eva went straight to Clive's office after her aggravating conversation with Simon. Other than the puzzling note her father had left her, she hadn't been able to get any details, either about the informant or about her father's death, from the reticent lawyer.

She strode out of the elevator toward Clive's office. She needed to vent. She needed Clive.

"Is he free?" she asked Clive's secretary as she walked past her desk.

She placed her hand on his office door and just as she pushed it to open, Trish said, "No...he's out on a lunch meeting."

The surprise in Trish's tone was faint, but evident enough to cause Eva a stir. Did Trish think it odd that Eva didn't know Clive's whereabouts? Because...*should I?*

"Is there something I could help you with?"

"N—no, thanks. Just stopped by to say hello." Eva smiled and brought tentative relief to Trish's expression.

What was Trish hiding from her?

Trust no One.

Her thoughts drove her crazy. She didn't want to return to her office just yet. She couldn't concentrate on work after the morning she'd had. She texted her best friends, Izzy and Allie, while she waited for the elevator, in case they were available for lunch. Minutes later, the trio stood in the line to order their food at a nearby Mediterranean takeout café.

There were only two barstools for people to perch on as they waited for their food to be prepared. The cozy space, thrumming with an eclectic blend of pop music and an equally good-humored owner, had quite a welcoming effect. But nothing could soothe Eva's twitching nerves today.

"Claire and Mila are available to interview any day you are."

Interview? *Ah yes…* Clive's little sister and her makeup artist friend had dressed Eva for the Met Gala, and Izzy had promised to help advertise their business. Eva looked forward to the *Celebrity and their Stylist* spotlight article Izzy had planned to feature Claire and Mila in the upcoming *In Trend* magazine issue. "I can free up tomorrow afternoon."

"That works." Izzy grinned.

"Thanks for helping them."

"Oh, don't mention it. Besides, that dress and everything else you wore to the gala was such a hit, I'm thinking you should be on the cover."

"What? No." One thing to answer interview questions, but posing for the cover was most certainly not something Eva wanted to be a part of. The limelight from being with Clive had become too much to handle as it was. Reporters lurked around her too now, as they did around Clive. "You should definitely have Claire and Mila on the cover. Not me."

"Why not? We'll photograph you for the article anyway."

"I prefer living under a rock."

Izzy rolled her eyes. "We'll see."

No. Eva gave Izzy a sharp look. "We will *not* see. I'm not comfortable with this, at all. So, feature Claire and Mila, not me, and that's final."

"Let her be, *Izz*. She's doing the interview, that's good enough."

"No, it's not. Because, everyone knows her as *Clive Stanford's hot new girlfriend*, instead of *Eva Avery, the hot new owner of an interior design firm*."

"Frankly, where media's concerned, I'm perfectly OK being Clive's arm-candy."

Izzy made a face. "At least think about it."

"I doubt I'll change my mind."

"What can I get for you?" the café's middle-aged owner, dressed in black pants and white chef's coat, asked from behind the glass enclosed ingredient counter.

"*Falafel* wrap, please," Izzy said and glanced back at Eva, "All I'm saying is—"

"Spicy?" he asked as he spread out a *lavash* on to a sheet of silver foil.

"Yes. Thank you." She side-stepped to move along the counter. "All I'm saying is give it some thought. Cons we already know, but there are benefits to being on the cover."

"What can I get for you miss, the usual?"

"Yes, please," Eva smiled, "thank you."

"One mezza plate," he shouted to another food preparer to handle Eva's order.

She too sidestepped, following Izzy.

"What can I get for you?" he asked Allie.

"Same. Thank you."

"One more mezza plate," he shouted again.

The chef rolled Izzy's *lavash* stuffed with falafel and several other ingredients into a silver log, while two compartmental take-out boxes were filled with a medley.

"Besides, you already know I'm camera shy. Without Clive, no way I could have walked that red carpet."

"I know, and you have nothing to worry about. I've booked an excellent photographer for this shoot, he'll take your picture before you even know it."

They paid for their food and walked back to Stanford. As they approached the luxuriant spire, Eva tilted her head back letting her gaze follow the length of the magnanimous, greenish-blue, all glass building that tapered into the sky. Shimmering like a crystal in the noon California sun, the vibrant color matched Clive's stunning irises.

She dropped her gaze, only to be riveted by the sight of the very man. Her breath jerked to a halt when Clive stepped out of the Stanford building. He looked superbly sexy, insanely rich, and yet perfectly casual.

She'd gawked at Clive as he'd dressed for work that morning. Other than a shave and a quick shower, he'd fussed little with his appearance. The only accessories he used to tame his erratic, dark, wild hair with were his fingers. His long, manly, skillful in many ways, fingers.

Laid back, yet chic for a billionaire looking to add more to his wealth, he'd worn beige pants, tucked in a white shirt, top button undone, brown belt, expensive watch and a sports coat which he seemed to have now abandoned as he'd rolled up the sleeves of his shirt showing off his strong arms. His gaze, his gait, amplified his finesse.

Her heart leapt into familiar and much welcome fluttering.

And *he* loves *me*.

Her longing for Clive rose steep as he approached. She ached for the warmth of his embrace, the scent of his crisp breath as their faces would near, the brush of his stubble against her sensitive skin as he'd kiss her in that unique way of his, only to make her desperate for more. And the lustful way he'd look when he wanted more of her…and the way he now looked as he opened the passenger side door of his Maserati for…Silvia…*Silvia*?

Perfectly set blonde waves framed Silvia's gorgeous face. Her tall, sleek body beautifully hugged by dark pants, a blazer and a hot red, cleavage baring, top.

Eva's stomach hardened at the site of the model, who was also Clive's ex.

Silvia splayed her hand across his chest. *Thank you.* Eva read her lips.

Silvia flashed Clive a glamorous smile, but when she turned to get into the car, she shot Eva a look...a *catty look.*

What the hell for?

Silvia caught her stare, Clive didn't.

Paaaannng...the earsplitting honk of a cement truck that almost hit Eva, followed by a series of soul shaking, shrill screeches from the urgent ramming of its breaks, stopped Eva in her tracks.

Stupefied by Silvia's sickening game, Eva hadn't noticed the red warning of the pedestrian walk sign and stepped into oncoming traffic.

"Watch it Lady." A harsh pull to her upper arm caused her to stumble backward. She would have yelped had her voice not already dried out from both, the stinging, and unfamiliar, hatred Silvia's gaze provoked followed by the deathly cement truck. She turned and stared, dazed, at the middle aged gentleman who'd come to her rescue. Dark sunglasses, a thick mustache, and a beard covered most of her rescuer's face.

Her heartbeat thrashed in her ears. "Thank you." She exhaled, shaky from all that unfolded in a matter of minutes. Several judgmental, accusing eyes glared at her, including Izzy and Allie, their expressions horror stricken, mouths agape, pale.

"God, Eva. Are you OK?" Allie held her.

"What happened?" Izzy grimaced.

Their questioning could wait. Eva turned around to look at Clive and Silvia, and of course, they were gone. She stared a moment longer at the empty spot where Clive's car had been parked, as though she could rewind time and see them again. But what could she do even if she could rewind time?

"Eva?"

Eva's breathing remained unsteady. "I'm fine."

"Are you sure? Because you look like you've seen a ghost."

"More like the grim reaper." Izzy chuckled.

"How is this funny to you?" Allie winced at Izzy.

"Really, I'm fine." Eva started to walk. Izzy and Allie followed while they continued to bicker.

They made it across the street just as the pedestrian walk signal turned back to a blinking red.

Eva couldn't get Silvia's pestering look out of her thoughts. Her walk through the turnstiles, through the lavish Stanford lobby, and up the elevator to the 37th floor remained a blur while her mind raced to decipher the meaning of that one look. What was Silvia up to, other than triggering Eva to pick a fight? Which she'd tried to instigate before, on the Met Gala night, but Eva had avoided an altercation.

She stepped out of the elevator and turned toward her office.

"Where you going?" Izzy asked.

She jerked to a halt and turned to her friends. She forgot they were even there. "Huh? To my office." Where else would she be going?

"Thought we were eating at Izzy's?"

"Yeah, didn't you say you needed a break from work?"

Ah yes, she had. Yes, *had*, at the time she'd texted them to meet for lunch. But how could she explain any of the day's happenings to her friends? The FBI situation, being confidential, remained off limits to conversation. And any discussion about Clive and Silvia would only lead to speculation, making matters worse.

All that had unveiled since morning threw her into a labyrinth of *what ifs*. Though every bend eluded a finish, she only moved deeper into the maze.

Challenged and riddled by her recent troubles, she first needed to wade through the ferocious waves of uncertainty that brewed in her mind. Until then, she wouldn't be ready to share her worries with anyone, not even Izzy and Allie.

Her pulse still pounded from that honking cement truck. She would do anything to avoid any further anxiety. "I remembered something I need to get done right away. I'm going to have to work through lunch." She disliked changing her plans with her friends, but she needed the reprieve. Besides, she hadn't lied. She needed to catch up from being away from work all morning. Sure, her friends weren't thrilled about her abandoning them, but they'd understand.

Chapter 3

Endearing, enraging and exhausting. That summed up Clive's day.

It started beautifully when he woke up next to the girl of his dreams. The warmth of her soft feminine body against his when he hugged her tight after an intense round of lovemaking made him want their togetherness to last forever.

Sex with Eva was mind-blowing, even when he'd selfishly woken her from her deep slumber. Her soft moans, her light gasps, perfectly in tune with his wants. He loved her for it. She'd given herself to him freely and entirely, and he wanted nothing more than to relive the same moments with her over and over again. He would have seduced her into doing just that today. They could have played hooky from work, had he missed Trevor's text message. *Silvia*.

As lunchtime neared, Silvia sat across from him in a red-seated booth of a French restaurant in the Stanford Tower. If it weren't for her insisting on meeting at the restaurant, Clive would have preferred to talk in his office. Did she imagine she could restrain his anger if they met in a crowded place? Regardless of her many tricks, he would never forgive her for leaking false information about him to the media, which nearly caused him to once again lose Eva. Public or not, he could read Silvia right through. His dislike for her grew every second he spent with her.

Tears rolled down her blushed cheeks, but her expression didn't change. Her eyes didn't turn raccoon-y. Her words didn't match her look. She kept her posture prim and proper. Something she'd learnt in prep school. The longer she talked, the faker she seemed, and the faster he wanted to end their conversation. How he wished he could spend this time with Eva instead.

"I'll tell them whatever they need to know. Would you go with me?"

He would, but not because he cared for Silvia. After all, her latest gaff topped the list of reasons why he disliked her.

A reporter had handed her an envelope containing compromising photographs of her and threatened to publicize her sex tapes from her pre-modeling days unless she'd break up Eva and Clive.

Clive suspected the reporter as none other than the informant, and the FBI could use any information Silvia could provide about the guy. In return, Clive would get her the tapes.

Although Silvia promised to tell the FBI anything they wanted to know about the reporter, Clive didn't trust her to go through with it.

She sniffed and brought a tissue out of her purse to dab under her eyes. Something shifted in him when a woman cried, even for despicable Silvia.

"I'll go with you." *At least, for Eva's sake.*

She smiled. "Thank you."

The sooner he got this mess sorted out, the better. Especially since he blamed himself for the informant contacting Silvia. That he'd gotten together with her a few times before Eva returned to his life was no secret. The informant missed no opportunity to get to Eva. Knowing that Clive kept the contract with S. F. Designs, the only way for the informant to break the renewed partnership between the two companies was to bring in a domestic disturbance. And who better than Silvia to do the dirty job?

"I think about us all the time." Silvia tried to touch his hand from across the table, but he aptly pulled it back. She stiffened. He didn't care.

None of the envelopes from the informant the FBI had run fingerprints on resulted in conclusive findings. The probability that the envelope Silvia would hand over to the FBI would be evidence free, was high. Although, Clive hoped the informant slacked on his caution this one time.

As always, Silvia had dressed to entice. Trevor gave Clive a sly grin when he opened the door to a conference room for Silvia to walk in. He leaned in, only for Clive to hear. "Remind me to thank the informant."

Clive sat through another round of Silvia's story while she recited it to Trevor. They saved her the embarrassment by not viewing the photographs. Sure Clive was experienced in ways of sex. He'd seen it all and done it all at one point or another. Videotaping, however, remained a fetish he'd never understood.

As Trevor prepared to conclude Silvia's statement, the conference room door opened, and McKenzie peeked in. He gave Silvia a double take. Who wouldn't?

But looks could be deceiving, especially Silvia's.

"Could we talk?" he asked Clive.

Chapter 4

Alone in her office, seated at her desk, Eva stabbed a plastic fork at the food in the takeout box, uncomfortably aware of how quickly she'd become envious of Silvia. How had her day gone from a terrific start to this puzzling state? After an incredible night's sleep, followed by a blissful morning when she woke up to Clive's luxurious love making, she had an awesome hair day, which in itself indicated brighter things in life.

And yet, she sat moping in her office, ignoring basic reasoning as she compared herself with Silvia. Silvia had a body to die for, while Eva could never be a model. Eva liked to eat. Food made her think positive thoughts. And she too was svelte in her own *not skinny but womanly* way.

She slathered a dollop of *hummus* onto a triangular piece of pita and took a bite. *Umm…*

And she worked out. She went running thrice a week and practiced yoga on weekends. No matter how much she exercised, her curves were always fuller. And she liked her curves more now than ever, because Clive liked her curves.

She smiled. *Clive.*

Then why did she compete with Silvia? And in comparison, why did she think of herself as a shapeless lump of dough? Not like her to think that way. She'd never let anyone get to her in the past, and she wouldn't let anyone in future either. Then why did the incident with Silvia still prickle at her? Why did she feel like Silvia had punched her in the gut?

Maybe because her heart ached upon noticing what a perfect match Clive and Silvia made. They looked like they belonged together.

How did he ever fall for me? Her insides twisted. *Because you're different*, her mind whispered the words Clive had said to her in St. Barth.

She bit into an olive. Umm...*buttery...*

Why had Clive met Silvia at all? Where did they drive? And why hadn't he mentioned any of it to her? No wonder Trish seemed puzzled that Eva knew nothing about Clive's plans. Not like Eva would have wanted to anyway, because she trusted Clive plenty. Silvia's intentions, however, she didn't trust. Silvia might have planned up something vile. And Clive probably had no clue. *Did Clive really have no clue?* Silvia was his ex after all.

Did she overthink it all? Maybe Clive had to meet a client and saw Silvia at the street corner, because *that's* where one would find a woman like Silvia. She snorted a laugh as she closed the lid of the now empty take-out container and tossed it into the wastebasket next to her desk. Yes, food *did* make her think positive thoughts.

She'd talk this over with Clive. It would end up being a silly misunderstanding. Because Clive loved her. So yeah, she had nothing to worry about.

And yet, Silvia's conniving gaze continued to niggle at her.

By mid-afternoon, her mood worsened. Her meetings flew by without her hearing a word. She needed to pay attention to these team discussions, to prepare for their upcoming meeting with the Marinos in New York. And she especially needed to pay attention after the conversation with her uncle that morning, particularly, after having read her father's note. Speaking of, should she suspect everyone in her office of espionage? Could that be her father's advice? And whom else should she not trust?

She sighed. She needed distance from this endless speculation over everything that bothered her today.

"Tina, need a break?"

"Oh my God!" Her secretary groaned. "I *so* need it."

Thankfully, Tina no longer addressed her as *Miss Avery*. Eva always felt it made their relationship too formal anyway. During their breaks, they chatted about all, except work. Eva loved their mid-day detachment from routine.

They walked to the coffee shop in Stanford Tower's lobby, bought their drinks and sat at the same table where Eva had sat with her uncle numerous times over the years.

Eva took the lid off the disposable cup and puffed a long breath to cool the piping hot tea. She took a sip. Creamy. Sugary. She needed this.

"That friend I told you about, from college?" Tina said.

But Eva remained distracted. From the corner of her eye, she saw her rescuer. The same bearded man who'd pulled her back from walking into traffic. She should buy him a drink as a *thank you.* She darted her gaze around the coffee shop to look for him. Where did he go? Had she imagined him being there?

"Eva?"

She looked back at Tina.

"Who are you looking for?"

"I thought I saw someone I knew." Well...guess she hadn't. "So, go on, Thomas right? He lives in San Diego?"

"Yes, Thomas." Tina bit into her lip suppressing a grin. "He's coming over for the weekend. He'll be here tomorrow night, actually."

"Nice. Any special plans?"

"None yet. Just hang out. Maybe go hiking. But mostly stay home. We have a lot to catch up on." She sipped her coffee. "How about you? Doing anything fun with that smoking hot boyfriend of yours?"

Umm...he's that. "Don't know yet."

Tina shook her head. "You're so lucky, Eva"

"I am." She grinned wide. "He makes me happy." And she genuinely felt that way. All the more reason why she worried that Silvia would destroy it all. But she wouldn't let her.

As soon as she returned to her desk, she messaged Clive.

Eva: *What are you up to*?

Chapter 5

Clive sat in McKenzie's office. His muscles tensed from the uncertainty their conversation raised.

"I've pulled back all surveillance on Miss Avery."

Clive's chest hollowed as though wind had vanished out of his lungs. "Why?"

"There's strong opposition from headquarters about this case. They think FBIs intent is jeopardized."

Clive exhaled a humorless laugh. "Jeopardized how?"

"Given the recent media madness, we have reason to believe the informant is aware of our surveillance. He's since gone underground."

"Reason to believe?" Clive's voice rose, altered by the mounting disbelief in McKenzie's decision to abandon Eva. McKenzie had to know the informant wouldn't remain in hiding for long. And when he reemerged, he might no longer resort to sending paper messages. Clive's muscles coiled when he imagined the endless, and possibly dangerous, intentions the rogue might return with. He couldn't bear to imagine Eva as his target. "What reason, Mac?"

McKenzie eyed him in silence from behind his desk.

"You have no reason, do you? Beyond *your* men looking bad because they're unable to catch the guy in all this while—"

"You're forgetting, my men are FBI agents, not personal bodyguards." McKenzie leaned in toward the table, his jaw tightened. "They were all over the news that day, when they escorted Miss Avery away from those reporters, after that magazine incident Silvia had caused. And it won't be long before someone finds out who the men protecting her were. Can you imagine the mess this case will be in then? It's important they step away for a while."

"Her life could be in danger."

"You don't know that, unless you have intel we don't."

Clive's head throbbed. He raked his fingers through his hair. He didn't discredit McKenzie's stance on the matter, but that didn't mean he liked the situation one bit. His pulse raced. His breath heaved. "I have a bad hunch."

"A hunch?"

"What if it's a ruse? He's hiding only so you'd pull your men out?"

"And what if he's not?"

"How can you do this, Mac? You know she was threatened in St. Barth, you know about that car chase, you know her father was murdered—"

"Allegedly."

"Whatever. You know my hunch is right."

McKenzie leaned back into his chair, his arms folded, his gaze dropped. After a moment of thought, he exhaled heavily and met Clive's gaze. "You know how such cases work. We have no evidence proving the man Trevor and Jason followed to St. Barth was the same guy who sent her that letter. Just like we have no evidence it was the same man in the car chase. Hell, we don't even know if it was a chase at all. Maybe it was a reckless drunk driver my men followed. We have no evidence, none whatsoever, about any of this. All we have is a rough sketch from Eva's descriptions of the man she saw in the park. We have no further leads."

"What about the guy who handed Silvia the envelope."

"Yeah, what about him?"

"You have yet to fingerprint that material."

"Even if we do find prints, we cannot implicate him for blackmail. Unless our rogue resurfaces and does something really foolish, this case is bone-dry." He paused. "So yes, I cannot send my men on a wild goose chase because rich kid here has a hunch."

Of course, he'd throw that in.

"Tell me you don't have a hunch."

"It doesn't work that way, Clive."

"Say it then."

McKenzie stared, silent for a long moment. He shifted in his chair. "Damn it, man. Yes, I have a hunch, and it's a bad one, but there's nothing I can do. My hands are tied. You know that."

A knock on the door ended that conversation. Trevor walked in and they talked about Dave.

Imagining FBI interrogating Dave in front of Eva wrung Clive's heart. She shouldn't have to deal with that all by herself. He dearly hoped she knew he'd protect her from it all.

"Tell Eva I'm sorry, will you?" Trevor said.

***

"Why is it that you're calling me only now?" The voice snarled.

The informant had begun to get tired of the gruff and cruel tone in which his employer bristled at him each time they conversed. "I didn't ge—"

"And why the hell were you among the reporters? You can't be *that* stupid to not realize you'll be all over the news?"

"But I was wearin' a reporters badge and—"

"Stop talking."

He hated to be spoken to that way. Especially, by a man…or a woman? *The voice…that voice.* A vein throbbed in his temple. He massaged the familiar spot with his forefinger. He didn't know whom that voice belonged to. But did it matter? Because some day, he would strangle that voice, and how he would love to hear it squeal for mercy.

"Who were those men escorting her?" The voice asked.

"Private security, I think."

"You *think*?"

"Well, who else could it be?"

"We wouldn't know now would we? Because *you* didn't bother to find out."

"You know somethin'? I don't like your tone. Neither do I like your accusations, because I—"

"Shut-up. Listen."

The rough grunt made the informant pull his head away from the phone's earpiece.

"Find out right away who…"

If it weren't for the promised money…

He tightened his fists as he imagined the warm neck of his employer in his hands as he squeezed it to the last breath. How much he loved the choking game. He'd played it a lot with the hookers, and they seemed to like it too.

He smiled, remembering Candy. He'd choked her last night. Her struggle for air, violent at first, followed by a state of calm and peace. Her eyes turned distant. Her skin grew pale. He took pride in freeing her that way. Liberating her from everything she'd ever known, even if her freedom lasted only for a few seconds.

He'd never pushed her, or any of the other girls he'd been with, beyond.

He licked his lips.

He wasn't a murderer, like his mother was.

His heart pounded; his breathing hastened.

His mother had asked him to watch as she stabbed his father to death.

You are exactly like your father, his mother used to say. His father was a drunk. His father was filthy. *Your father is no good…*his mother used to say. He never wanted to be his father. He wanted to be his mother—superior…powerful…*but a murderer*?

Because if he could be a murderer, why did he save Eva today from being run over by that cement truck? Why did he pull her back instead of pushing her ahead? There were so many people at the intersection; no one would have had a clue how she'd fallen into oncoming traffic.

Eva's father died that way. He was crossing the street when a white van ran him over. He'd seen it all. The van. The driver. The dead man. He hadn't spoken of it to anybody. Especially not to his employer, because for all he knew, his employer might have driven the van that day. His employer might have killed Eva's father.

His swiped the perspiration from his forehead with the back of his hand.

No, he was no murderer. But the more his employer taunted him…he was tempted…*very tempted*.

Chapter 6

Over half an hour ago she'd texted Clive, and he still hadn't responded. Despite her best intentions, her concentration on the discussions in the present meeting remained non-existent as she kept checking her phone for his response. Not like her to be a stalker. Yet, when she returned to her desk, she called Clive's office. He hadn't returned from that lunch meeting.

She glanced at her wristwatch. It showed half past three. Was he still with Silvia?

Her phone buzzed from an incoming message from Clive. Just like that, her muscles weakened, her tension released, but only until she read his text.

Clive: *Busy. Anything urgent?*

Well, not when he asked like that.

Eva: *Nothing urgent.*

Clive was a busy man. With all that he did on any given day to maintain and further add to his staggering net worth, she couldn't imagine how he found time to sleep. Yet, evident since they met in the elevator over a month ago, no matter what required Clive's attention, he always gave Eva top priority. Miraculously, despite his impossibly busy schedule, he still somehow made space for her. Except today, and it added to her puzzlement, when his text lacked the affection he'd gotten her accustomed to.

Nothing made sense today, from Clive's clipped text, to the note from her father, that the FBI suspected her uncle of foul play, the uncertain impending turmoil her company headed toward, the informant, and…*are you still with Silvia? Urg! Why can't I stop thinking about her?*

That last thought plagued her for the rest of her afternoon. Finally, nearing five o'clock, Clive texted again, this time to say that she shouldn't wait for him and that Tom would take her home.

Had he meant to come by her house later? Did Trish tell him she'd been looking for him? If he did spend all afternoon with Silvia, she no longer cared, because something was wrong and, once again, he was keeping her in the dark about it all.

She stood by her office window with the view of the blue bay. She stared, looking at nothing in particular as she contemplated how to proceed next. And instead of replying to Clive, she sent a message to Izzy. *I'll do the cover*. It might be a placebo effect, but her decision made her thoughts lighten. Because Izzy was right; Eva wasn't simply Clive's arm candy. "Nor am I a shapeless lump of dough!"

"I'll say." A manly voice interrupted her thoughts.

Oh. Did I say that out aloud? She turned around to find Ryan, her friend from her childhood years, walking into her office.

"A *very shapely* lump of dough, if anything." He grinned.

Her face heated, she froze in her stance. "What are you doing here?"

"I called earlier. You were in a meeting. Didn't Tina tell you?"

"Y—yeah, she did." Of course she did and Eva had meant to return Ryan's call. But...how did she forget?

"Thought if you're not busy maybe we could grab a drink? Clearly you need more than *a* drink, because what are *you* doing here, Eva?"

She sighed. Her shoulders sagged from the weight of the unresolved issues she'd mulled over all day. She walked toward her desk. "Trying to find solutions to my ever mounting troubles."

"See, that's what happens when you date a Stanford." Ryan plopped into a chair opposite her desk.

His comment rubbed her the wrong way. Her mind raced through everything she knew about why Clive and Ryan didn't get along, which was...a quick recap, because she didn't know much at all. "Why do you dislike him?"

"Let's just say, I don't like the way he treats his women."

Despite her afternoon, her basic instinct to defend her lover kicked right in. "What?" She laughed. "We're speaking of the same Stanford?"

"Yep, the one and only." He leaned his elbows on the armrests and intermingled his fingers. He smiled, and now his smile rubbed her the wrong way.

"No, we aren't. Because sure, he's shrewd and a powerful businessman and has uncompromising control over us all—"

"Not on me, he doesn't."

Ignoring him, she continued, "But he's also very friendly and has never once been disrespectful to me, or to anyone else for that matter."

"You'd be surprised."

Everything about Ryan rubbed her the wrong way. Why did he antagonize her? She gripped the edge of her desk. "Go on, enlighten me then."

A slow grin appeared on Ryan's face. "You really like this guy."

"Yes, I do, very much so. But I like you too, Ryan. You're one of my closest friends. It bothers me that you two don't get along. And I want to know, once and for all, what caused the rift between you both?"

"OK, but I'd rather not have this conversation sober." He stood from the chair.

She raised her eyebrows. "Chickening out?"

"No." He sounded surprisingly unaffected. "You seem too wound up, and I think you could use some relaxation first, don't you? Don't want to make matters worse, especially because, for some unimaginable reason, you seem to like him." He paused. "Also, Izzy and Allie are waiting by the elevator, eager for a night they won't remember tomorrow." He grinned that grin again but this time, it bothered her less.

Ryan was right. She was in knots and needed to ease up before learning any new and probably inflammatory information about Clive. All energy left her. She should have a nice long soothing bath when she got back home. Light some candles, pour herself a glass of wine…She brought her hands to the back of her neck and massaged down its length. *Oh that feels so good…* "I'm sorry if I sound teed off. I could use some forgetting today." She grabbed her purse, and as she picked her cellphone from her desk to toss into her bag, it buzzed with an incoming message.

Clive: *Dinner at 8?*

Yes!

Her heart fluttered. Though she'd questioned Clive's intentions all afternoon, she missed him terribly too. Her longing for him teemed.

No!

He'd kept his day a secret from her, and in all fairness, she should give him the same treatment.

Eva: *Sorry, have plans.*

She kept her text short, not wanting to give out details, hoping he'd be bothered.

Clive: *OK, have fun.*

And once again her attempt to draw his attention failed.

Have fun? Didn't he want to know whom she was dining with? What happened to his overprotectiveness? What if… Renewed fear clawed at her. He'd passed his one-month, one–woman timeline. What if he had lost interest in her? Was this

his way of shooing her off? Her insides twisted further into a tight mess. She pressed her hand to her stomach.

"Is everything OK?"

"Yep." She forced a smile.

Overburdened and over influenced by erratic emotions, the back of her neck stiffened again. She brought one hand to it and rubbed, but her attempt no longer worked. For her own sake, she needed to let go of thinking about her day. She *so* needed to forget.

They stepped out of the Stanford Tower onto the pavement, which almost seemed non-existent given the two-way traffic of throngs of people walking hurriedly to their destinations. Public transportation too altered into a riot during rush hour. Cars and buses stood huddled in winding, lengthy lines. One car honked. She flinched remembering the cement truck. She cut the driver a quick look. *Tourist.*

A cold evening breeze brushed past. She fastened the top button of her trench coat and plunged her hands into its pockets. She looked around for the FBI car. She hadn't seen it by her home that morning, nor did it wait for her here now.

Well, good. Less people reporting her whereabouts to Clive, the better.

Except for that one person she definitely wanted to be noticed by, Tom, Clive's driver. Seeing her approach, Tom smiled and opened the passenger side door for her to enter. She too smiled and waved casually as she walked past him. "Thank you, but we're going to walk."

His mouth opened, and before he could tell her that Clive had ordered him to take her wherever she needed to go, she hurried toward her friends and disappeared into the crowd. *Go tell Clive whom I went to dinner with, Tom.*

Minutes later, they snagged a high bar table just as the waitress cleaned away the last of the empty glasses and plates left over by its former occupants. Ryan pulled in a couple extra all steel bar stools. Before they knew it, they were already sipping their second pisco sour at the Peruvian restaurant's happy hour lounge.

They ordered their favorites, plantain chips, ceviche and sliders. Though the first drink had blurred away the storm that consumed her day, Eva was still too coiled up to ingest any food. But their order wouldn't be wasted, because Allie ate for them all.

"I don't know…guess being in love makes me hungry," Allie justified with a half shrug, and drained her drink.

Izzy reached for a plantain chip, but Allie beat her to it. She glared at Allie. "My point, before Allie eats that too," Izzy took a chip and dipped it into the Aioli as she spoke, "What's wrong with making education free for all, I mean…"

Such were the conversations with her friends. Limitless topics of discussions about practically anything they could think of. Anything but work. Anything but her troubles. Anything but *why did Clive meet Silvia today*? That last thought, occurred to her only once in all this time. She downed her drink and ordered another one. Spending time with her besties was exactly the pick-up she needed.

"Eva, why aren't you eating?" Allie broke a long chip into two with one crisp snap. "Thought these are your favorites."

"They are, but not today. I have a photo shoot tomorrow. And I'm," she raised her glass, "On a liquid diet."

"Not that kind of liquid." Izzy pointed.

"The only kind I'm on prior to a shoot."

"Oh, booze will flow plenty tomorrow. Kevin, the photographer I mentioned, he home brews this alcohol. It's sweet and absolutely delicious. He'll definitely bring some in to ease you girls."

With the twist her mood had taken by then, she needed no easing…because after two and a half pisco sours, was being camera shy even a thing? She might see it differently when she sobered in the morning. But she wouldn't worry about that now.

When Izzy and Allie stepped away to the ladies room, Eva jumped right in to conclude the mystery between Clive and Ryan. "So, I'm pleasantly tipsy." She grinned. "Ready to talk about Clive?"

Ryan scrubbed his chin. His glanced in the direction where Izzy and Allie walked and returned to look at her. "You should probably hear it from him first."

"Oh c'mon! Why do you keep pushing this away?"

He remained silent.

"Ryan?"

"I don't entirely dislike him, Eva. But there are things…from his past…that bother me when I see you with him, that's all."

"Things like what?"

"Like Olivia, the only girlfriend he ever had, before you came along. Did he talk to you about her?"

"Well, yes and no. He did say he had one serious relationship. But we didn't discuss the details about how it ended or anything. Why?"

He leaned away from the table shaking his head. "I don't think I should tell you this then."

"What the hell, Ryan? You're my friend, you said you were going to tell me, now tell me already."

He dropped his gaze to his drink and moved his glass in a circular motion stirring the liquid within. A moment later, he set his glass down. "Fine. I'm warning you though, it doesn't end well."

Chapter 7

Clive shifted his attention from his phone in the direction of garbled voices and muffled footsteps. Ryan and Eva approached. Seeing them together took him back to that first time he spoke to Eva. He would never forget, fifteen years ago, in his home, at a New Year's Eve party...

Is that...her? That girl he'd seen at school. That girl he'd avoided talking to because she made his insides jump. Like she did right now when she shot him a quick glance. She didn't immediately look away as he had expected. Boldly, she held his gaze. And just like that, all except her grew blurry. All except his heavy heartbeat, muted. He'd never reacted this way to anyone before. He liked how his mind, his body, reacted to her. Then why did his insides clench? Why did his chest tighten? Why did her stare make him uncomfortable? Because she didn't give him a *stop looking at me* stare; she gave him an, *I think I like you too* stare. And he'd never wanted anything more than to find out if Eva found him as irresistible as he found her. Then why did the moment become too difficult to handle? Why did he tear his gaze away from her only to be overcome by his overwhelming fascination toward her?

She diverted her attention to the guy standing next to her.

He said something.

She smiled, at *that guy*.

That smile, Clive would never forget. So pretty, *she* was pretty. And now he wanted her to return to staring at him again.

The guy nudged her shoulder.

She giggled.

Something twisted within Clive. His jaw clenched. His hands formed to fists. He'd never felt this way before. And he didn't like how he felt. All because of *that* guy. Clive didn't know him, and he didn't care to get introduced, because he already didn't like *that* guy.

"Clive?"

"Hmm…"

"Clive?" The harshness in his brother's voice demanded attention.

Clive forgot Carter stood right next to him. "W-What?"

"I said, go talk to her."

Talk? To her? She laughed now. Something *that* guy said. *That feeling* that Clive didn't like feeling worsened.

"No." He picked up a pre-filled glass of red liquid and took a huge gulp. *Ugh! Disgusting.* Sweet…fruity…*disgusting… disgusting* punch.

His stomach churned. Not because of the awful drink. But because he couldn't bear to look at Eva when she was with *that* guy. Why was she with him anyway? And why did he care that she was?

"Why not?"

"What?"

"Why...not?" Carter dragged his words.

"Because..." he started off, his response strong, but he had no words to describe how turbulent and incomprehensible his thoughts became. His shoulders slumped. His heart sank. "I don't know what to say to her."

"Ask her if she wants some punch."

"What? No." Clive gave his brother a pointed look. Of all the things he could offer Eva, punch wouldn't even count as the last. And Carter knew that. Without giving the drink in his hand another chance, Clive channeled his frustration to crumple the plastic cup and hurl it into a trashcan.

"Why not?"

"I don't know her, Carter. She'll think I'm crazy."

"No kidding. The way you're looking at her, she probably already thinks that."

He'd had enough, between first *that guy* and now his brother. He turned to face Carter, to tell him off.

But a delicate voice reeled his attention, "Hey." It was Eva, sans *that* guy.

"Punch?"

She smiled, *that* smile, and held up the glass in her hand. She already drank that unpalatable drink.

Carter...

"Stupid." Carter shook his head and laughed as he walked away.

Clive sighed silently and glanced back at her.

She smiled—*at him*—and her smile put him to ease.

He spoke some, and she seemed interested.

He spoke some more, and she seemed intrigued.

He joked, and she laughed.

And just like that, his confidence returned. That pleasurable pain she caused in him exploded further. His excitement amplified from her being there. *With him*.

They chatted by the punch table for a while, until the voices and distractions surrounding them became far too many. He wanted to take her away some place where he could have her all for himself.

Minutes after, they were in his room. *She* was in *his room*. His *messy boy's* room as his mother would call it. All those things his mother had asked him to put away, his dirty socks, his scattered cleats, that unfinished sandwich, his unkempt bed...

What did he think bringing Eva here?

He cringed because he couldn't undo what she'd seen.

But, maybe she cared for none of that, because she walked around his room and looked intently at his things, as if reaching out to him through them.

She touched his medals. "How long have you played soccer?"

"Since I was five."

"Really? So has my brother. I go to all his games."

Her eyes glistened when she talked about her brother.

"The guy I saw you with, is that your brother?"

"No, that's Ryan, Joey's friend." She shifted her gaze to his bookshelf.

Talking about Ryan didn't make her eyes glisten, yet Clive's jaw tightened again as an image of her with *that guy* flashed his mind.

"Ryan too plays soccer."

Clive's jaw tightened farther. He didn't know why, but he couldn't bear to imagine Eva watching Ryan play soccer.

She touched his books and pointed out her favorites. She had read a lot of the same. She pulled one out. "Twenty Thousand Leagues…I'm reading this now. Yours has a different cover than mine." She flipped through the pages and pulled out a pink, quilled flower, bookmark from within.

He'd forgotten he'd left it in there.

She glanced back to the shelf and ran her fingers over the bookmarks that stood out from several of the books. She cleared her throat and gave him a strange look. "You collect *pink* bookmarks?"

Whatever she might have thought made her grimace too comical and made him laugh. "My sisters made them for a class project, a charity they were raising money for. I bought a few."

She looked back to the shelf. He could no longer see her face, but when she turned to meet his gaze again, her expression mimicked from earlier when all else around him, except her, turned blurry. *She likes me.*

54

She flicked her gaze away to his guitar and slid her fingers over the veneer. She picked at the strings, and they hummed at her touch. "Play something."

He did.

She sat in his chair and pressed her palm against her cheek as she watched him. When the first song ended, she wanted more. "One more. Please, please?"

He played one more. She pleaded with him to play another. He played another. And then another. And another…

A crackling explosion reeled them back. *Was it midnight already?*

They stood by the window. He stood close behind her but not close enough. As though she'd sensed his silent plea, she leaned backward into him and loosely laced her fingers with his. Caught unprepared for her provocation, his pulse raced, he grew breathless. He looked at her, and she smiled. Her face glowed in the gleam from the fireworks. She stared, mesmerized by the lit up sky. He stared, mesmerized, *by her*.

Glasses clinked. People cheered from the lawn that sprawled outside the window. Some hugged, some kissed, and he didn't know how he got himself to ask, "May I?"

Her smile receded. She stilled.

Shit. He shouldn't have asked.

She turned around to face him. Once again, her expression blurred all else but her. She nodded lightly, giving him the affirmation he needed.

He bent his head, and she tilted hers. Their lips met. Her lips were soft and warm, and her breath reminded him of punch. Now his favorite drink, that punch. Though a quick kiss, his lips tingled from it for a long time after. It was the first time he'd kissed a girl. And this wasn't just *any* girl.

"Happy New Year, Eva."

"Happy New Year—"

"Eva." Ryan stood in the doorway to Clive's bedroom. Had he seen them kiss? Because he glared at Clive, and of course, Clive glared right back.

Eva introduced them, so they shook hands. Ryan gripped his hand tighter than usual. Tension radiated from Ryan as much as it did from Clive. Why? Did Ryan like Eva? *His* Eva? Clive's insides twisted. He didn't want to know.

"We're leaving," Ryan said. Eva complied. Why? Ryan was her brother's friend, but what was he to her?

He stared at her, hoping she'd give some indication that she didn't want to leave with Ryan. But she didn't. Just like that Ryan took Eva away from him.

Clive came across her a few times in school after that night but each time he hid away from her. He didn't know what Ryan meant to her. And he didn't want to know. Because what if she thought of Ryan as more than simply *her brother's friend*?

Days passed. Months passed. Almost a year passed before his father had another one those office parties in their home, this time a few days before Christmas.

Once again, Clive saw Eva and didn't talk to her. He watched her as she stood with Ryan by the Christmas tree. Ryan chatted. She only nodded.

Something seemed different about her. It was her smile, or the lack of. Her eyes looked vacant. Her spirit and her radiance had diminished.

What's wrong, Eva?

As though she sensed him watching, she turned and caught his stare.

"And here's Clive." His father's large frame blocked his view of Eva. "Do you remember John Smith?"

He did not. And frankly, he couldn't care less about John Smith or anyone else except Eva for that matter. He wanted to be with Eva. Because seeing her sad made him sad. He would fix it. Whatever might have her bothered, he would fix it all.

"Hello, son." The burly Mr. Smith shook his hand. "You're a lot taller than I remember. Soon, you'll take over your father, and his business too perhaps?"

"Clive's not interested in what we do at Stanford. He wants to be a cop."

"Special Forces," Clive corrected.

"Ah, yes." His father grinned.

"I see. And how about you, Carter?"

Carter shrugged. "I don't know yet."

"I don't care what my boys choose to do, as long as they're happy," his father added.

Yes. Happy. The exact emotion neither Clive nor Eva shared at that moment. Eva's sadness haunted him. His insides tumbled. His reasoning for staying away from her for all those months no longer made sense. Why hadn't he already walked over to her and broken his silence? Unable to focus on the present conversation, he shifted uneasily on his feet. He wanted to get back to looking at her. Maybe tonight he would build up the courage to stop avoiding her.

His mother joined in on their conversation.

"Mrs. Stanford, it's so lovely to see you again. You have a very beautiful home," Mr. Smith said.

As mostly always, knowingly or not, his mother came to his rescue.

Seizing the opportunity, Clive sidestepped and veered back to the visual his father had blocked. He looked toward the Christmas tree. Eva wasn't there. He darted his gaze around the room for her. *Where did you go?*

"Outside," Carter whispered.

Clive gave the adults a quick glance, then left them to continue with their niceties. He tried hard to remain composed, regardless of how much his heart hurried. He snuck away from the group, from the room full of people, out into the garden where he found her.

Eva sat alone on a bench. Her gaze remained locked at the dark bay beyond.

Clive hadn't spoken to her for close to a year. Was this a good time to talk to her? Did she want to be alone? And if he would talk to her, what should he speak about? For one, he should definitely pretend like he hadn't woken up today dreaming about her with him in his bed, again. Like he hadn't wanted to kiss her every day since their first and only kiss. Like he didn't even know she'd come to the party. Like he hadn't thought she was the only one in the whole room full of people, though in truth, he couldn't take his eyes off her...because how could he...why should he?

She covered her face in her hands.

His insides twisted. *Is she...crying?*

Her soft sobs touched a nerve. His heart crumpled further.

He would do anything, *anything*, to make Eva smile *that* smile again. He took a deep shaky breath to ready himself and started to walk toward her.

She brought her hands down and stiffened. One moment she looked at him and in the next she looked away and wiped her tears. She didn't want him to see her that way. And he wouldn't want to make her any more uncomfortable than she already was. He slowed his steps. He should turn back. As he began to do just that, she looked at him and scooted over making space for him to join her. He stilled, and she smiled...*that* smile. He joined her on the bench.

Unlike earlier with Ryan, when he'd seen her only nodding to whatever *that guy* said, she actually talked to Clive, and they talked for a long time. Not about her troubles, but about everything else. And he didn't mind, because at least for the moment, she seemed to let go whatever had her bothered.

She smiled at him, a *real* smile. Once again, time and place didn't matter with Eva around. What had he thought, staying away from her all this while?

They watched the city lights that glimmered beyond the bay. They sat close enough that their hands touched. He curled his fingers around hers. She let him.

"Eva."

Ryan's voice made them both flinch. Clive didn't let go her hand. She didn't tug away either, until Ryan went on to say, "Your parents are looking for you. It's time to go home."

Once again, Clive stared after Eva as Ryan took her away from him. Ryan walked a little distance with her, then asked her to continue on, while he turned around and walked back to where Clive stood.

"You made her cry." Ryan spoke through gritted teeth.

What? "I did not." Clive's hands formed to fists by his sides. He'd never resented anything or anyone more than he resented Ryan.

"Then why does she look sad?"

Clive wished he knew why. But he'd wait for Eva to tell him. He couldn't pry. She eased up during that brief time they'd spent together tonight; he didn't have the heart to remind her about whatever had her grieved.

"What kind-a-guy makes a girl cry?"

He'd begrudged Ryan then. A surprising twinge of envy struck him even now while he watched Eva and Ryan approach. But, *she* loves *me*.

Eva had her head tilted down as she walked up the steep climb to her house. She hadn't noticed him yet, until Ryan said something. She looked at Ryan and laughed, and saw Clive, seated on middle of the five steps that led into her white Victorian. Her laugh morphed into a coy smile when her eyes met his. She kept her gaze steady, and once again, time and place didn't matter when Eva looked at him that way. Yes, *she loves me*.

But just as quickly, she darted a look to Ryan and back at him. Her expression questioned.

After his last encounter with Ryan at her grandpa's house in Napa, she'd most certainly concluded the tug between him and Ryan had worsened.

Tom had informed him that she'd dodged his offer to drive them where they wanted to go. He hoped she hadn't thought he would mind her going out with Ryan. Sure he didn't see eye to eye with Ryan on *certain* matters, but Ryan and Eva had known each other since childhood, and Clive would never disrupt their friendship.

So, for Eva's sake, Clive greeted him, "Ryan." He tried hard to smile but settled for a nod.

"Clive," Ryan uttered back, his expression unreadable. "See you around, Eva." He kissed her on the cheek, turned and walked back down the winding road.

Good. He didn't want to talk to Ryan any more than he already had.

Eva smiled endearingly as she climbed the steps toward him. Unable to hold back any longer, he stood, slid his hand into her hair and tugged her to his chest. "I missed you." He kissed her temple.

"I missed you." She tilted her head back, rose to her tiptoes and placed a light kiss against his lips.

He kissed her back. Their kiss was soft and warm. He wanted more of that kiss. He wanted more of her. He'd wanted her all day.

A cold gust of wind swept across the steps, making her shiver in his arms. He tightened their embrace.

"Let's go inside." He loosened his hold just enough for her to dig into her handbag for the key. She pulled it out and stared at it for a moment, then looked up at him. Her lips parted in surprise. Only now had she noticed he'd attached the small, rectangular, silver access card for his apartment to her key chain.

He kissed her on her cheek and something shifted in her expression. She looked as though he'd melted away all else, except this moment she shared with him. Did she have a good day?

He took the keys from her hand and opened the door. They walked into her house. He was there once before. What a memorable evening that had been.

Leaving him in the living space, she walked toward her kitchen, then stopped by a writing desk. Dropping her bag there, she dug into a miniature wicker basket and returned to him. "Sorry, I should have given this to you sooner." She handed him a spare key to her house. "Were you waiting outside for long?"

He should have replied, but more than that, he wanted to return to their kiss. Yes, he had waited for her for the longest fifteen minutes of his life. He had glanced at every person that walked past her house, hoping to see her. But none of that mattered now that she was with him. He pulled her close and slanted his mouth over hers.

After a long moment of kissing, he pulled back for a quick breath. "You are *so* tasty…and lemony."

"Pisco sour." She rushed a breathy answer and went back to kissing him. She missed him too. Had she longed for him as much as he had for her since they'd parted this morning?

As though she'd read his mind, she went on to say, "I needed to be with you Clive." She spoke between kisses. "I've wanted you all day," she whispered against his lips. "But you weren't there."

I wasn't there? "You went to my office?"

"Yes."

"When?"

"Noon." She looked puzzled. "Didn't Trish tell you?"

No, because he hadn't talked to her since he'd left for lunch with Silvia. He brushed her lips with his. She let him.

"I've been busy."

Just as he yearned to get to kiss again, she pulled back. He didn't understand why. He tugged her to him.

"Let go of me, Clive." She looked anywhere but at him.

What? Why? Something was wrong, *what did I say*? "What's wrong?"

She remained silent.

"Eva..." he cajoled. The depth of persuasion in his voice helped force her to meet his gaze. Creases formed between her eyebrows. And despite looking troubled, *damn she's hot*! He really should have more restraint. But what else could he think when she looked at him like she...*wanted him*?

Like she wanted to return to their kiss.

Like she wanted to rip off his clothes.

Did his imagination trick him to believe so, because that's all he had wanted all day?

"H-How was your day?" Her expression relaxed.

She might as well have told him to get his mind out of the gutter and that she wasn't going to answer his question. Why wouldn't she say what had her troubled? His jaw tightened. "Not good. I was at the FBI office."

"Oh."

He wished she'd say more, but she remained silent.

"Trevor says sorry."

She gave him a look and again tried to pull away. She forced against him with harder effort this time, but he didn't budge and continued to hold on to her. "You haven't answered me, Eva." He hadn't meant he'd let go of her if she did answer him, though.

She gave him *that* look, a look he knew well from having two sisters and a mother, and he knew better than to provoke her further when she gave him that look. He would return to his question later.

"How was your day?" He cleared his throat, skirting around the obvious, hoping to ease her into telling him what had her bothered.

"Busy." She gave him half a shrug. "Trevor and Jason talked to Uncle Dave, but you already know that."

He nodded. "I heard Dave didn't take it well."

"No, he didn't. I felt guilty at first, not having told him about FBI's involvement, but..." Her gaze dropped. He loosened his hold on her waist and brought one hand to cup her face, tilting her head gently to look at him.

She relaxed into him. Though eased that she did, he knew she wouldn't like the consequences of his

64

discussion with McKenzie. "They won't be following you anymore." He tried hard not to sound worried.

"Oh." She winced a little. "That's…good, right? Does that mean there's no threat from the informant anymore? Or whoever was following my father, or me for that matter?"

Unsure how she'd take what he would say next, he proceeded with caution. "It means we're going to set up security for you. A few bodyguards—"

"What? No."

He expected her to say that. "Eva…"

"No, Clive." Again, she tried to tug away from him. Again, he didn't let her.

Before he angered her further, and she'd kick him out of her house, he had to convince her that she needed protection and he was her only hope "Why not?"

"Well, why yes?" she fired back.

He would do anything to avoid worsening her already troubled mood, but he had no choice. "Because I don't want anything bad to happen to you, *damn it*." He took a step back and settled his hands on his hips.

Her expression shifted again, and if he doubted her intentions earlier, she definitely wanted him in that moment. She looked like she wanted to jump him, kiss him hot and wild and let her hands mess up his hair. And if she'd do any or all of that to him right then, he wouldn't protest. Because she looked too sexy in that button down white shirt, and that skirt that hugged her perfectly, and those heels. Yes, they could totally return to this conversation later, and maybe not until the morning. Because the way she looked at him right then…

"Nothing will happen to me."

Guess they were back to talking.

"Because you'll always be around, and when you aren't, I have Izzy and Allie."

"Izzy and Allie?" He threw his head back and laughed. She couldn't be serious, thinking her friends could protect her from…wait, *is she serious*?

Of course, she didn't consider his reaction all that amusing as she proceeded to contest, "Why not? We all have air horns and pepper sprays. I'm trained in self-defense and Izzy has a Taser."

"A Taser?" He continued to laugh. "For self-protection?"

"A-Among other things." She nodded, her infectious smile slow and difficult to conceal.

She was *so* cute right then, he could eat her alive.

"You know what, I don't want to know." He shook his head. "I've seen enough kinky stuff for the day."

Her mouth fell open.

Just the reaction he'd wanted to evoke. Good. They'd returned to being their usual selves; him teasing her, her stumbling at his every trick. Why do men ever joke about how difficult it is to understand women? He bit into his lip, the only way to contain the happiness from his triumph.

"With *Silvia*?"

Silvia? He sobered at that. Shocked at her unexpected comment, his breath caught.

"What?" he snapped. And did she not mean to say that out loud? Because, she grimaced, her eyes

66

shut tight. "Eva?" He really needed her to start talking.

"What?" Her eyes popped open.

"Silvia?"

"Yes." She inhaled and trembled a little as she did. "I saw her with you today."

"Silvia is not your problem." How could she still be bothered by Silvia?

"Like Ryan's not yours?"

"Ryan is not a problem for me." He sounded oddly unaffected given how grim he really felt after realizing what had her troubled. "Because I trust you."

"It's not *you* I don't trust." Her voice softened. "I was almost run over by a truck when I walked into oncoming traffic watching you and *her*…and…the look she gave me…*that* look…" Tears shimmered in her eyes.

He mumbled a curse. His heart ached. He tugged her to him. Surprisingly, she let him.

"I don't like her, Clive."

And there, she revealed what had her disturbed.

"Neither do I." He gazed into her brown, hazy eyes and willed her to believe him. "Silvia is *not* your problem. Not now, *not ever*." He tangled one hand into her hair, and circled the other around her waist. He held her close. He held her tight. "I thought we'd cleared this out already."

"Yes, we did." Her ear pressed against his chest.

He hoped she heard his heart battle for her. He hoped she'd know how much she meant to him over anyone else, especially Silvia. "Then where did I go wrong today?"

67

She pushed back slightly, until their eyes met.

"My past will catch up with me, *a lot*. But, it's my past, Eva. And you're my present, my future, and if you let me…you're my forever." If she'd thought the worst, he wouldn't let her. He would prove to her that her apprehensions were needless. And he wouldn't let this conversation take a nosedive, because there was no reason to, because he loved her more than he'd ever loved anyone and because he'd do anything to make her see that.

What might have crossed her mind since she'd seen Silvia and him?

Her eyes glazed.

What did she think now?

"Why did you meet her today?" She sounded softer than usual, as though she half-wished he wouldn't reply.

Given a choice, he would have eased the day's happenings to Eva.

Given a choice.

He brought her up to speed on the reason he'd been to the FBI office.

She went completely silent. Again.

She distanced her thoughts from him. Again.

Please, talk to me.

"I don't want security."

"Why not?"

"I don't want to be restricted if I don't have to be restricted."

His stomach curdled, because he disagreed. But he got that she wouldn't give up her freedom. He, of all people, could relate to her reluctance. Since the moment he had taken over the Stanford business from his brother, privacy had become a luxury of the past, and certainly forgone for the rest of his life.

Silence lingered between them again, until he gave in. "Fine, have it your way. But know that I'm only saying this because *you* want it this way. I'm still extremely unhappy with your decision."

And finally, *finally*... she gave him a sweet smile. "Thanks for understanding, Clive."

"I'll be worried sick for you all the time."

"Well, see, there's no reason for that. I'm not in any danger, am I?"

He didn't want to touch that. Because danger or not, she made him want to lock her away until they caught the rogue. And since that was obviously not an option... "I'll be with you whenever I can. When I'm not, would you let Tom take you wherever you need to go?"

"I said, *no* security."

"Tom is not security. You need someone to get you away from those reporters."

She opened her mouth to protest, but he didn't want to hear it, because he couldn't hold back any longer. He kissed her. Her words muffled by his mouth capturing hers with strong dominance. Surprisingly, she didn't hold back either. She responded with a matched desperation that he'd fantasized about all day.

He kissed her until he was once again in danger of pushing off their conversation until morning. Whether she saw it his way or not, he would do whatever it took to keep her free from harm.

He wouldn't let anything bad happen to Eva, especially so, after what happened with Olivia. He should have protected Olivia. He didn't. He should have stopped Olivia that night. He didn't. He should have at least warned Olivia. He didn't. And he could do nothing to reverse the consequences now.

He loved Olivia. Or so he'd thought until he met Eva again. What he had with Olivia was a strong connection, but what he had with Eva couldn't be compared with anyone or anything he'd ever loved before.

Eva was precious, Eva was his life…there never was and never could be a substitute for Eva. And if anything were to happen to her…

He broke their kiss and pulled back, his breath ragged. "There's no negotiating this, Eva. Tell me you'll let Tom drive you around."

Her breath shook. Otherwise, she remained silent. Was she not going to answer, again?

She rose on her tiptoes and slid her hands from his shoulders into his hair, just like he longed for her to do. Their faces neared. If he got anything right today, it would be that Eva was as hot for him as he was for her. He feared their argument would turn her away. Gladly, he was wrong.

He smiled. "Tom will drive you around then," he whispered against her lips.

She nodded lightly and moved in to kiss, but he held back, continuing to hover only an inch or two away.

"Say yes, Eva."

"Yes." Her voice was barely audible.

"Yes to what?" He tilted his head slightly back, making her unable to reach him to kiss.

"You're provoking me."

70

"You're encouraging me."

He continued to hold back.

"Yes to whatever. Now kiss me, damn it."

Chapter 8

His grin...*hot.*

His breath brushed her cheeks...*hot.*

His lips met hers...*hot.*

He fisted her hair and pulled her to him. He craved this too.

She shouldn't fight her longing anymore. Being away from him all day tortured her as it was.

He tasted her with decadent leisure. The way he took over the kiss, he'd vanished all the horrid thoughts from her day. Slowly, yet forcefully, he quenched the hunger she'd carried since morning, from the moment she had seen him walk out of Stanford Tower, *with Silvia.*

And before she knew it, they peeled off each other's clothes, him gentler than her. A button ricocheted off the hardwood. His mouth curved in a smile. "What got you this eager?"

"You did."

His lust-filled gaze held hers, exciting her without words. He was as turned on by her as she was by him.

"Bedroom?" he asked, gruff and slightly above a whisper…*hot*.

It would be the first time they'd spend the night at her place. A quick signal with her finger was all she could manage. She moaned into his mouth when they got back to their heated kiss. She let him sweep her away to her bed. Gently, he tossed her on to the mattress. He got on top of her…and…"Eva…" The way her name rolled off his lips…*hot*.

Eva woke the next morning to her erotic fantasy, *her* Clive. A routine she loved. In the night she'd sleep cocooned against his strong body, by morning he'd lay partially on his stomach. Her gaze traveled over his sculpted arms and bare back. The sheet had drifted down to his hips showing off his…*pants*? He slept *in his trousers*?

Then it all rushed back. How tenderly he'd consoled her. He cared for their relationship. He cared for her well-being. He cared *for her*.

And she…

She cringed, her eyes tightly shut.

She'd gone off to sleep…*while they were making out.*

His light snore brought her to flutter her eyes open. She hushed the temptation to wake him up to her pleasuring him. He looked peaceful. She couldn't disturb him. She crept out of the bed, freshened herself and tiptoed out of the room.

In the living room, she found his brown leather weekender. She opened to peek. He'd brought along a few of his things. She smiled. Their relationship had progressed far. She hung his clothes in her closet and set his toiletries bag on the bathroom vanity. Leaving him to sleep, she walked to her kitchen and made herself some tea.

The first sip stimulated her mind, making her look forward to a lovely day. The second sip, however, reminded her of the conversation she had with Ryan, about Olivia, Clive's first girlfriend. What luck she didn't bring that up last night in her inebriated state. Should she speak to Clive about Olivia, or should she wait for him to tell her?

By the time she finished her tea, she'd made her decision. Had Clive wanted her to know about Olivia, he would have told her already. But he hadn't. So she'd wait until he did.

She sighed, adding one more secret to the ever piling list. It had only neared eight in the morning, and she'd sighed a few times already. She would find it difficult to keep a secret such as that from Clive. Especially because the harder she tried not to think about Clive's past, she only thought about his past. She must mute yesterday's clatter from her mind. She must suppress it all before Clive woke. And the only way to do that…

A brisk whisking of eggs in a stainless steel bowl erased the innumerable frustrations and apprehensions that had plagued her. Now more than ever, a comfortable warmth returned to her heart from having at least one avocation that took her mind off almost anything.

The aroma of lavender and milk chocolate melting in a double boiler, coffee she had freshly ground to brew, steeping jasmine tea, and the orange she had peeled…shed away all other thoughts except these moments she spent in her kitchen.

Minutes later, Clive joined her. He stood shirtless but wore a pair of black silk lounge pants she had picked out of his weekender and left for him on the bed. He caught her to him and placed a tight kiss to her lips.

"I want to take you away someplace, Eva. Away from work, computers, cell phones…just you and me."

"I want that too." She smiled.

"This weekend then?"

She loved spontaneous getaway plans. "Where are we going?"

"It's a surprise."

"What do I pack?"

"Nothing."

"Nothing?"

"It will be just you and me, so yeah, *nothing*."

"Not even my toothbrush?"

"Nothing."

"Well, OK then." She loved anticipating the surprise as much as its revelation. She kissed him lightly on his lips. He kissed her back, his kiss stronger, hotter, wetter and longer than hers.

"The way you are looking at me right now, as though nothing and no one else matters, *I love this look*. I'm addicted to this look." He went back to kissing her.

His words and the thoroughness of his kiss had a predictable effect on her body. Her heart leapt. Her toes curled. Her mind and her body belonged to him. *She* belonged to him. Just as much as he was hers. Despite Silvia. Despite Olivia. Despite any other woman in his life before her.

The coffee machine beeped. Breathless, they pulled back.

"Coffee?"

"Yes, please."

"Let go, Clive." She laughed.

He held on to her for a long moment before loosening his hold.

She clicked a button on the Barista machine and brewed him a cappuccino. Handing him his cup, she led him to the breakfast table by the window.

Beyond the window, beyond the patio, blue bay glittered in the morning sun. He admired the view, although not of the bay, but of the breakfast she'd laid out. "You made this?"

She nodded. "Uh-huh, double chocolate, pistachio, lime pancakes."

He rounded the table and set his coffee cup onto it.

"I—It's beautiful." He pulled his phone from his pants pocket and took a picture of his plate. She had mesmerized many with her presentation skills, but to see Clive react to her creation was a delight of its own. She dragged out a chair and took a seat.

He tapped his phone a few times, then set it on the table between them and took a seat.

"Go on, dig in."

"It's too pretty to eat, but so are you." He brought her hand to his lips and placed a light kiss.

He shoved a forkful of the breakfast into his mouth. She focused on his expression to gauge his reaction.

He chewed, slowly. He swallowed, slowly. He met her gaze, slowly. "Wow. It just melted in my mouth ...it's..."

Speechless.

She too started to eat, umm...*yes, wow*.

Seconds later, his phone screen lit up with a message from Trevor. *Bastard*. Clive's lips curved, smug. His slid his phone into his pants pocket.

"You do plan on going back to being a chef again, right?"

Sure, she'd thought about returning to pursuing her dream someday, but given the present circumstance... "I don't think I can."

"Why not?" He took a sip of his coffee.

She shrugged slightly. "It's too much already...this company...all its problems..."

"I'll take care of the company for you," he stated with the effortless confidence of a self-assured powerful businessman.

How easy he'd made it seem to command a business like hers. Could she ever be that fearless about leading S. F. Designs?

She set her fork and knife onto the plate. She leaned back in her chair, and traced her fingers around the rim of her teacup.

"Eva?"

She sighed. *Again*. "Be right back." She pushed her chair back and rose. He didn't move, but he watched her. She went to her writing desk to find her handbag and brought back the letter her father had left her.

"What do you make of this?" She handed him the envelope.

He read it. Like she had, he too flipped it over. He seemed as puzzled as her, the first time and all the many times after that she had read the note.

"That's all there is. Unbelievable right?" She shook her head.

His gaze caught hers. His confidence shone again. "Your father didn't know you'd have me."

No, he didn't. Her heart wrenched that he didn't. She imagined the gleam in her father's eyes, the thrill in his smile, when he would have found out about Clive and her. Her father liked Clive, her uncle had mentioned to her a few times.

"What am I supposed to do now?"

"Nothing different." Determination simmered under his sullen tone. "Continue reaching out to new clients, keep things moving. Leave the informant to the FBI. They're on the case, although not as aggressively as before, they're still looking for leads."

"What about my uncle?"

He ran his teeth over his lower lip. "Dave's involved somehow, but there isn't enough evidence, *yet*, to make a case against him. All you can do is stay vigilant and try not to raise suspicion."

A heavy sunken feeling settled deep in her stomach. "How am I to not trust my uncle? I mean, pancakes, clearly no mentor needed, but leading the company without my uncle…"

"You have me." Clive reached across the table and held her hand in his. "I'll *never* let you fail. *You have me.*"

Once again, his assurance, the power in his expression, the determination in his voice gave her strength. Her gaze dropped to stare at the table between them.

"Eva?"

She forced a small smile and nodded. "Thank you."

He locked his gaze with hers, looking as though attempting to read her thoughts. "Busy day today?"

"In the morning, yes, and in the afternoon I'm meeting Claire and Mila for the *In Trend* article."

"Meet me for lunch then. My office. Noon?"

Chapter 9

"Do you ever get bored of this view?" John Smith, Clive's father's lawyer, gawked at the bay beyond Clive's office window.

"I'm in awe every day I walk into this office."

They watched a long container ship pass from under the Bay Bridge toward the Oakland docks.

"This is prime property. I still remember the day your father bought this building." John turned to face Clive. His chubby face dimpled when he smiled. "You were a little boy then. And look at you now. Owner of Stanford. You've done well, son." He patted Clive's arm, then walked over and sat on the couch.

Clive followed him with heavy footsteps and sank into a seat opposite him. His world had come to a halt when he'd learnt the reason John had wanted to meet him today. "After all these years, who could want to re-investigate Olivia's death? It can't be her family. They knew she was troubled."

"That's what the evidence points to, anyway." John shifted deeper into the seat. "So, I say, let them rehash it. There's not much else left to investigate." He paused as though he questioned the validity of his statement. He stared at Clive in silence.

Clive's mood darkened that John paused at all. *I killed her John. Just say it.*

"I know what you're thinking, Clive. I knew it then. I know it now. You didn't kill her."

"Then why the hesitation?"

He shook his head. "There's no hesitation. We were thorough. There's nothing else they can find that we haven't already."

"Then why are you here*?" What is it that you haven't told me yet*?

John exhaled audibly before he spoke. "It's not a police investigation. The case is still officially closed. We think it's a reporter."

"You think? You're not sure."

"We don't know which news agency is going through all this trouble. All we know for now is that someone is asking a lot of questions."

The timing of the investigation just didn't fit. "I'm beginning to think this is not related to Olivia at all."

John gave him a bleak smile. "Inherited your father's enemies too, have you?"

Yes, Stanford Enterprise did have enemies. But none like the informant, who also happened to be the only person Clive suspected over this new turn of events.

He had used Silvia to tear Eva and Clive apart. *Unsuccessfully.* What would stop him from attempting to bring Clive's long buried past to light? Especially the wounds Clive had only shared with a few people, and Eva wasn't one of them, *yet*.

Clive couldn't bring himself to reveal his past to Eva. He quivered from self-hate each time he recollected his last encounter with Olivia. Her grim expression that night, her battered face, her alcohol-ridden breath…every second of those final moments he'd spent with Olivia would haunt him for life. He would never forgive himself for what he let happen to her, the girl he'd once thought he loved.

"The reporter is using a private investigator, Ryan Cohen."

Ryan…

Ryan resented him over his relationship with Eva, but looking for kinks in Olivia's death hit a new low, even for him.

"You know the guy?"

"I'll deal with Ryan—" Before he could say further, the buzzer beeped, and Trish announced that Claire wanted to see him.

"I suggest we keep this hushed for now, Clive."

Seconds later, Claire walked into his office. Clive hugged his little sister. She looked jubilant, as always, until she saw John.

"John, wow, it's been a while." They shook hands. She darted Clive a *why is he here* look.

"Yes, it has. I saw you at the Met Gala. Clive mentioned you were building your clientele, so I thought I should leave you to socialize."

"Thank you. Yes, I got a lot of leads that evening. Thanks to Eva, especially." She grinned. "She's Clive's girlfriend. Have you met?"

"No, we haven't met." He looked to Clive. "You should come over one of these days. Martha is obsessed with celebrity news. She'll be delighted to meet Eva." John stood from the couch. "I'll let you know a day that works." He shook hands with Clive and then with Claire. "It was wonderful to see you again, Claire."

The moment the door closed behind John, Claire folded her arms across her chest. "*Why* was he here? Is it about Olivia?"

"Why are *you* here? Shouldn't you be at your photo shoot?"

"I should be, but I wanted to stop by to say hello and see what you were up to. And what luck I did, because, really, Clive…is this about Olivia?"

"Drop it, Claire."

"Fine. I'm also here to ask if you'll ever get Eva and mom introduced. Mom's really unhappy that you haven't already."

His mother worried for him, so did his siblings and his father. Since Olivia, they'd longed for him to find that special someone again. Someone who wouldn't remind them of Olivia.

Chapter 10

At noon, Trish buzzed Eva into Clive's office. "He might be on a call," she informed.

Eva entered the room, and the door automatically closed silently after her. Clive stood by the floor to ceiling, glass wall overlooking the cityscape and the bay. His back to her, his hands shoved into his pant pockets, he spoke into the mouthpiece of a headphone. "Fix it."

Something about the way he spoke. He sounded angry somehow.

He casually turned around and caught her gaze. His expression reset from a frown to being pleasantly aware of her presence. His sensual eyes raked her length, intensifying the lingering heated anticipation she'd carried from the moment he had zipped her blush lace sheath dress this morning. *Would rather be unzipping, Eva.*

Unwilling to suppress her need for him any longer, she unzipped her dress as she walked toward him. After letting it fall to the floor, she hopped up to sit on his desk.

His eyes set on her. "Get it done." He removed the headset and tossed it onto his desk.

"Eva." The way he said her name, her insides did a quick leap. He pushed an inconspicuous button on his desk phone, and she heard a light click. He'd latched the door.

"This has been my fantasy since I saw you that day in the elevator. You here…like this…eager for me…" The low gruffness in his voice sent heated sensual waves through her.

It's been my fantasy too.

She nestled her hands around his neck and pulled him closer. She took his mouth in a heated, wet, hungry kiss. One moment he groaned a wild sound into her mouth, and the next, he'd taken over the kiss. His hands rushed to grip her hair. That was his thing, to grip her hair like that. He caressed her ears, felt down her neck, her collarbone…he tugged down the cups of her bra. He squeezed and teased while he continued to kiss her with a rough, deprived, aggressive want. His teeth bruised her lips, sending an electrified signal to her core.

He pulled back, just for a moment, and looked at her. His breath sped, and so did hers. He smelled *so* wild, *so* good. The lust in his expression amplified the desire his nimble fingers had roused as he rolled and tugged her hardened nipples.

"You want me. Right here, in my office."

"On your desk."

"Fantasy is one thing, but this is not something I'd ever do at work."

Of course not, and neither would she, for that matter. But with Clive… "With me?"

"You're the only one."

He knew his past bothered her, and he conveyed how insignificant his ethical dilemma stood in comparison. Typical Clive. He'd set her at ease before all else.

Touched by the sincerity of his words, she whispered, "Thank you."

"Thank you, Eva. I really needed this today."

Why especially today?

His hand slid beneath the edge of her thong and touched her exactly the way she craved for him to touch her. Her gasp from their contact brought a wicked smile to his gorgeous face.

"And we're only getting started." His playfulness fed into her pleading need, making her desperate to be sexed by her lover.

He pumped two fingers into her, and she tightened around him. His eyes scorched with desire as he watched her. His thumb viciously rubbed her clit, his fingers sliding in and out. The more he touched, the wetter she got. Waves of pleasure gathered restlessly, waiting to be dispersed where his thumb met her clit.

"I want you…now." She freed the button on his fly and unzipped, then pushed down his pants and circled him in her palm, deliberately, tenderly. He groaned. He was hot, smooth, ready…*for her*.

He slipped his hands around her. Cupping her behind, he pulled down her thong. He lifted her off the desk, then sat on his chair and pushed the armrests away for her to straddle him.

"Take me then." He leaned his head against the seat back to look at her.

She placed her hands on his shoulders and rose. His magnificent erection brushed between her legs. Her insides throbbed simply from that feeling. He positioned himself, and she lowered, taking more of him until she had stretched to a point of pain...*pleasurable pain*.

"You feel *so* good, Eva." His voice, almost a desperate plea for her to *take him*. She didn't know what roused her more, his words or the return of his thumb to her clit. She clenched her thighs and lifted, sliding over him. The more she undulated the more he thickened. He mouthed her breasts surprisingly gently. His hands gripped her hips, angling her and moving her along his length. She rolled her hips, over and over until she exhaled...she moaned...she clenched, on the verge of her approaching release.

He mumbled something, but she lost all focus as if she'd ached far too long for him to make her feel that way. He angled her hips farther, pushing him in deeper. Her muscles tightened, her nerves tingled. He hastened the pace of his thumb and ultimately shattered and freed her.

Weak and spent, she leaned her head against the side of his face. He picked her up with him, laid her carefully onto the desk and continued to move with deliberate commanding strokes. His strong hands held her hips in place to meet his every dive. The carnal authority of his expression built her up again. A few more intentional thrusts and he took her with him. Their minds and bodies became one as they clung to each other.

Chapter 11

Her body still hummed from being with Clive when she walked into the all white dressing room at the *In Trend* magazine office. Several vanity mirrors, each rimmed by numerous bright light bulbs, covered one wall. Wearing white bathrobes and seated in their makeup chairs, Claire and Mila chatted with a heavyset woman, dressed all in black and decked in beaded jewelry.

When Eva entered the room, Claire and Mila sprung out of their chairs to hug her.

"Thank for doing this for us, Eva."

"Thank you more. I can't imagine how I'd have dressed for the gala without your help."

They introduced her to Mystique, an astrologer, who was also there to get her picture taken for the monthly column she wrote in *In Trend*. Her choice of clothing indicated her prediction for the month. *Dark and dangerous* for all signs, she explained.

Mystique wore numerous rings. Eva's gaze especially caught on the oval-shaped, transparent one on her middle finger. Blood red liquid moved around when Mystique moved her hand.

"You a believer, Eva?" Mystique asked.

"No. I'm not. Sorry, no offense." She laughed.

"Oh, that's OK. I get that all the time. But believe it or not, I've changed a lot of lives for the better."

"Yes, you have." Mila grinned. "I read your article every month and follow your every advice. It always works."

The dressing room door opened, and a youthful man dressed in a black T-shirt and jeans peeked in. "You ready?"

"I sure am." Mystique rose from her chair and checked herself in the mirror. "Nice to meet you ladies. And Eva, give me a chance to turn you into a believer, will you?"

"Why not?" Eva shrugged.

They said their goodbyes, and Mystique left the room.

One of the makeup artists handed Eva a plush white bathrobe wrapped like a present with a pink satin bow. Moments later, Eva too began to get her hair and makeup done.

"Nice blush, by the way," Mila said.

Blush? She stared at her face reflected in the mirror in front of her and *oh…* "Thanks." She left it at that. She still tingled from her hot and heavy session with Clive.

By the time they were halfway done with their hair, a combination of purple and pink jumbo curlers crowned their hair. Izzy brought Kevin, the photographer, to meet them. Kevin, too, wore a black T-shirt and jeans. He'd knotted his hair back into a miniature twist. As if the room wasn't bright enough, Kevin switched on two lighting umbrellas and placed them a few feet away from each other.

Like Izzy had mentioned, Kevin brought a couple of bottles of homemade honey wine. Such an easy drink, that wine, and before they knew it, they'd downed the first bottle. He opened another.

The room door opened again, and the guy who'd taken Mystique away peeked in. "You ready?"

"Not yet, Larry. Come back later." Kevin waved him off and shut the door after him.

They laughed and chatted, and Eva didn't realize until she'd heard a series of clicks that Kevin had photographed them all that time. *He'll take your picture before you even know it.*

"OK, where's that holy-grail-of-a-dress?" Kevin asked.

"Right here." Izzy walked to a metal rack of hanging clothes. She picked out the pink dress Eva had worn on the gala night and brought it to Eva.

Just as Eva took the dress from Izzy, Mila walked across to grab her drink.

And... Mila's four-inch stiletto heel tore an enormous gash in the dress.

They gasped.

They glared at the tear.

Then...they looked at Kevin. Click. Click. Click.

Slowly, Kevin brought down his camera. His expression remained stark, as he stared at the dress.

He blinked a few times, turned around and walked out of the room, shutting the door after him.

"H—He gets like that sometimes, don't worry about it," Izzy comforted, yet continued to grimace while she too stared at the dress. "This article needs to go out soon, Eva. If you don't mind, we'll have to find you something else to wear." She indicated the metal rack full of designer clothes.

The room door opened, and heads turned to see if it was Kevin.

"You ready?" Larry peeked in.

"NO!"

He flinched and quickly shut the door.

"Oh. My. God." Mila's eyebrows came together. "I am *so* sorry, Eva."

"It's OK. Don't worry about it. It's only a dress."

"Yeah," Claire added. "And there are many others here." She moved one dress after another on the metal rack as she perused each before moving to the next.

"Exactly." Eva smiled, but Mila did not, so Eva continued, "A-And we can fix this." Not like she knew anything about sewing. "I think…" She pulled up the torn cloth to patch the gash. "See, it's barely even noticeable." Not really, because, *God that looked terrible*! She tried not to wince.

She glanced at Claire.

Claire shook her head.

She glanced at Izzy.

Her lips pressed together, Izzy tried hard to contain her laughter.

Eva started to giggle, and they cracked up laughing.

After the interview, Eva and Claire sat in the *In Trend* lobby while they waited for Mila to return from the dressing room.

"About that cover picture, should we come back another day?"

"Yeah, I think so." Izzy said. "I really do want Kevin to take that photo, you know. Let me check on his availability." She left to talk to the woman behind the reception desk.

"Eva…" Claire cleared her throat. "I have something to ask, and I hope you won't mind. And… you don't have to answer if you don't want to."

"Please, go ahead."

"Are you…and Clive…doing OK?"

What? "Yes, why?"

"I went to see him before I came here. He seemed…distracted."

Of course, he seemed that way, after all he'd waited for Eva. She smiled. But, *fix it*, he'd said. Fix what? *Get it done*, he'd said. Get what done? "Your brother is a busy man."

"Yeah, *that* he is." She rolled her eyes. "But, that wasn't it. I think it was John. It was odd that he met him today, you know?"

Not really. "Who's John?"

"Oh yeah, you two haven't met. But you must have heard about him from Clive. You know John, the lawyer who helped him with Olivia."

Eva blinked, unable to explain to Claire that Clive hadn't spoken to her about Olivia yet. Nor had he spoken to her about John.

Claire gasped. "He hasn't told you about Olivia, has he?" She brought a hand to her mouth.

Should she tell her she knew? But what would she say if Claire asked how she had come to find out about Olivia?

"Please, don't tell Clive I told you about Olivia." Claire bit into her lower lip.

"I won't."

"What was I thinking? I'm blaming Kevin's alcohol for this." She bit her lip again. "Is it all right if we don't talk about Olivia then?"

"It's all right." Eva forced a smile. Well, not entirely all right, because Eva brimmed with curiosity to know Claire's version of the events.

Claire smiled. "I'm glad it's going well between you and Clive. He's only had one serious relationship in the past, so we worry for him, you know?"

She worried for him too. From what she'd heard from Ryan, it had to have been difficult for Clive to move on after Olivia. Why hadn't Clive talked to her about Olivia?

Chapter 12

Twelve years ago…

"What do you think?"

Clive looked at the photographs Olivia had spread out on his bed. "Stunning." He picked one up. She looked like a fairy in her outfit. Olivia was a budding gymnast. She'd already made it to sports news and trained to compete at a National level next season.

"I look fat, don't I? In that one, especially."

He peered at the photograph she'd pointed to, and the only word that crossed his mind, *beautiful*. Why would she ever doubt her looks? "You look perfect."

"Thomas said I looked fat."

"Thomas is an idiot."

She gave him a look. "Thomas is a professional photographer."

"And also an idiot."

"He's going to make me a star, Clive"

"You already are a star, all by yourself. He's using you to get ahead, that's really all he's doing."

"You doubt him a lot and he hasn't done anything wrong."

She always defended Thomas.

"You know what I think, you love me, and you're jealous." She began to stack the photographs.

"Yes I love you. And yes, I'm jealous of anyone who spends more time with you than I do on any given day."

"He's going to send these pictures to several magazines and news channels tomorrow." She grinned and covered her mouth as though to contain her thrill. "I cannot believe this is happening, Clive. Can't you forget about Thomas for a while and just be happy for me?"

He pulled her to him and gave her a chaste kiss. "I'm more than happy for you. Buy you dinner to celebrate?"

"OK, but I only want a smoothie."

"A smoothie is not dinner."

"I have to look good for tomorrow's try out. Thomas wants to re-take some of these." She stared at one photo in particular, the one she thought she looked fat.

Thomas…

"How about Sushi?"

Minutes later, they walked to a nearby sushi restaurant. As they waited to cross the street, Olivia's head turned away from him and remained turned.

"What time is your try out tomorrow?"

95

She didn't answer, so Clive looked in the direction she had. In the distance appeared a faint outline of a man dressed all in black and nearly unnoticeable as he stood in exactly the shadow the dim street lamp didn't light. He lit up a cigarette, and that's when Clive caught his gaze. Clive's gut twisted at the way the man stared at Olivia.

He tightened his hold on her hand. "Do you know that guy?"

"Not particularly." She looked straight ahead of her and began to walk.

He squeezed her hand making her look up at him.

She exhaled. "Jessica buys from him."

Jessica, Olivia's best friend, lived on the edge. Drugs floated plenty at those parties she had in her house when her parents were away. Like Clive, Jessica knew her limits. They had fun in moderation. They'd made Olivia try too. And what a bad idea that had been. She'd passed out at her first inhale. It was the scariest five minutes, until she finally regained consciousness.

For a long time after, Olivia refused to do drugs again, for which Clive was thankful. She aimed to be a world famous gymnast and wouldn't jeopardize years of training. Clive admired her willfulness. He loved her for it.

All the more reason why that man's stare troubled Clive. "You went with her to buy?"

"Once."

How had he never before questioned where Jessica got her drugs? "He could be dangerous, Olivia."

"I didn't know we were going for a pick up. I almost fought with Jessica about it."

He held open the door to the restaurant letting her walk in first. "It was one time and one time only. So can we drop it, please? We're here to celebrate, remember?"

Olivia ate little. Thomas's comment bothered her, regardless of what Clive said about her photographs. He should have known. Olivia wasn't one to budge.

Chapter 13

Clive steered the car over the highway that curved along rough surf beaches and rock face cliffs.

"Look at all those kites!" Eva rolled down the passenger side window. Her hair moved erratically from the uneven breeze that blew in. Innumerable kites of various shapes, sizes and colors, from a dragonfly, to a mermaid, to a shrimp dotted the blue California sky.

"Aww…Nemo."

"Have you ever flown a kite?"

"No, never, but I'd love to."

Half an hour later, Eva and Clive's kites strained against the strong coastal breeze. Hers was a colorful butterfly, and his a blue quadrilateral. The longer the tail, the better for this sort of wind, she learned. They soared her kite first, and then his. They sat on the white sand beach, on a blanket he'd pulled from the trunk of his car. Surfers waded the tide in expert precision. Occasional seagulls clamored along the winds.

Eva cleared all negativity from her thoughts, her neurosis, about her father's note, about the informant, about her uncle, about Olivia... at least for the moment.

She laid flat on her back. Her gaze followed the numerous kites and one airplane that drew streaks of white contrails in the clear sky. Clive laid on his side facing her. He held his head up with one hand and played with a tendril of her hair with the other.

"Do you surf?" she asked.

"Yes. Less now than I did during my college years though. Do you?"

"No."

By now, she'd ogled Clive enough to guide a sculptor to carve him to perfection. Yet, she found herself checking him out as though looking at him for the first time.

Clive, *the surfer*. Tanned, chiseled body. Board shorts. Holding a surfboard in those strong biceped arms. *Biceped*? Was that even a word? *Whatever*. Windward hair. Bluish-green ocean eyes...*Hot. Hot. Hot*.

"Thinking dirty thoughts, Eva?" He leaned in and placed a light kiss on her lips. His breath, fresh and seductive, and the fervor with which he said her name added to her already pulsing senses. Her want for him increased, instantly, exponentially.

"Always."

"Good," he stated simply, grinning...*that* grin, she lost her focus again.

"Can't wait to see you surf." She steadied her thoughts.

"You could now if you'd like, but only if you'll join me."

Join him? She blinked. She shivered imagining herself in a four foot swimming pool, let alone the sea. Though she knew how to swim, and there was a time when she'd swam fearlessly, regardless of the depth of the water, the last time she'd ever swam was the time she'd nearly drowned in the lake by her grandpa's house, when Ryan had come to her rescue. A familiar tremble shot down her body. Her skin heated. Her stomach churned. Her mouth grew dry. *Breathe, Evie. Breathe.* Her grandpa's compelling words echoed in her mind. She breathed a couple of deep breaths and slowly alleviated her anxiety.

So, no, she didn't want to surf. *Ever.* Just like she didn't want to swim. *Ever.* View of the ocean, *fine.* Thunderous waves crashing onto the beach, like they did now, *fine.* And Clive surfing…*so…so fine!* Because…look at him. Her vivid fantasy returned, and just as simply, all her fears vanished. She stayed entranced, until Clive shook his head and started to laugh.

"W-What?" *Shit.* Did she speak her fantasy out loud?

She side-flicked her eyes to dodge his penetrating gaze. But whom was she kidding? Her betraying heart swiftly lured her back to Clive. Where were her sunglasses when she needed them? On the blanket, behind him, he'd taken them off, because *I want to see your eyes, Eva.*

"Dirty thoughts," he said with mirth, and then asked, deadpan, "Do you swim?"

Do I swim? Really? Why were they still talking? He knew where her mind was at that moment, and at every moment since they'd left home that morning. Then why did he ignore her obvious lust? Unless…he'd stalled on purpose? She narrowed her eyes. His eyebrows rose a little, and he looked entertained. Yes, he'd stalled, on purpose.

"Yes," she too replied, deadpan.

He grinned at her plight. He cleared his throat. "And yet you're scared of water." He circled the tendril of her hair around his finger.

How did he know?

A slight glint in his eyes told her she'd silently confirmed his guess. Humor vanished from his expression. His jaw clenched. He let go of her hair, cupped her face with his warm hand and stroked her cheek. "What happened?"

She told him. He didn't mind her talking about Ryan, which was a relief, but would he take it just as easily if she told him about the one time they'd kissed? Should she ever tell him about it? Clive and her weren't together then. And speaking of past relationships, he had yet to tell her about Olivia.

As fast as that thought crossed her mind, it fled again, because she grew distracted by Clive's tender touch. His thumb now brushed sensually over her lips.

"OK, no surfing or swimming." His gaze focused intently on hers.

And just like that all else around her turned hazy, only Clive and the excitement he'd incited prevailed. "What do you want to do then?"

"Same thing *you've* wanted to do all this while." He rolled on top of her.

She loved his mindreading skills. They always came into action at the perfect time. The sensations he'd already provoked amplified by the weight of his body, his leisurely touch, and the desire in his eyes…

She brought her hands around his back. His mouth slanted over hers. Their lips met slowly at first, but the longer they kissed, the hungrier they became.

His tongue did all the tricks she loved. He gripped her hair with one hand and caressed down her body with the other. Despite her clothing, willfully he awakened every inch of her skin, from her breast to her waist to her hip, where he now gripped.

"Clive." She whispered, breathless, while he continued to trace soft kisses along her jawline to the side of her neck.

"Hmm…" He nibbled on her ear, and her body rushed into a quick shiver.

She gasped and laughed.

"What?" he whispered by her ear, causing another wave of tingling.

"We're on a beach…a *public* beach."

He stilled. He stared, almost invasive. Then his expression sobered and he rolled off her. They lay there for a long moment or two. She gazed at the sky. The kites fluttered. The airplane had left the sky and the lines it left in its wake dispersed into foggy waves.

"Ready to go?" He sounded serious and gruff.

"Yes." She didn't bother holding back her grin, because, what ever happened to his stalling?

He got up, shaking his head and laughing. "I'll have to pick up a new workout routine just to keep up with your *needs*, Eva."

"Don't see how that's bad for you."

He held his hand out for her and pulled her up.

They reeled down the kites and minutes later arrived at a vacation villa overlooking the ocean that Clive had rented for the weekend.

She gawked in awe at the spectacular view. The setting sun reflected off the now orange sea, while a few cruise ships floated on the horizon.

He hugged her from behind. "We can always come back," he whispered, placing a light kiss on her shoulder before nuzzling her neck. They watched the sunset.

"Dinner?"

Dinner? He returned to stalling, *again*? She turned around in his arms to face him and glared.

"I'm not stopping once we start."

Her insides leapt at his fervent tone. How could she eat when she was that turned on?

They walked over to the patio table. Clive removed the dome shaped lids from the heated plates already set for them with food.

"Smells delicious."

"Thai. Resort's specialty."

Though the food was delicious, she ate little, she drank little, and so did he. They both wanted one thing and one thing only. So, she got up from her chair.

"Where you going?"

"To the Jacuzzi." Keeping her gaze connected with his, she began to pull down the shoulder straps of her romper, slowly, seductively, and purposefully. He leaned back in his chair and watched as the fabric slipped down her shoulders, then her chest, revealing her black satin lace bra. She loved how quickly his expression turned dark. Her choice of lingerie was no fluke. She knew he liked her in lace, especially when it barely covered her.

His gaze, heated, followed as she pushed the romper down her legs, letting it slip to her toes. Just when she was about to undo her bra, he reached for her, and carried her to the bedroom. Of course, she didn't complain, though warm water strategically jetting to soothe her tightened nerves sounded like a great idea, the satisfaction from which could come nowhere close to the gratification that bolted through her with Clive. His seizing hands, his skillful mouth, his stubbled jaw, teased along her neck to her heavy, needy breasts, down to her stomach, to between her legs...

She longed for this all day, she'd longed for Clive.

"I wish I could take you with me." Clive threw a T-shirt into his suitcase.

He had to be in Miami for the rest of the week, and they would meet again, over the weekend, in New York. Five days without Clive...*five mornings, five afternoons, five evenings, five nights...without* Clive. Her heart drowned in pain just seeing him pack, how could she be without him for five whole days?

"I wish it too." Emotions welled. Her throat got scratchy.

He looked heartbroken too. If it had to be more difficult for the one who's left behind than for the one leaving, it most definitely didn't seem that way with Clive. He longed for her too.

"Have Tom take you wherever you need to go. And if anything, anything at all, out of the ordinary happens, you tell me right away. Please, Eva."

Chapter 14

Twelve years ago…

It had been a few months since he'd taken Olivia to that sushi restaurant to celebrate.

How much she'd changed since. He'd changed too. Who could have imagined the downward spiral Olivia's life would take once she met Thomas? Who could have imagined she would lose track of her goals? Who could have imagined she would become a drug addict? Who could have imagined Clive and her would break up and also make up so many times?

They argued, a lot. He wanted her to go to a rehab. She didn't see the need for that. He wanted her to avoid Thomas. She didn't see the need for that. He wanted to reach out to her family to help her. That angered her the most. "All they want is for me to be famous, Clive. They don't love me like your family loves you."

He didn't understand why she would think of her family that way. The few times he'd met them, they seemed genuinely affable.

"But *I* love you. And I don't want to lose you."

"Well…I don't love you," she finished.

She probably wasn't thinking straight. After all, she was once again heavily doped from whatever drug she'd injected. But something in her expression told him she'd meant every word.

His fear was realized when she went on to worsen the stab. "The constant pressure, from my family, from the public, from you…"

"From me?"

"Yes, *you*. You're suffocating me, Clive. What I choose to do with my life is my choice. And you don't seem to get that. Thomas is the only one who truly understands me."

They broke up that night once and for all.

Clive didn't hear from Olivia for weeks, until one evening his phone flashed with an incoming call from her.

He hadn't erased her number or her pictures from his phone yet. They weren't together, but…he still missed her.

"You need to come get her," husky manly voice spoke through Olivia's phone.

Guess she hadn't erased from her phone either. After all that talk about how only Thomas understood her, she still had Clive on speed dial, and as her emergency contact.

Clive arrived at a dingy hidden bar. He couldn't believe they'd let her into that joint. He found her unconscious in one of the restroom stalls. A nearly empty bottle of alcohol stood next to her. She reeked of it.

"She's eighteen," he told the bartender.

"She pays well."

His parents had been away that night, so he took her home. She woke up in his bed, promising to refrain from all forms of intoxication for life.

Yet, he brought her home several times since that night. His heart crumbled each time he found her passed out, in a party or a bar or the drug dealer's house. Until one day, he'd had enough. Whether they were together or not, he cared for her plenty to get her the help she needed. He took her home...*her home*.

"Why would you do this to me? I thought you loved me, Clive...why would you take me home?"

For several weeks he didn't hear back from her. Then, one day, he received an incoming call from a number he didn't recognize. He answered anyway.

"She ran away from the rehab. Do you know where she might have gone? Please help me find her Clive. Please."

The desperation in Olivia's father's tone charred Clive's insides. They went to all the run-down places Olivia frequented. After hours of searching, they found her, once again unconscious, at the dealer's house.

Although this time, she had no pulse. They rushed her to the hospital. They waited frantically as the doctors brought her back to consciousness.

"Why did you do this to my daughter, Clive? You gave her that first drug. You did this to her...*you* did this to her..."

That was the first time he'd seen a man cry.

Clive stared at Olivia. Her eyes were closed, her face was pale, and though luckily brought back to breathing again, she lay almost lifeless on the hospital bed.

Yes, I did this to her. The guilt stung him deep.

Chapter 15

As every weekday morning, Izzy and Allie arrived at her townhouse to walk to the train station with her. But as Eva promised Clive, "Tom is driving us to the office. He should be here at eight, so we have…" She glanced at her watch. "Five more minutes."

"Oh, thank God!" Izzy moaned. "Could we wait for him by the coffee shop? I'll die if I don't get some caffeine in me right now." She yawned.

They walked a couple of blocks from Eva's townhouse, down the steep road to the quaint neighborhood coffee shop.

"You look beat, Izzy. Rough weekend?" Allie probed.

"Don't even get me started. Carter and I met for dinner last night, and guess who we bumped into at the restaurant?"

Allie widened her eyes. "No way. Your ex, Stan?"

"Yep. He followed me home. Drunk. Refused to leave. Threw up all over my doorway. It was so bad." She shook her head. "Carter took him to his place for the night."

"Carter's so nice."

"Yeah. But that's not the end of it. Stan woke up in the middle of the night, disoriented, imagining he was taken advantage of—"

"He thought Carter made out with him?" Allie started to giggle.

"Well, Carter did take off his puke stained pants." Izzy rolled her eyes. "Anyway, then he got into a fistfight with Carter and cried when realization hit him. Of course, he threw up some more." She shook her head. "What a nightmare!"

Eva pulled out her phone to dial Tom and ask him to pick them up by the café. Izzy and Allie stepped into the shop.

"Excuse me, Miss Avery?" Eva turned to face the man who knew her name. The shop's door closed behind her, leaving her alone on an almost deserted sidewalk with the same man who had saved her from walking into oncoming traffic, the same man she'd later imagined seeing in the coffee shop, the same man she should have looked forward to meeting again. Instead, something about him irked her. Because, *he knows my name…*

Once again, dark sunglasses, a thick mustache, and a beard covered most of his face. The glasses seemed needless, given the thick fog. Odd that he'd be wearing them at all.

After all the danger that surrounded her since finding about the informant, she couldn't trust this man even though he had saved her life. Besides, that he knew her name bugged her far less as she became increasingly aware of his resemblance to the creepy-guy from the park in New York. Though not a one to one match in their appearance, the creepy-guy had a deep scar on his cheek and this man wore a heavy beard. Sunglasses or not, they both had the same iciness about them. Her pulse picked up pace. The hair at her nape rose.

She shoved her hand into her coat pocket and held the canister of pepper spray within, readying it for attack. Her other hand she tightened around her phone. Her brother's words rushed to her mind. *You have no one to help you…no mom, no dad, not even me.*

"Why are you following me?"

He smiled. "I'm Adam Lavato from the Local Chronicle."

"You're a reporter?"

"Yes." He indicated his badge hanging in a long loop from his neck.

That's what was off. He was a snoop. Clear now why he had followed her, she didn't bother to take a closer look at his badge, because she wouldn't indulge him anyway. She loosened her grip on both, the phone and the pepper spray.

"Look, if this is about my relationship with Clive—"

"No, it's 'bout your company."

*His accent…*wait, *my company*? She tightened her fists again. "What about it?"

"You know, 'bout that informant. That's why you have cops protectin' ya', right?"

She froze. Did he mean Trevor and Jason from when they took her away from the media? Or did he mean Tom? But Tom wasn't a cop. And more importantly, how did he know about the informant? Her mouth dried. She couldn't think of an appropriate response.

"They were cops, weren' they? Rescuing you from them reporters. Undercover cops were they?"

Trevor and Jason. "Bodyguards," she lied, hoping to avoid a front page story about her company and the FBI's involvement in finding the informant.

"What do you need bodyguards for, if I may ask?"

Shit. She shouldn't have called them her bodyguards. In fact, she shouldn't be talking to this man at all. "We're done here, Mr. Lavato." She turned and walked toward the shop.

"Is someone threatenin' you, *Miss Avery*?" At the eerie way he said her name, a cold chill shot from her shoulders to her toes.

But she didn't fear him. Her blood boiled at his boldness. She turned around and gave him her full attention. "No, but *you* most certainly will be, if you don't leave right now."

Self-defense tricks her brother taught her looped her mind giving her the needed confidence...*I'm your kidnapper. Hit me. C'mon.*

Her phone vibrated in her hand, startling both her and Lavato. Clive's picture flashed on the screen, which luckily, Lavato noticed.

Something shifted in his stance. He took a quick step back and then one more. Without another word, he turned and hurried away from her toward the intersection and disappeared around the corner.

She swiped her phone to speak but Clive beat her to it.

"Eva." His endearing voice hit her with relief.

Her nerves uncoiled, her head dizzied from her struggle to return to normal breathing. She exhaled.

"What's wrong?"

How did he know her temperament just by listening to her exhale? She was tempted, at first, to blurt it all out to Clive, because what had occurred was *out of the ordinary*. But the reporter had left, at least for now. And she would only be worrying Clive.

"Is Tom with you?"

Just as he asked, a black SUV did a U-turn and pulled up by the curb next to her. "Yes, in front of me, in the car. We're by this coffee shop, waiting for Izzy and Allie." Given her strange encounter, though impossibly difficult, she still managed to fake normalcy.

But he didn't sound convinced. "Are you OK?"

They'd dated for hardly over a month now, but Clive already knew her well. He read precisely, her every gasp, every grimace, every gesture. Nothing...*nothing* slipped by him.

"No, I'm not OK," she said softly. "I miss you." *That* she most certainly didn't fake. They had returned from their weekend getaway only yesterday, and yet it seemed like an eternity since she last saw him.

"Eva." The loving way in which he said her name consoled her. "Can't wait for Friday when I see you again."

"Me too." She paused...hold on... "How come you're calling me? I thought you wouldn't be available most of the day."

He too paused. Something was wrong. Before she could probe, he went on to say, "Can't stop thinking about you...wanted to say hi."

"Hi." She smiled.

He too sounded like he might have smiled as they hung up.

Tom got out of the car and walked toward her. "Morning, Miss Avery." He grinned and opened the passenger side door for her.

"Morning, Tom." She smiled, silently thanking the god of perfect timing. "How did you know where to find me?"

"Mr. Stanford called."

And how did Clive know where she was? *He's tracking me.*

Tom brought the car to a halt by the entrance to Stanford Tower. Eva tugged at the latch to open the door, but it wouldn't budge.

She shot Tom a look.

"Please, let me." He got out of the car and closed his door. He locked the doors.

Locked the doors?

"Eva...did your driver just lock us in the car?" Allie's eyes widened.

Tom circled around the hood. He looked left, he looked right, he looked all around. *What is he looking for?*

Izzy gasped. "If he rolls us a carpet we're totally having him drive us to work every day."

Eva gave Izzy a strange look. Speechless. Because really...a carpet?

"What?" Izzy half shrugged. "People do all kind of things with their money."

Tom reached her side of the car, unlocked the door and held it open for them to step out.

Eva glared at him as she got out of the car.

He shrugged lightly as though to say, *sorry, Mr. Stanford's orders.*

She narrowed her eyes. *We'll see about that.*

"Thank you, Tom." She forced a smile.

"You are welcome." He smiled back. "I'll be right here if you need me."

"Right here? But I won't be leaving the office until five. It really makes no sense for you wait here all day."

"It's no problem." He laughed, seemingly kindhearted. "Have a nice day, Miss Avery, Miss Millbrook, Miss Zimmerman."

He knew Izzy and Allie's last names? More importantly, he must have other things to do besides needlessly waiting there for her. Fun things, like maybe hang out with his family. Wait, did he have a family? A girlfriend perhaps? Other than his first name and that he didn't wear a wedding ring, she knew nothing else about Tom.

Although she couldn't let him spend his entire day waiting for her, and could have argued endlessly for him to find something else to occupy his time, he wouldn't steer an inch without Clive's permission.

And speaking of, she had to talk to Clive about this. His tracking her to the coffee shop and Tom's over protectiveness simply wouldn't do. It was worse than having the FBI following her.

"Thank you, Tom." She meant it this time. She turned around to walk to her friends who waited by the building's entrance.

"You know," Izzy went on, "though I don't mind what Tom did there, it is a little odd, don't you think? I mean who is he looking for? Reporters?"

"Right? Or someone else?" Allie paused. "Wait, are you in danger, Eva?"

Yes, in danger, of being smothered by her lover, that is. She shook her head. "Don't ask."

"Is this another one of your secrets you aren't supposed to talk about, like that contract with Stanford?"

"Yes."

"How many such secrets do you have?"

"Don't ask."

"Oh c'mon, clearly you need to vent. Do you not trust us anymore?"

Eva sighed and hit the elevator button. "Of course, I trust you. But, there's too much going on, and…"

They walked into the car, and Allie pushed the 37th.

Her friend's expressions riddled with concern for her. Yes, she needed to vent, and nothing could bring her as much relief as sharing all her troubles with her besties would, but… "Like I said, don't ask."

Silence ensued until the elevator doors opened on their floor and they stepped out. Just as they said their goodbyes, it occurred to Eva, "Izz, do you have connections at the Local Chronicle?"

"I do, why?"

"Could you…" She cleared her throat. Her question might invite more trouble. *Oh, what the heck.* "This reporter, Adam Lavato, could you find out whatever you can about him? Please?"

"Sure."

"Thanks."

Before Izzy could probe, Eva turned around and walked to her office.

Tina, beamed from behind her desk as she stood, looking brighter than usual.

"What's up?"

She spread out her hand in front of Eva and wiggled her fingers.

Eva gasped. "You got engaged?"

"Married!" She glowed.

"What…when?"

"Friday. He asked and, obviously, I agreed, and we went to the city hall and…well…" Tina's eyes glittered.

Obviously? Regardless… "I'm *so* happy for you." She circled Tina's desk, and hugged her. "Why are you here today? You should take some time off."

"Thank you, but, he already left."

"Left?"

"Yeah, he flew back to San Diego this morning."

118

That's right, he'd gone back to pack his things. "Is he going to move up here?"

"N-No, not for a few months at least. He's in last year of law school. So, he'll move here after his exams, or maybe I'll move to San Diego, who knows?" She shrugged. "We don't know." She shrugged again.

From meeting an old friend for the first time after many years of living apart, to proposing and getting married, all in one weekend. How could one make life altering decisions that fast? Could she do that with Clive?

"Oh, and my friends are having a bachelorette party for me. I know, it's all reversed, but, why not, right?"

"Right."

"I would love for you to join us. You could bring Izzy and Allie too."

"Of course, we'll be there. When is it?"

"Tonight. It's a last minute plan. Well, it was a last minute wedding, so…"

"Tonight works. Just let me know when and where."

"Yay! Should be fun."

"Yes. Can't wait." Tina's happiness was contagious. Eva almost forgot about Lavato and also about Clive smothering her. "I still cannot believe you got married."

"Me neither!" She almost screamed and covered her mouth with both hands.

Just as Eva was about to push her office door open, Tina announced, "Oh wait, I almost forgot." Tina's expression forewarned Eva about the danger that lurked behind that door. "Silvia's in there. She was already in your office when I arrived. I asked her to wait here in the lobby, but…"

Silvia… Did she know Clive was travelling? Is that why she dared to step into Stanford Tower at all? Clive had asked Silvia to stay away from them. *Why is she here?*

Eva nodded. "It's OK." Her palm still splayed on the wooden door, she halted to gather her thoughts. After her last encounter with Silvia, when she'd given her *that* look, after her conversation with Silvia at the Met Gala…Eva could never be too cautious when dealing with Silvia. Eva dragged in a deep breath and pushed the door open.

"Silvia, hey! Wasn't expecting to see you here." She forced a smile.

Silvia turned her gaze from the bay window when Eva walked into the room. She gave a genuine looking smile and also gave Eva a quick once over, her gaze lingering a little too long on Eva's skirt. Her favorite skirt.

Eva set her bag at her desk. "Would you like something to drink?"

Silvia walked casually toward the couch. "No, but I bet this plant could use some water." She plucked out a yellow leaf from the nearly dead plant and let it glide into the planter.

Eva didn't have a green thumb. Neither did Tina, it would seem. She'd only kept the plant because it had lived in this office for years. In many ways this was still her father's office.

Though Silvia wasn't entirely wrong, she could have simply said *no* to the drink. But Eva had prepared, she would play nice and wouldn't let Silvia's snide comment affect her.

She plopped into her chair behind her desk. Silvia however, sat graciously on the couch. If this were an advertisement, that couch would be sold out in no time.

"I met Clive the other day. But you already know that, you saw us."

Play nice, Eva.

"Yes, Clive told me about the tapes." She hadn't intended to say that last part, but seeing Silvia's posture slump ever so slightly soothed the little part of her that wanted to scream *get out!*

"Look, Clive and I had a good thing going, until you came along."

She made it hard for Eva to play nice. "Why are you here, Silvia?"

"You're destroying Clive."

"What?"

"I'm certain whoever contacted me to break up you and Clive did so because of you, and not Clive. I, for one, would never make Clive suffer because of me."

Oh please!

"Bet you wouldn't want Clive to be in danger because of you, either."

Dammit. Despite all her attempts to avoid Silvia getting into her head, Silvia got into her head. Eva had stressed incessantly about Clive being in trouble because of her. He'd left Tom to take care of her. But who would protect Clive? He'd told her once that Stanford had enemies. And now she had enemies. If their enemies were to catch up with Clive… That

121

thought send a sharp shudder through her. Her chest tightened, her toes curled.

A slight knock on the door brought relief to Eva's tightened nerves. The door opened and Tina leaned in. "Your nine o'clock is here."

Tina walked back into Eva's office after Silvia left. "Are you OK?"

"Yeah... I'm fine. Thanks. Who's my nine o'clock?"

Tina shook her head. "No one. I assumed you wouldn't want to talk to Silvia for more than ten minutes."

Eva smiled. "Thanks." Her gaze drifted to the plant. "Could you get that out of here?"

Tina gasped. "Oh no. When did the last leaf fall?"

Chapter 16

Olivia
YOU KEEP ME AFLOAT

Clive stared at the sparkly pink letters painted on the side of a white boat. Olivia loved pink. Olivia loved glitter. All her gymnastic costumes were sparkly pink.

He'd sat in his car for over ten minutes. His knuckles pulsed from how hard he gripped the steering wheel, yet he couldn't let go. He should turn back. Why had he thought meeting Olivia's mother after all these years was a good idea? The look of hatred in her expression when he met her last, at Olivia's funeral, flashed through his mind. *You could have saved her, but you let her die*, were June's last words to him. What else should he have expected from a mother grieving her teenage daughter's death? Besides, she had it right. Clive could have saved Olivia, but he'd deliberately chosen not to.

It had been twelve years since her death. His guilt would never wane.

But June's words had affected him deeply. He needed closure. Did June need it too?

It had taken him a long time to adjust to the fact that Olivia was gone. Although, he did struggle with memories of her, even today. He couldn't forget his past, but he would do anything to not be reminded of it. He had only now begun to move on. And that was because of one person, and one person only, who had ever caused him to forget...

Eva.

Lonely. Boring. Meaningless. Such were his days after Olivia. And then he met Eva again. The turn his life took from that moment on, was a turn he'd never imagined possible.

How he longed for Eva to be with him in that moment. He should have told her about Olivia. He should tell her now.

He swiped his phone to call her but held back when the GPS tracking he'd set up on her phone showed her walking from her house. She promised she'd let Tom drive her to work. *Where are you going? Please tell me Izzy and Allie are with you.*

He called Tom and gave him her location. He called Eva immediately after.

Hearing her voice pulled him right out of sorrow. He couldn't bring himself to talk to her about Olivia. But speaking to Eva did give him the confidence he needed to step out of that car and walk toward June's boat. At least, for Eva's sake, he needed to sort out the investigation before it hit the media. Had June appealed to re-investigate her daughter's death? Had she hired Ryan?

His heart raced, and his palms got sweaty. He didn't know how he brought himself to knock on the door, but he did.

The door opened...

"Clive." June blinked. "Is that...you?" Her voice trembled. "Are you really here?" She shook her head. "I—I can't...believe..." She sprang into his arms and hugged him tight. Impassioned, he hugged her back.

His shirt turned wet from her tears. All lingering apprehensions he'd had about their meeting lifted.

Her reaction, astonishingly unexpected, freed him, liberated him...at last. Only now did he realize how much he'd waited for this moment. How long he'd waited to be forgiven.

Though he would continue to blame himself for not having prevented Olivia's death...*this*...right now... he needed this... *God he needed this*!

June fished the tea bag from Clive's cup and the one from hers too.

"Cream and sugar?"

"No, thank you."

She led him out of the tiny kitchen onto the boat's deck. "He was tall, brawny, good looking...*like you*." Her smile reminded him of Olivia. "I cannot believe I forgot his name. He said he was a private investigator."

"Ryan." Clive's teeth almost lost some enamel. Because...no, *Ryan and I are nothing alike.*

"Yes, Ryan, that's the name. Ryan Cohen. How do you know that name?"

"He did some investigative work for the FBI."

After hearing from John about Ryan's probing into Olivia's death, Clive put his men to track Ryan. Ryan had visited June. Naturally, Clive suspected June had hired Ryan. But when he found Ryan's visit had surprised even June, it became evident that someone else had led Ryan to her. *The informant*.

"He said he was helping a reporter who claims there is more to Olivia's case than what was disclosed." She looked away for a moment. Despite the years since Olivia's accident, it had to be hard for June to talk about her passing. Clive loathed Ryan for ruffling her wounds.

June's eyes filled up and she closed them for a long moment.

When she opened them again, creases formed between her eyebrows. He'd seen her more times sad than he'd seen her joyful.

Her hands shook as she brought the teacup to her lips, but lowered the cup right back down to her lap without taking a sip. "Our lives changed drastically after Olivia. You left for the army. Olivia's father and I separated. I moved here." Her laugh held no humor. "I live on a boat because Olivia had always wanted to live on a boat." She sighed. "I've made my peace with the changes in my life. I think you have too, though only recently." She looked at him. "I've read a little about you and Eva. Childhood sweethearts." She gave him a faint smile. "I'm happy for you."

Her smile receded when she dropped her gaze. "I like to read about you…so I can…" She dragged in a deep shaky breath. "I can imagine what my daughter's life could have been had she…" Heavy beads of tears rolled down her face. "I don't want Olivia's last days to be brought back to discussion, Clive." She wiped her face with a tissue. They said nothing for a few minutes. She stared at the tea in the cup she held in her lap.

His throat closed. He stared beyond her shoulder toward the horizon at nothing in particular.

"I told Ryan just that. He said he wouldn't bother me about it again, and I believe him. He seemed like a decent man."

Clive almost laughed. *Asshole*? Sure. *Decent*? Not a word he'd associate with Ryan.

"But, I'm concerned about that reporter, whoever he is. I mean, who is he to go looking for clues about my Olivia? *My* Olivia, Clive…*our* Olivia." Her chin trembled. She brought her hand to her chest. "I really don't want him to…I don't want this…" She shook her head.

He raged, no longer for Olivia's drug habits, or for Thomas, or toward himself for not saving Olivia from dying… He raged for that *asshole* Ryan and his *jackass* reporter friend. "I'll find the reporter. I'll stop him. I assure you, June. Don't think about any of this anymore. I'll take care of it. I promise."

She wiped the last of her tears. "You were always a gentleman." Her smile reminded him of Olivia.

Chapter 17

Eva and her friends, and Tina and hers, each downed a shot of Tequila, then shoved limes into their mouths, shuddering from both the alcohol burn and the tang of the lime. They set their glasses on Tina's kitchen counter.

"All right, let's go dancing, ladies." Giselle, Tina's best friend, announced, and they headed out to the limo she'd hired to chauffeur them for the night.

Tom had dropped Eva and her friends at Tina's.

"It's a bit much, Clive. Almost suffocating," Eva had complained the first chance she got to speak to him after Tom had dropped her off at work.

"I worry for you," he said sweetly.

"I love that you do, but what I don't love is losing my freedom."

"Fine, I'll ask Tom to ease up a bit. But, that only means I'll worry for you more."

"And what about tracking me via my phone?"

"That I'm not willing to budge on, Eva." The starkness in his voice conveyed there was no debating that, at least not over the phone.

Another topic not to discuss over the phone? *Lavato*.

When they approached the limo, Eva looked around to see if Tom had waited for them. As Clive had promised, she didn't find the black SUV.

Lust, a recently opened club with a huge line of people waiting to get in, was their third stop for the night. Giselle walked to the bouncer by the door, showed him a pass, and he let them in.

When they entered the small lobby, a model-like woman, dressed in a strapless white mini-dress, welcomed them. "Tina's bachelorette?"

"Yes."

A tall, brawny man, his suit and shirt all black, hair slicked back, and an ear piece with a wire that disappeared somewhere behind his neck, said something to the hostess.

She smiled. "Sure."

She said to Giselle, "Please follow this gentleman. We have the VIP section open for you."

"The one across the skywalk?" Giselle asked.

"Yes."

"I thought it was reserved for private guests only?"

"It is." She shot Eva a quick glance. *Why*? "Since it's a bachelorette, we thought to make an exception."

"Sweet." Giselle looked back at her friends, and grinned wide. "Thanks!"

They followed the man into the club. Seductive music pounded as Eva entered the darkened space that overflowed with dancers and multihued lighting. The ambience was swanky and cool, young and fresh. The interior looked far superior to the other clubs they'd already been to. Something about the place reminded her of Clive. Not like she needed any reminding. Her longing for him worsened with every passing minute she hadn't either texted him or called him. Sure, she loved a girl's night out. But for whatever reason, given a choice, she'd rather have spent her evening with Clive.

They walked around the rim of the dance floor, weaving past shimmying, swaying dancers, some with drinks in their hands. They reached a set of metal stairs. Another man, dressed similarly to the one they had followed, unhooked a silky red rope allowing them entrance to the second level of the club. They walked across the skywalk, also packed with dancers, to the VIP section. He led them to a huge U-Shaped velvet couch, which they settled on. They ordered a round of fiery red colored shots. Downed them. Ordered another round. This one a neon blue, they downed those too. Giselle led the way, and they hit the upper level dance floor.

Beats thumped. Bodies moved. Lights flashed. Fueled by alcohol, at least for the moment, Eva let go off all the worries that had her trapped.

Music raged on, and at first they all danced together. But as the songs smoothed into each other, Tina's friends moved on to dancing with other

130

people. Allie gestured to Eva, signaling to get a drink. They left the dance floor and went back to the VIP section. As soon as they approached the large couch, the waitress, dressed similarly to the hostess they'd met in the lobby, stopped over to get their order.

Moments later, Eva sipped a gin and tonic, reveling as the cold drink washed down her heated body. She hadn't mentioned the extra lime part to the waitress, but surprisingly her drink had the exact amount of sharpness she loved. The more time she spent in the club, the more she suspected their evening there was somehow influenced by Clive. She pulled out her phone and tapped *Lust SF* into the internet search. Of course, Stanford Enterprise owned the club.

Finding that bit of information put her to ease. Though she hadn't feared being accosted either by Lavato or by the creepy-guy from the park in New York, just in case, she'd remained vigilant of her surroundings all night. And now, knowing that Stanford owned this club, she no longer scanned around her like she'd done at every bar they'd visited through the evening. The drinks had begun to further soothe her, and she missed Clive more than anything she'd ever missed.

Unable to spend another second without reaching out to him, regardless that he'd be asleep given the time difference, she texted him.

Eva: *Sleeping?*

A second later her phone buzzed. It was Clive, on video chat.

"Was hoping you'd text me." He wore a simple white T-shirt, his hair mussed as always. The way he gazed at her through her phone screen…*damn he looked sexy*!

"How come you're awake?"

"You're out without me. I worry."

"Clive…" she started to say, but she could never convince him to not worry for her. "Thank you," she said and leaned deeper into the couch.

"For what?"

"For everything."

"I wish I was with you right now."

He sounded melancholic. He looked adorable when he longed for her.

"Are you having fun?"

"Not as much as I would if you were here."

He gave her a faint smile. "How long do you plan to stay?"

"Not sure. Izzy, Tina and her friends are somewhere in the sea of dancers. Allie and I are VIP-lounging." She turned the phone around to show Allie propped up on the couch.

"Hey Clive." Allie waved.

Eva turned the phone back around. "This club totally rocks. The drinks are fucking awesome. Why we haven't been here already, I don't know, but we sure as hell will return, many, *many* times. Yes?"

"Yes, yes, yes!" Allie screamed.

"Yes." Clive laughed. "Never heard you curse before."

"No? I've quite a potty mouth."

"You have a *very* kissable mouth."

She bit into her lower lip. Odd how they'd made out a gazillion times by now, and yet, his every advance jolted her like it were the first time they'd flirted.

"Eva…" The desire in his tone was evident. He paused, as though unable to finish his sentence. "Video chat when you get back home?"

"What? No. It'll be hours before we get back. Don't worry about me."

"I like worrying about you."

Which was sweet and all, but… "Please, go to sleep."

"*After* that video chat."

She glared.

He clarified, "I have to catch up on work, anyway. I'll be awake for a few hours, at least."

Allie leaned in to avoid having to shout. "I miss Marc."

"I miss Clive." Did he ever take as luxurious care of himself as he did of her? Neither time nor place held any meaning to Clive as long as he ensured her happiness. Her longing for him turned ceaseless again. Didn't she only just talk to him?

"And *I* miss…" Izzy joined them. "I don't really know whom I miss," she stated flatly. "I'll have the…" She scanned the drink menu. "*Bartenders Lust*, thank you," she told the waitress, who was obviously extra attentive per Clive's instructions.

Izzy leaned in close to Eva and Allie.

"How about Carter?" Allie gulped down the last of the water in her glass, dunked her fingers in, pulled out an ice cube, and dabbed it across her forehead.

"We met a few times after Napa."

Eva picked up her drink and sucked at her straw.

"Made out...*a little*." Izzy pursed her lips looking playful.

"A little?" Allie dropped the cube back into the glass and began to dab her face with a tissue.

"Well, whatever...the point is, we don't miss each other."

"You don't see him every day, Izz, and you don't see anyone else either. From all the years we've known you, fidelity is not your thing. You must feel *something* for Carter."

Izzy appeared to contemplate, and then she said, "You know what, I *do* feel something for Carter...and it's achingly wet." She winked.

They laughed. It was fun to be lighthearted with her friends.

"No, but seriously, Carter is really...*skilled*."

Eva's thoughts drifted to Clive's skills. Now she too was achingly wet.

The waitress handed Izzy her drink. She tasted it. "Umm... This is *so* good. The drinks here are excellent."

"They are!" Allie picked up her drink and started to sip. She stared into her glass when she asked, "Do you wonder if you could be as spontaneous as Tina?"

Izzy snorted a laugh. "I most definitely can't."

"Even if it was someone you've known for years?" Allie asked.

"Regardless. The thought of marriage has never appealed to me, you know?"

"Oh, I know." Eva set her drink down. "Nor has it to me, seeing how my parents' marriage turned out."

"Exactly, and I've heard too many such stories. I'll never get married."

"Those who say they won't almost always do. And it's almost always spontaneous." Allie said.

"I don't know. Cannot see the future, so, cannot comment." Izzy shrugged.

Future…with Clive…

"I wish I could see my future." Allie sounded dreamy. "Marriage, children, house, a dog…with Marc?"

"If that's what you both want, then what's stopping you?"

"Nothing is, but you know, he's in New York most of the time now because of those condos." Allie glanced at Eva. "And he'll return only when they start their construction here. Which won't be for another few months at least."

"I'm meeting him next week by the way." And speaking of work… "I *so* wish I could see my future, my company's future, that is."

"Aren't you a little too wound up about work lately?"

"I am." Eva tightened the hold on her glass.

"Anything we can help you with?"

She loved her friends. "Thank you, but no. There's a lot going on, and I can…" She sighed. "*Trust no one.*" She shook her head. "I'm becoming my father."

They sipped their drinks in silence while the music thumped loudly in the background.

"You know what? I wish I could see my future, too. And come to think of it, maybe I can." Izzy grinned mischievously.

"How?" Allie narrowed her eyes.

"Mystique."

"Mystique?"

"Yes, Mystique." Izzy looked to Eva. "You met her."

Yes, she had, and she would never forget that red liquid that moved around Mystique's ring. She shivered when that image flashed her mind. "I'm *not* meeting Mystique."

"Wait, who's Mystique?"

"Tarot Card Reader," Eva replied.

"Also a Medium," Izzy added.

"A medium?" Eva laughed. "As in, she talks to dead people?"

"Yeah."

"Do they talk back?"

"Of course, they don't talk back, Allie, they're dead," Eva stated.

"Then whom is she talking to?" Allie was too cute when she was drunk.

"There's only one way to find out," Izzy suggested.

"What, go see her you mean? Now?" Allie's eyes widened.

"Yeah." Izzy took another sip of her drink. She looked for the waitress, and within seconds she arrived by her side. "I know this drink is a secret house specialty, but do you think the bartender would share the recipe?"

"Oh, he absolutely can. Let me go ask him for it."

"Gosh, this place is too nice. Right?"

Right. "Thank Clive for that."

"Why Clive?" Izzy asked.

"He owns the club. And he's been taking care of us all this time."

"Aww…" Allie placed her hand to her heart. "Wait. Isn't he in Miami?"

"Yep."

"Then how…?"

"Don't ask." Eva's drink gurgled as she sucked the last of it through the straw.

"I can't take any more of your *don't asks*, Eva." Allie pouted.

"Sorry, but, that's how it is for now." She set her glass on the table.

"Yeah, we know, you have *trust issues*." Allie shook her head and darted her gaze to Izzy. "But you know whom I don't trust? That Mystique person."

"Let her prove it, then?" Izzy finished her drink and set the empty glass on the table. She looked at Eva.

Eva shrugged a *why not*.

They looked at Allie. "Let's." She also finished her drink.

"All right." Izzy sprang from the couch. "Let me see if she's available." While she stepped away to make her call, Giselle, Tina and her friends returned to where they were lounging.

"Time to leave, ladies." Giselle announced.

"Why? I love it here." Tina groaned.

"Because, I've made reservations."

"Where?"

"Men of Exotica."

"What? No," Tina winced, "I don't want to go to a strip club."

"Well, it's your one and only chance, Tina. After which, you're officially and, hopefully, forever happily married."

"I'd rather stay here," Tina finished.

"How about another round of shots and we'll decide then?"

"Yes to the shots, no to the strip club for us." Eva indicated Allie and Izzy. "We've got to get going."

"Oh…why?"

"I've got an early meeting tomorrow." It wasn't a ruse. Eva did have an early meeting with Marc, and Tina knew that already. Besides, that lover of hers would stay awake all night unless she reached back home.

"OK, shots first." Giselle ordered them another round of the club's signature miniatures. Orange colored this time, they grimaced from the tang of the sweet, minty, lemony liquid.

Giselle hit her glass down on the table. "Is it just me, or is every drink here *really* delicious?"

Chapter 18

Eva and Allie followed Izzy's lead into a dimly lit, deserted street a couple of blocks from *Lust*. For the first time all evening, Eva second guessed her decision not to have Tom around. Once again, she dug her hand into her coat pocket and held the pepper spray in position. She scanned their surroundings intently, ensuring they weren't being followed. She especially looked for that bearded reporter.

They teetered on their high heels across the cobblestones, the din from which echoed through the darkness. They halted by a red brick building with emergency exits mounted on its façade. A series of horizontal, grey, steel platforms connected by ladders ran along each story.

"So," Izzy exhaled a heavy breath, "We're here." She indicated a flight of stairs leading underground to what appeared to be a basement home with a bright red colored door. Other than the turned off, neon pink *open* sign on the window, there was no indication of it being an entrance to an astrology parlor. They stood staring at the door for a long moment, as though none of them wanted to take the lead.

"I don't know why, but this is stressing me out." Allie bit her lower lip.

"Last chance to turn back." A deep voice startled them all. They turned to find Mystique grinning at them. "Afraid you'll become a believer, Eva?"

"Not gonna happen." She shook her head.

"We'll just have to see now, won't we?"

Yes, we'll see. Eva believed in what could be proved by science. And Mystique's tricks had no scientific proof whatsoever. Regardless of what would happen in that parlor, it would simply be another one of those funny episodes for Eva and her friends to muse about later.

"And you must be Allie."

"Yes." Allie's eyes widened. "How did you…?"

Was she serious? Allie's expression and her ridiculous question were way too comical. Eva looked at Izzy, and they started to giggle.

Mystique, too, threw her head back and laughed. Her chortle echoed. "I'm not *that* talented young lady." She continued to laugh as she walked past them down the stairs. "Izzy called to say she was bringing you here. *That's* how I know your name." She inserted a key, opened the door and disappeared into the darkness beyond.

"Stop it," Allie snapped, her voice slightly above a whisper as she gave Eva and Izzy a pointed look. She followed Mystique down the stairs. "Yes…of

140

course," Allie said out loud and cleared her throat. "I knew that."

A light turned on, and Mystique reappeared by the doorway. "I'm glad you're here. Please c'mon in." She waved them into a foyer with two doorways, guiding them toward the one on the left. "Make yourselves comfortable, I'll only be a minute," she said and disappeared through the other doorway.

As they entered the room, the sweet smell of incense engulfed their senses. Other than the dim light from a red crystal chandelier that hung from the ceiling and the countless lit candles pooling in wax drippings that stood on side tables and on the window ledge, there was no light in the room. The window remained partially hidden by a blood red velvet curtain. The walls were covered in empty black photo frames of various shapes, sizes and textures, giving the place a hollow, ghostly look. Mystique had clearly decorated the parlor on purpose to indicate the unnatural. Eva didn't fall for the ruse one bit, and neither did Izzy, apparently, as they exchanged glances and snickered. Allie, however, looked apprehensive.

"Allie," Eva whispered.

"What?" She flinched.

What was wrong with her? "Jeez, are you OK?"

"Yes, why?"

"You look spooked."

She licked her lips. "I *kinda* am. What if she channels someone I know?"

"You're kidding, right?"

"No, I'm not." She looked sincere.

"Allie, seriously, you know there's no such thing as channeling the dead, right? It's not real, none of what happens here is," Eva pressed on.

"I know…" she whispered. "But what if it is?"

"But it's not," Eva and Izzy whispered in unison.

"Please, take a seat." Once again, Mystique startled them. She had a deep, raspy yet cordial voice. A voice that could easily be mistaken for a man's over a phone. How long had she been standing there? Was she snooping on their conversation?

They pulled out the wooden chairs and sat around the circular table covered in a black velvet cloth, on top of which were three tarot cards placed face down.

"If this is your first time, please, try to relax." Mystique smiled, looking at each of them one by one.

"Allie, you've been to one of these before, haven't you?"

"Ah—" she cleared her throat. "Yes." She smiled, looking faint.

She has? Izzy and Eva looked at Allie.

"But it never worked or anything." She half shrugged.

"I see. Well, many times it doesn't work, but many times it does."

Well, yeah, whatever. Eva suppressed a yawn. Speaking of, what time was it? Poor Clive. He'd stay awake until she returned home.

"OK, then, let's all hold hands."

Eva held Mystique's, Mystique held Izzy's, Izzy held Allie's and Allie held Eva's.

142

Mystique closed her eyes.

Eva darted hers to Izzy. Izzy's uncontainable grin was contagious, and Eva bit into her lip and tried hard not to giggle. Izzy appeared to be doing the same. They glanced at Allie, and though Allie looked somewhat uncertain, she most definitely believed Mystique's abilities.

Silence ensued for a lengthy minute or two. How long would this take? If they weren't holding hands, Eva could have texted Clive about their whereabouts. Maybe even mute videoed with him. Mystique's eyes were closed, anyhow. What a laugh he'd have. And, why not? She tried to wiggle her hand out of Allie's, but Allie met her with a strange stare, as though she thought Eva had lost her mind. Alert and intent on evoking the dead, Allie tightened her hold.

Ouch, Allie. Eva made a face and, just as she shot a look at Izzy for a *what the hell is wrong with Allie* eye roll, Mystique started to breathe heavily. An audible inhale followed by an audible exhale, another inhale and another exhale, and so on. Until Mystique too tightened her hold on Eva's hand.

Mystique opened her eyes and dropped her gaze to the table.

"Allie..." Her raspy voice grew deeper, androgynous, and almost mannish.

Allie gasped.

Eva's insides jumped. *That voice...*

"He misses you..."

Allie's eyes widened, "W-Who?" Her tone became an anticipated whisper.

"He misses you, Allie..."

"Who?" The way Allie gawked should have been comical, but Mystique's large body, covered all in black to match her *dark and dangerous* forecast for the month, towered over them. Numerous beads hung around her neck, and *that* ring on her finger...*that* red liquid...moved close to one of Eva's fingers, which she couldn't move given Mystiques strong hold. Her deep virile voice amplified the obscured effect of their surroundings, and very quickly it all became hair-raising.

Before she knew it, Mystique let go of her hand and shot up from her chair, causing it to hit the hardwood floor with a loud thud. She hit her hands flat on the table. "I miss you...damn it. Can't you tell? Don't you recognize me?" Her voice raised a few decibels.

Allie's mouth fell open. She paled.

What just happened?

Eva cut her gaze to Mystique, and when Mystique's infuriated gaze connected with hers, she leaned hard into the back of the chair.

Mystique's voice grew louder. "*Evie...*"

Evie? Eva froze. Her blood ran cold. She most definitely stopped breathing.

"Trust...NO ONE."

Eva wanted to scream, but her voice had abandoned her.

Mystique glared at Allie. Her eyes almost bulged out of her face when she whispered, "Bubba."

Allie screamed, a loud shrill cry.

But Eva didn't know why, because she fled that very moment, and had already opened the front door. She raced up the stairs, two at a time, tripped and grasped the railing just in time to regain her balance. Her heels tattered across the cobblestones, echoing loudly. A few feet away from the parlor, realization hit her. *What am I doing, leaving my friends behind?* She stopped abruptly and turned around, when Allie bumped into her. Eva hadn't realized Allie had taken off right after her.

Eva would have fallen, if not for two strong hands that held her up. "I've got you. I've got you." Of course Tom had followed them around all night. And what luck he had, because her legs were too wobbly to stand, let alone walk. *Thank you Clive, for tracking me, for sending Tom…Thank you. Thank you. Thank you.*

"Eva." He'd never called her by her first name. "Please, get in the car. Its bullet proof." He reached to his side. From under his jacket he pulled out a gun. *A gun?* What the…Shit! Shit! Shit!

They stared in the direction he pointed the gun, toward Mystique's Parlor.

***

The informant raised his hands when Eva's bodyguard pointed the gun at him. He hadn't seen the man before. He wasn't one of those men who'd escorted Eva that day away from the reporters.

Besides, how had the bodyguard spotted him at all when he'd made sure to hide in the darkest shadow the building had cast?

Seconds after, Eva's blonde friend emerged from the basement parlor, laughing, shaking her head, "Oh my God," she cried out aloud. "I cannot believe you morons fell for that." She laughed more. "Oh. My. God!" she yelled again, throwing her head back, talking to the sky. Her voice echoed. She brought her gaze down and stopped in her tracks. When her hands slowly went up, it occurred to him, the gun wasn't pointed at him, after all.

The blonde spoke hurriedly, "It was a joke, I promise, it was only a joke."

He couldn't believe his luck. Because once again he came too close to being caught, and once again he'd gotten away. He liked that he got away, just as much as he liked that he got close to Eva. It had become a game now…a game where only he called the shots.

And for that reason, he'd watched Eva and her friends all evening, bar hopped with them. He'd made a note of each of the girls she'd hung out with. She had way too many friends. They liked to have fun. He liked to have fun…in his own way…he liked following Eva. The last club she went to, however, had a long line of people waiting to get in. And he couldn't have gotten past those bodyguards. Guards always made him twitchy and fidgety. So he waited outside the club for over an hour, scanning the club entrance and the street, ensuring Eva and her friends hadn't walked out and he'd missed them. His vigilance lifted when he did see them walk out, and not toward the limo this time but toward him.

Eva walked past him.

Eva saw him.

Eva didn't recognize him. Maybe because he'd dressed like himself tonight. He glared at her. She didn't even flinch.

Eva did not fear him.

Like that time in the park in New York, when she'd run past him unbothered by his staring at her.

Like that time outside the coffee shop, when she threatened him to leave.

And now…

Should he take offense? All his attempts to make her fear him had clearly failed.

The bodyguard continued to point his weapon at the blonde but cut his eyes to look at Eva. "Are you OK?"

"Yes." She nodded fast.

"Is she telling the truth?"

"I guess." Eva replied.

The bodyguard glared at Eva.

"YES, yes, she's telling the truth."

The bodyguard stared at the blonde for a long moment before straightening his posture. Slowly, he drew the gun down. Clicked it to safety and put it back in its holster.

He exhaled, hard. "Not like you owe me any answers, Miss Avery…but…what just happened?"

Yes, what did just happen? What does Eva fear?

***

After explaining everything that had happened to Tom, they got into the car and started to drive.

"Let me make it up to you all by buying you a drink?" Izzy offered.

"*A* drink?" Allie hit Izzy with a fierce gaze.

"Fine, however many it takes for you to crawl back home."

It took a bit of convincing for Tom to join them. He'd insisted on remaining sober while on duty. So, Eva called Clive, and minutes later, Tom sat with them at a gastropub, chugging a local brewed lager.

Eva took a huge gulp of her drink. Still feeling the shakes from the incident, she set the glass down heavier than usual. "Didn't I say Mystique wasn't a medium?"

"No kidding." Allie shook her head.

"How'd you come up with this anyway?" Eva asked Izzy.

"Seriously? Have you not seen a single supernatural movie? Medium's channel the dead all the time." She, too, set her glass down. "Mystique played the part really well, don't you think?"

Mystique's acting skills aside, Eva couldn't figure how Izzy came up with... *Trust no one.*

"What else could I have asked Mystique to say to you? Haven't you been doing exactly *that* lately? And you said so yourself, you're acting like you father." She mocked Mystique's voice, "*Evie.*"

Eva brought her glass to her lips and gulped another wave of beer. *Trust no one.*

"Bubba?" Allie shook her head. "It's inexcusable."

"Inexcusable?" Izzy made a face. "If anything, it's genius and laugh-out-loud hilarious."

"Inexcusable," Allie said deadpan.

"Who's Bubba?" Tom asked.

"Allie's gold fish."

"Oh yeah..." Eva recollected.

"A *very* dead one." Izzy snorted a laugh.

"Bubba's not dead. He was sent home." Allie gave them all a look.

"*Flushed* home, you mean," Eva corrected.

Allie exhaled. "So Tom, tell us about you. You have a girlfriend? Kids?"

"A talking gold fish?"

Chapter 19

"So the men escorting her that day from the reporters were bodyguards after all. How'd *you* ever find out?" the voice sneered.

His employer's rough tone enraged the informant. And his anger only grew worse with each piercing word of disbelief in his abilities his employer conveyed to him on every one of these phone conversations they had.

"I asked the building's security."

"The security guards at Stanford Tower spoke to you? About Eva? That easily?"

"I flashed them my press badge and paid them a few bucks."

Silence…and then came the words he never imagined would be said to him, "Nice work."

He smiled, glad he'd chosen to lie and not tell his employer that he'd talked to Eva by the coffee shop. He especially hid the part about how he once again ran away from her. All because of that phone call from her boyfriend. What if she'd answered the phone and alerted Clive and he'd alerted the bodyguards? He'd so far seen three of them around Eva. And all three looked able. He could at the most take down one of them. But all three, at the same time? He wiped the sweat beaded at the top of his lip with the back of his hand.

"Tell me again, how did you get the press badge? You got it from a reporter?"

"Well, that stupid son-of-a-bitch left it at Candy's."

"Candy?" The voice stiffened.

"One-a-them hookers I visit."

The voice reverted to that familiar and unwelcome, unhappy grunt. "Does she know you stole the badge?"

"Who?"

Another heavy groan. "*Candy*, you idiot."

"I don't suppose so."

"Don't suppose so?" The voice rose. "She either knows or she doesn't. Now which one is it?"

His anger seethed. "No. She does not know."

Silence, again. And then a heavy sigh. "Fine. You have the next delivery. *Try* not to mess it up."

No, he wouldn't mess it up. And he didn't think about the delivery, because how difficult could it be to drop off another one of those envelopes, this time at Eva's house? But his new plan to meet Eva again, that's what he wouldn't mess up. A plan he wouldn't share with his employer just yet. And before he did anything else, he needed to find out what made Eva run out of that astrology parlor. What did Eva fear?

Chapter 20

Damn, it was amazing to have her with him again. Through the week, though surrounded by friendly faces, Clive wanted to avoid them all. He'd missed an integral part of life. He'd missed Eva more than he'd ever missed anything else.

But now, as he drove her from the airport to his condo, his isolation vanished, and his life returned. No words could describe how soon how precious she had become to him.

He locked her fingers with his, tugged her hand to his lips and placed a kiss on the back of her hand. She smiled, *that* smile. He held her hand through the drive, and through the time they spent at the fair. They drove past it at first, but turned around because she wanted to ride the Ferris wheel, eat cotton candy, and make a wish at *Zoltar*. He topped it off by winning her a paper rose.

Life with Eva was real. Life with Eva was right. Life with Eva was the life he never imagined he'd live someday. He wouldn't let go…he'd never let go of Eva.

He brought her to his apartment by Central Park.

"Go out for dinner, eat in, or…"

"Or." She tipped up on her toes and kissed him, greedy, possessive, and desirous.

He kissed her back with a matching drive. He loved the feel of her smooth skin beneath his rough fingers. Her soft body was plush against his hard ridges. The sweetness of her breath mingled with his, darted an electrified rush through him. Never before did he turn that giddy from being with a woman. He did not know how he'd waited the slowest and the lengthiest five days for her to return to him, because more than anything else he'd ever wanted, he needed his hands all over her. He needed to see her blush from the litany of pleasures he whispered in her ear. He needed her fingers to grip his hair, like she did now. He needed to hear her light moan, like he heard now…as he played his fingers between her legs and she gushed into a blissful orgasm he just unleashed.

She placed her hands on the one-way, bay window overlooking the park and bent over for him to sex her from behind.

His senses heightened with her every deliberate request. Uninhibited fiend, *his Eva*, she made him break all his rules. Like when she'd wanted him to take her in his office, on his desk. Like when she wouldn't stop touching him in the car as they drove back from their weekend getaway, needing him to detour to a secluded view point for a gratifying finish to what she'd started.

Her body awakened with a contagious delight, each time he drove into her. The savagery of his passion grew increasingly hard to control, but he made sure it wasn't too much for her to handle. There was a fine line between pleasure and pain, and he'd never forgive himself if he ever crossed that line with Eva.

She came again, screaming out his name. Never had his name sounded better. He brought his pace from slow to a stop. He turned her around to kiss her. She kissed him back, tenderly, endearingly, playfully. He picked her up into his arms, laid her on the couch and got on top of her.

"You OK?"

She smiled. "That was exactly what I wanted."

He pushed into her again. Deep. She liked deep. She scorched against him. She'd climaxed twice already, yet their connection was tight. "Stop me if I hurt you."

She smiled again, nodding slightly.

He clenched her hips, because he just had to. He dug his teeth into the side of her neck, because he just had to. He drove fast and powerful inside her, because he just had to… He continued on until pleasure crashed through them. Panting, shaking, they held each other…through the night.

Chapter 21

In Clive's bedroom, in his New York apartment, like the last time she was there, Eva woke up refreshed, but to a dark room and a cold bed. She felt around her for Clive, and he wasn't there. She turned the knob on the bedside lamp and winced when the light pierced her eyes. She rolled out of the bed, freshened up and headed out to the living space where she found him by the breakfast table, typing on his laptop while speaking into a headset. She didn't know he'd be working over the weekend.

She hugged him. He flinched. He hadn't heard her approach. She kissed his cheek to soothe him.

"Hold on," he said into the phone, muted the line, pulled out the headphone, and tossed it onto the table. He tugged her around and pulled her into his lap. He kissed her.

"Did you sleep well?" He moved a stray strand away from her forehead.

She nodded. "Did you?"

"Yes and no, early meeting...might last another hour."

"OK." She gave him a sweet smile. "As long as I can keep looking at you."

He placed another tight kiss to her lips. Leaving her tingling for more, he returned to his call.

She poured hot water from the kettle into a cup, dunked in a tea bag and picked up a croissant. Letting Clive concentrate on his call, she went to find her phone. An hour and a half later, she'd attended to her emails, replied to a few text messages, read the news, searched her favorite online clothing store for sales, and...Clive had still not finished his call.

She peeked out of the bay window. Sunny. Bright. She changed into her exercise clothes and walked to where Clive worked. She mouthed, *park*, and put on her GPS watch. He raised a finger, asking her to wait. "Hold on," he said into his headset and muted the line.

"How long is your run?"

"One hour."

"I'm almost done with this call. Go ahead, and I'll join you after I'm done."

"OK, ten minute, extra slow, warm-up run, just for you."

He kissed her hand and returned to his call.

She plugged her headphones, turned on her music and headed down. When she exited the elevator and walked into the building lobby, she looked around for Mr. Gomez, the building concierge, and found him by the door. She paused the music.

"Miss Avery. Good Morning! It's lovely to see you again."

"And you, Mr. Gomez. How've you been?"

"Better than ever. My daughter graduated this week." He grinned wide.

"Congratulations. Does she know what she wants to do next?"

"Yes, she wants to be an interior designer."

"Really? Well, I run an interior design company myself. If she's interested, tell her she has her first interview."

His eyes softened. "For real? Oh, she'll be thrilled. Thank you."

"Please, don't mention it. I'd be happy to help."

"Going for a run?"

"Yes."

"Gorgeous day."

Yes, it was. She started off with a slow walk leading into a light jog, slower than usual, so Clive could catch up.

She recollected the last time she'd run in that park. Today too there were several people scattered about. And *that* creepy-guy...she looked to the direction where she'd spotted him the last time...and...she blinked. Because...was that him in the distance? A tight alertness awakened through her. The creepy-guy stood in the same place as he did the last time. Once again, he looked through binoculars in her direction. He was watching her. *He* was most definitely watching *her*.

She paused her music, so she could think. Her heart beat picked up pace and drummed in her ears.

Like the last time, as she neared the man, he brought his binoculars down and stared at her.

Yes, she identified the man. White male, dressed all in black, completely bald, no facial hair, but *something's missing...what's missing*? That deep scar, on his left cheek, was no longer there. And she didn't know how, but her mind connected him to Adam Lavato, the reporter from Local Chronicle. Creepy-guy had neither the beard, nor the mustache, but he wore those sunglasses again. With similar body structure as Lavato, the resemblance between the two men was uncanny. Besides, she could never forget that icy stare. *Yes, it is the same guy*. Or...is he not?

Her first thought was to run toward him. Her second thought begged her not to be a fool. Her third thought agreed with her first, and that ended that debate. One moment, she jogged, and the next, she took off full speed toward the man.

Did she have a plan as to what would she do when she reached him? *No*. Did she have a plan as to what she would do if he wouldn't move an inch and continued to stare her down? *No*. Did she have any plan as to what she would do if he started to run toward her? *No*.

His stance shifted from being threatening to being threatened, as his jaw dropped and he took one step back, then he turned on his heel and began to run, *away...from her*.

What are you doing? And more importantly, *what am I doing?* Running after a man, probably a dangerous one, at that, in Central Park with all its horrific gory secrets, murders, rapes, crime...

But his reaction gave her all the confidence she needed because now she had a plan. She'd catch him. She'd confront him.

She chased him farther into the park, through a winding trail. People became scarce. Yet, she ran after him. Their footsteps grew louder. Their footsteps echoed. He disappeared into a dark tunnel.

Her determination reset. She'd chased the man in broad daylight. She'd gotten away with it. But to follow him into darkness…*not the greatest of ideas*, her mind whispered.

She slowed her pace. Significantly. Suddenly. She came to an abrupt stop. Her muscles quaked. Her stomach ached. She bent over and placed her hands on her knees and tried to catch her breath. When a strong arm grabbed her shoulder and pulled her up, she almost shrieked.

"What the hell, Eva?" Clive too panted, but not as heavily as she did. "How am I supposed to catch up with you if you run that fast?"

Speechless, she blinked. She'd forgotten all about Clive joining her.

He studied her, and his expression altered to concern. A crease formed between his eyebrows. Though cautionary, he sounded surprisingly soft when he asked, "What's wrong?"

She wanted to tell him, but where should she begin?

"Eva, what's wrong?"

She licked her lips. She told him what happened.

"You did what? Are you out of your mind? Running into *that* tunnel, *alone*, after *that* man." His voice rose.

"Well, not exactly *into* the tunnel. I stopped. You saw."

Clive's jaw twitched. He shoved his fingers through his hair and rested his hands on his hips. His gaze cut to the tunnel. "What were you thinking?"

"I wasn't at first, but…"

His gaze locked with hers.

"It wasn't the smartest thing to do, I know, but…it felt good, Clive…*Fuck,* it felt good!" Exhilarated, she was unable to contain her grin.

He glared, his glower so intense, her grin vanished and her insides did a tumble. Not the nice kind of tumble she'd gotten accustomed to with him around, the kind that made her shrink into her shoes not wanting to be on the receiving end of his wrath. Maybe he'd ease up a bit if he knew the reason she'd acted the way she had. "It felt good to threaten him back," she clarified. "He's threatened me enough already. In the park, in St. Barth, and that coffee sho…" *Oops.* She pulled her lips together as tight as she possibly could.

Shit.

She hadn't told him about the coffee shop incident yet, because, until only moments ago, she'd believed Lavato was a reporter and not the creepy-guy. But now, most certainly, they were one and the same man. Why had she not told Clive about this already?

"What coffee shop?"

She gulped. She licked her lips, again.

He tilted his head down slightly. His greenish-blues narrowed. "Explain," he said in *that* tone, the interrogation tone she recognized from the last time she evaded discussing the creepy-guy. Unfortunately for her, this time, they weren't talking over the phone.

"Explain…what?" Of course she knew *what*.

His expression hardened.

"Oh…You know, the coffee shop." She cleared her throat. "Where you buy coffee, and pastries, and speaking of, you've got to try the pastries in this shop by my house…" She shook her head. "Out of this world good."

His eyes gleamed mad, stark raving mad.

If only she could vanish at a snap of a finger. Like vaporize into a purple haze, *poof*! If only they'd succeeded, Izzy, Allie and her, in inventing that witches' vanishing brew they brewed many times during their childhood years in her grandpa's backyard. Of course, they always tested the potion on Allie. Of course, they lied and told her she did actually vanish. Of course, Allie believed them. *Oh, Allie.*

"Eva?" Clive said harshly.

"Hmm…"

"*What* are you thinking?"

"That you weren't asking what a coffee shop was, because obviously you know." She rolled her eyes, snorting a laugh. But he wasn't tickled. She found it difficult to come up with a reasonable explanation for her actions when he took it all so seriously.

His expression remained unchanged. His eyes continued to bore into hers.

She cleared her throat. "Remember, when you were in Miami?"

His hands still on his hips, he raised his eyebrows. "Yeah, like it was only yesterday." He cocked his head a bit. "Oh wait! It was."

Knowing her question was stupid, she only cringed more at his sarcasm. She changed her approach. "He's always in disguise, Clive. I know it, because today, his scar is missing. He posed as a reporter the other day at the coffee shop, and he wore this ridiculous rug—"

"He wore a rug?"

"Yeah, a mustache, a beard, there was hair everywhere…"

Clive ran his teeth over his lower lip. Did he stifle a smile? Did he not? Maybe not.

"Well, anyway, so I asked Izzy to find out from her connections at Local Chr…" Before she could finish, Clive sighed, a heavy audible sigh. He took her by her arm and began walking toward Clive's condo. She talked all the way, till they reached the inside of the apartment. Sure enough, all that time, he didn't say a word.

He tapped a screen to activate an alarm for the front door.

Unable to hold up her defense any longer, she gave in, "Are you angry with me?"

He pulled her into a tight embrace. His heart drummed fast against her ear. His familiar strong body had tightened and tensed. He held her close. He held her snug.

"Anything…*anything* could have happened today," he whispered, as if any louder and his fears would actually come true. "He could have had a knife, or worse, a gun. Maybe he had an accomplice or two, waiting for a cue to kidnap you."

"Well, he ran away from me," she spoke against his chest. "He probably didn't have a weapon on him, right?"

"Wrong." Clive eased his hold on her, and she tilted her head back to meet his gaze. "It could have been his plan all along, to lure you into that tunnel."

Well, when he put it like that...

"I'm setting up security for you."

"Why...Oh, I understand, you need Tom back. He's probably tired of listening to all our girly talks anyway."

"I meant, in *addition* to Tom."

In addition to Tom. Whether she liked to admit it or not, that coffee shop incident did have her on the edge. Additional security did seem like a great idea.

"I agree, extra eyes to watch out for me won't hurt. But let's back up a little." And she literally took a step back from Clive and met his gaze in earnest. "What did happen today? I ran after a man, who may or may not be the informant, may or may not be the reporter, who may or may not have been intentionally staring at me in the park, but who most certainly ran away from me. For all you know, right now, he's probably setting up security to protect himself...*from me.*" She almost grinned.

"How is any of this funny to you?"

"How is it not to you?" She laughed. He didn't. So she continued to explain, "The guy ran away, as fast as he could...from me, Clive. I mean, who would run from a five foot six, pink tank, white shorts, ponytail wearing, not that great of a runner?

163

Look at me. I've never even killed a fly, really, it always gets away. So, yes, it *is* funny." She went on to giggle but right away sobered. "Oh, but one time, I did break Joey's nose." She nodded.

His eyebrows shot together. "Glossing over how you broke Joey's nose, what happened today is no joke. Because what if *he is* the informant, what if *he is* the reporter, and what if…" He paused and his tone softened. "What if he's the guy who killed your father?"

Clive's intense stare twisted her insides.

"My instincts say the man you chased is our guy and he's dangerous. He had a ploy devised, otherwise he wouldn't have let you see him today."

Her father's killer…

"I'll let the FBI know that the informant might have resurfaced." His eyebrows lifted as though to ask if she had any objections.

No, she didn't. Because Clive was right, because, *what if…*?

What would she do without Clive? "Thank you." Her voice slightly over a whisper, a thick lump formed in her throat, and she could barely speak.

The familiar heavy, sunken feeling returned to the pit of her stomach. Her goofiness in making the situation light vanished. Her awareness of the deeply concerning reality soared.

"And *no*, I'm not angry with you."

She exhaled a sigh of relief.

He tugged her back to him and placed a tight kiss to her lips. "I don't want anything bad to happen to you. I love you, *damn it*."

"Thank you," she said again.

"For loving you?"

"For everything."

He hugged her for a long moment.

He went to his phone and called Trevor. They chatted for many minutes, after which he called Tom and chatted some more. He returned to the kitchen table, where she sat sipping warm chamomile tea Clive had brewed for her. Every sip soothed her more. He pulled out a barstool and sat next to her. "Eva, I need to hear everything you told me all over again, only this time, in greater detail. Let's start with what you saw on the way to the coffee shop. Oh, and you broke Joey's nose?"

He had many questions, and she answered them all to the best of her knowledge. He asked each of his questions multiple times in different ways, until it seemed as though he'd gotten the answer he'd been looking for. It surprised her how her answers changed depending on the way he phrased each question. Commendable how detectives ever found the right clues from all the gibberish that consumed each case.

They talked for half an hour or more. By the end of it her head throbbed from the concentrated interrogation, and she shrank into her chair. Clive studied her, her hand still held in his, and he rubbed his thumb across her skin. Her insides did the nice kind of tumble this time.

"I'll draw you a bath." he pushed back his chair and headed toward the bedroom.

She followed him, with slow steps, acutely aware of her tightly wound muscles, probably stiffened more from the mental strain than from the intensity with which she'd chased the creepy-guy.

She stared at the tub, remembering how she'd fallen asleep and dreamt of him. A quick shiver sprinted down her spine.

What if the guy hadn't run away from her today? What if he'd stood staring at her until she reached him and, like Clive suspected, pulled out a knife or a gun?

Clive turned off the waterfall that had filled the tub. "I'll join you in a minute." He placed a light kiss on her cheek and left the room.

Chapter 22

Eva sank into the water, the warmth soothing her wound up body. She slid in deeper, submerging all except her head in a layer of freesia-scented bubbles.

Moments later, Clive joined her. He held her from behind, while she sat cross-legged and melted into his embrace. His thumbs massaged the balls of her feet in a circular motion. She moaned, softly, and he tensed against her lower back. He kissed her shoulder, her neck, teased her earlobe with his teeth all the while kneading along her feet to her calves. She moaned again, because truly, his hands were doing magic. Her strained muscles melted at his touch. And he tensed some more. His fingers played along her upper thighs, and between them. She gasped when he cupped her mound. But he didn't touch her where she craved for his touch. *On purpose?* His head nuzzled her neck, and he laughed lightly by her ear each time she reacted to his touch. His nifty fingers drew circles around her stomach and moved up toward her breasts. As she prepared for another gasp, he circled his fingers back down toward her thighs.

What are you doing? Go back up…

His fingers once again intently played along and kneaded her thighs. But this time, she tried hard not to react as revenge for all his teasing. After all he'd not only deliberately left her craving for his touch but also enjoyed her misery.

He kneaded again. She remained unmoved, again.

He stilled. "You're holding back on me."

She turned her head to look back at him, grinning playfully. She kissed his lips. "Yes. But you deserve it."

"Get out."

"What? Why?"

"Get out, Eva."

His stern tone puzzled her. She looked at him for a second longer and then got out. He stepped out after her.

"But you started it."

He remained silent, pulled out a white fluffy towel, dabbed her dry, then dried himself.

"Sorry." She pouted.

"Are you?" He picked her up over his shoulder. She squealed at his unexpected move. He walked over to the bed, tossed her onto it, and hovered over her.

Ah…so he wasn't planning on stopping after all. She grinned, liking where they were headed.

He didn't grin. He didn't smile. He didn't even have that lusty look he always did when they were fooling around.

Their faces neared. The rub of his stubble against her jaw line evoked a pleasure like no other. His lips waited over hers. "Hold back on this one," he said, and before she could respond, his mouth met hers in a possessive, toe-curling kiss. His fingers found her warm, swollen cleft. He flicked her with a speed completely opposite of the tender fervor of their kiss. The persuading contrast of his actions provoked and pushed her to the brink of an exquisite climax. Then, he stilled.

She opened her eyes to meet the mischief in his features, an arrogant grin.

He moved down her body, caressing her, kissing her, kneading her, squeezing her, "Still not convinced you're sorry, Eva."

His warm mouth met the heated space between her legs. She moaned, a genuine moan.

"What happened to holding back?" he teased.

His breath, his stubble, his aggression as he pulled her clit between his teeth and started to pleasure her with his tongue, tightened her knot of engorged nerves further. A tremble ran through her and she arrived at the brink again, ready to explode, and again, he stilled.

"No," she almost shouted.

He stood up, laughing, and as if it were even possible, he grinned haughtier than before.

She narrowed her eyes at him.

Again, before she could conjure a response to his torment, he pulled her to the edge of the bed and pushed inside her in one merciless thrust. It was exactly what she wanted. She gasped from the pleasure of her sensitive flesh being stretched to the maximum. He began to move, gradually picking up his pace. Her heart beat hastened, while her desires grew strong, but she lay pinned to the bed. Her hands gripped at the sheet.

He stilled yet again. "Eva, you've got to relax." He kept his tone distressingly smooth.

"How can I, you evil s..." She hissed into his mouth as it dominated hers with a hungry urgency. He worked her breasts with both hands. It was exactly the stimulation she craved, and she surrendered to her innate need, to that aching desire he'd incited, to the immense pleasure he caused her...

"Open your eyes, Eva." His lips brushed against hers.

She opened her eyes and met his darkened gaze. His lust had returned.

"Not teasing this time. Please, relax. It's no fun if you won't enjoy it too."

His hands reached hers, coaxing her to let go of the sheet. She complied and weaved her fingers into his hair. She wrapped her legs around his waist and began to move with him. He groaned his pleasure into her mouth. His strong fingers gripped her hips, and he gratified her with a dominating force. Every surge, every pull, felt *so* good. Without warning, together, they shattered. They clenched. They satiated each other in a long, extended, ravishing bliss.

***

He watched as she slept, her hair, the color of dark brown autumn leaves, splayed in ringlets across the pillow. She looked peaceful, his, silly, funny, sexy Eva.

She had spunk, must be why her father had wanted her to take over the business after him.

Spunk like no other woman Clive had known before.

Spunk that made him want to brag to his friends about but at the same time also raced his pulse. Because if she wasn't careful, the same spunk could get her into a lot of trouble. As it almost did today.

His insides flipped at that thought.

She was typically innocent, denying danger until it threatened her life. He did not get why she didn't tell him about Lavato that morning when they talked. But how could he question her? He hadn't spoken to Eva about Olivia either, despite that being the reason he'd called her.

He suspected Lavato, the informant, and the reporter who'd searched into his past with Olivia, were the same person.

Meanwhile, one thing was certain. No matter how difficult the situation, Eva liked to fight her own battles. Independent, strong minded and stubborn…she was like him. And who better than him to know those traits weren't always a good thing?

He couldn't chain her spunk, but he certainly could provide her the protection she'd need when she pushed her luck to the extreme again.

He sighed. *Eva*.

He'd have to figure out a way to get her to depend on him. Over everything else she wanted freedom, and he'd always remember never to take that away from her. He'd set up security for her, but she'd never feel their presence. She would appreciate the distance, and he would appreciate that someone looked out for her when he couldn't.

She was confident, over confident at times, but she was also fragile, delicate... *precious*. And if anything bad were to happen to her...

The thought raised the hair at his nape, and his palms got clammy. He wouldn't let *that* man, or any other for that matter, get close to Eva again. He'd do anything and everything to keep her away from danger.

Izzy had confirmed that Lavato worked as a reporter at the Local Chronicle, but Clive's instinct told him Lavato wasn't the rogue the FBI was looking for. Thus far, the informant's actions seemed deliberate, and it made no sense that he'd give away his identity that easily.

A faint buzz brought him back from his thoughts. His phone rang from the living room. Must be Trevor. Letting Eva sleep, he closed the bedroom door and went to answer.

"Lavato was on vacation all last week."

"Alibi?"

"Strong. His wife and family. They celebrated their 30th wedding anniversary in San Diego."

"He isn't our guy then."

"No, he isn't. But he did lose his press ID recently. We checked. He got a replacement badge this week."

"Does Lavato look similar to the guy Eva described?"

"Yes. Heavy beard, mustache, middle aged man. Your girl's right, our crook likes to play dress up."

Clive smiled. Yes, his girl was right...she was also naughty, cute, smart...

"Anyway, so get this. Of course, Lavato appeared to be a perfect family man, until we left his place. We hadn't driven away yet, Jason and I sat in the car discussing the case, and guess whom we see...Lavato... rush out of his house and hurriedly drive away in his car. Naturally, we followed him, and guess where he led us? ...*Madam's*."

"What's that?"

"Gentleman's club. He argued with this chick outside the club and then got into his car and drove away. Jason followed him home while I went to talk to *Candy*. I paid her enough to get her to talk. Supposedly, the last time Lavato was with her, he left his badge. But she has no recollection of seeing a badge."

"So one of the guy's who saw her after Lavato took the badge."

"Yeah, but she doesn't keep a list of her visitors, and she couldn't really say who it might be, given the number of men she's serviced since then."

"How many?"

"Twenty eight."

"Aren't some of them repeats?"

"Supposedly not. But she offered to tip us off when a repeat from those twenty eight shows up. She gave us her schedule. Guess we'll be hanging around Candy for a while. Will keep you updated, anyhow."

"Also, you might want to check out Ryan Cohen. I have my men on him already."

"The PI guy? Your best friend?" He chuckled.

"Yeah, *that guy*. I suspect the informant has met him."

"Wait, why do you have your men on him?"

"Ryan's digging up Olivia."

Trevor said nothing for a second or two. When he did, he sounded serious and humorless. "I'll check out that son-of-a-bitch."

Again, they remained silent for a moment.

"How's Eva holding up?"

"Stronger than I could ever have imagined."

"Did I tell you I love her?" Trevor teased.

Trevor's attempt to divert him away from thinking about Olivia wasn't lost on Clive. And, yes, Eva most easily took Clive's mind off everything else.

Chapter 23

"We'll be done in about two to three months," Eva said to Marc, who sat across the table from her at a Dim Sum restaurant.

They'd toured the model condos Eva's team had designed. Impressed with their work, Marc gave them a go on their completion plans. After hours of discussions, Marc and Eva headed out for lunch.

As they sat at their table and waited for the waitress, Eva looked around for her incognito bodyguard. Clive had introduced her to him that morning. He came highly recommended by Tom.

"You'll know where he is when you begin to look for him," Tom had said on their drive to Marinos.

She scanned the crowded room and found the bodyguard seated by the bar. He looked at her the moment she looked for him, as though he waited for a cue from her. He watched her, and somehow it didn't bother her. She liked the distance.

"That's sooner than we planned," Marc said just when the waitress rolled along their aisle a cart full of dim sum specialties. They selected a few.

"Is that timeline a problem?"

"Not at all. The sooner the better." He paused and met her gaze. "Because the sooner these condos get done, the sooner I return to San Francisco." He smiled.

She caught his hint. "Allie misses you."

His smile faded. His gaze dropped to the table between them. "I wish things could be different, you know?"

"How do you mean?"

"If I didn't have to travel this much, especially now."

Especially now? What's special about now? She blinked, clueless.

"You know," he said again, but then stilled. "Shit. You don't know." His face paled. He set down the chopsticks. "Allie hasn't told you yet."

"Hasn't told me what?" She stuffed her mouth with a dumpling.

He leaned back into the chair. "I don't know if I should be telling you this." He paused. "But, we've known each other for years now, right? I think you know me well enough."

She swallowed her food and took a sip of the green tea. "Of course, we're friends before anything else." She smiled. "Now spill. What's going on between you two?" She plopped another dumpling in her mouth.

"I asked Allie to marry me."

She almost choked.

176

She cleared her throat. "That's fantastic!" She should call Allie on her drive back to Clive's apartment. Allie must be bubbling to tell her all.

"Well…" He laughed and brought the napkin in his lap up to dab his mouth.

Something about his laugh forewarned Eva with the slightest hint that *fantastic* might not accurately describe how Allie took Marc's proposal.

"It would be, had she agreed."

She should definitely close her eyes, because they'd pop out of their sockets any moment, because why would Allie ever, *ever*, refuse to marry Marc? "I-I'm sorry…I didn't know." She blinked. Her breath caught. "I'm *so* sorry, Marc," she said again, softer this time.

"Oh, that's all right. I don't think she meant to refuse." He laughed that not-so- much-of-a-laughter laugh again. Picking up his chopsticks, he began to eat. "I'm not giving up though, I'll ask her again when I move back to San Francisco. I think it's my travel that has her bothered."

He *thinks*? "She didn't tell you why she refused?"

He shook his head, "No."

Why would Allie do that, especially knowing how madly in love Marc has always been with her? "Do you want me to talk to her about it?"

He half shrugged. "I'm not sure. I'm surprised she hasn't discussed it with you already. I mean, you girls seem to talk about everything."

So she'd thought, but apparently, Allie had secrets she didn't want to share with anyone…*yet*. And of all people, Eva understood the need to keep secrets. She'd stocked up more of those in the few months she'd worked in S. F. Designs than she did in all the years before combined.

And yet, later, as she paced across Clive's living room, she called Allie. "Why did you refuse Marc?"

"*Why* did he tell you that?"

"He didn't. It just came up."

"How can something like that just *come up*?"

"Well, it did. But that's beside the point. You needn't tell me the reason behind your refusal, but he certainly deserves to know why, Allie. He's clueless and yet *so* in love with you."

"And I'm in love with him too."

This made no sense at all. "Then why did you refuse to marry him?"

She didn't respond.

Unwilling to give up on these two that easily, Eva went on, "When did he propose anyway? Was it over the phone?"

"No, he flew in Friday, stayed for a couple of hours, and then flew back."

"He flew in…all the way from New York…which is at least a five hour flight… and you refused without telling him why? *Why*?"

"Well…" She sighed. "All that talk during Tina's bachelorette with you and Izzy got me thinking about how marriages don't work."

Was this a joke? It had to be. "Not all marriages end up broken, Allie."

"Don't I know that? My grandparents married at eighteen and are together even today, and so are my parents for that matter."

"There you go!"

"But, all these divorce cases I work on daily, the ridiculous reasons why people split up…it's scary, Eva. And it only gets worse when children are involved."

"You've talked to Marc about this?"

"No. Because, he'll tell me that it won't happen to us."

"And how's that a bad thing?"

"Because, what's the guarantee?"

Seriously? "Seriously?"

"Really, Eva? What if Clive proposes to you, today? Will you say *yes*?"

Clive walked in just as she ended her call with Allie. Her friend's question echoed in her mind. *Will I say yes*?

He hugged her close. "What do you want to do now?"

His intent was clear. She grinned. "Not yet."

"OK…what then?"

"I'd love to complete yesterday's run, but its drizzling out."

"There's a gym in the building if you'd like to go?"

Minutes later, Eva ran her full pace on a treadmill. Clive ran next to her. He could have easily run faster than her, but he deliberately set his pace to match. *Sweet Clive.*

They stopped after a good hour of running. She was definitely more spent than Clive. Her legs wobbled when she stepped off the machine.

He held her. "Are you OK?"

"Yeah." She laughed.

"There's a heated pool on the top floor with a fantastic view of the city. Want to go for a swim?"

"Uh-uh." She shook her head and took a swig of water she'd pulled out from the communal fridge.

"It's only five feet deep."

She shook her head again.

He wiped a towel around his face and neck, then tossed it into a basket. "Do you wish you could let go of your fear someday?"

"Someday, yes."

"You let me know when that day comes, and we'll go swimming together." He wrapped his arm around her waist and tugged her to him. They walked toward the elevators.

She loved him for not forcing her into overcoming her fear. One more thing to add to the list of things she loved about Clive. Was there anything she didn't love about Clive?

When they were back in his apartment, "What do you want to do now?" he asked in the same sexual tone he'd asked her earlier.

She laughed, "this," she pointed to a play on Broadway she'd picked out from an events booklet.

She looked through the wardrobe collection Claire had put together that one time for the Met Gala event and picked out a white long sleeved silk shirt, tucked it into black skinny slacks and completed her look with ankle strap black sandals.

Clive looked delicious in a dark gray V-neck sweater, dark trousers and a sport jacket. Now, she questioned her choice to go out over staying home for a night of making out with Clive.

On the way to the show, she found it impossible to keep her hands off him, but he didn't seem to mind. On the way back to his condo, she found it impossible to keep her mouth off his. He didn't seem to mind that either.

"What do you want to do now?" he asked her again when they entered his apartment, as if he didn't already know.

She tipped up on her toes and pulled his face to hers.

"Excellent answer."

Chapter 24

Twelve years ago…

"Olivia? What's wrong? Where are you?" Clive gripped his phone wishing dearly that she'd talk.

She spoke between sobs. "Meet me by that sushi restaurant."

Minutes later, Clive stared in horror at Olivia. Her one eye was swollen and bruised. Her clothes were torn.

"Thomas?"

Tears trickled down her face and she dropped her gaze to her feet. She stood barefoot. She told him she'd hurled her shoes at Thomas to get away.

Clive pulled her to his chest.

How had it come to this? How could a sweet sensible girl with a relentless drive to chase her dream to be famous be abused by the very man who'd promised her that dream? Thomas had traumatized her mentally for months now. That he'd gotten physical with her came as no surprise. Clive had tried hard to drag her away from Thomas, but Olivia wasn't one to budge.

"You should get that bruise checked."

"No. I'm fine."

No, you're not. "You could have a concussion."

She touched the top of her cheek with her fingertips and winced. "It hurts like hell, but otherwise, I feel all right."

"You should report him, Olivia."

"In the morning. Not now, please. I cannot go anywhere looking like this." She picked at her torn clothes.

He couldn't take her to his home either. He settled her in a hotel for the night, promising to bring her painkillers, food, a change of clothes and shoes. By the time he'd returned, she was gone. The hotel receptionist described the man she'd left with. Thomas.

That moment changed it all.

Chapter 25

Work had picked up pace the moment Eva returned from New York. Her list of clientele remained unsteady, the informant had reached some of them again. Four more businesses terminated their projects with S. F. Designs all in the same week. Was it a consequence of her threatening the creepy-guy in the park? Was he the informant?

Added to that, the board members had found out about the FBI's visit to her uncle. Which only made matters worse because they demanded he step down until the investigation ended.

"What?" she snapped at a room full of people who glared at her with the same caution and doubt they had when she'd first met them and each time after.

The one difference, Uncle Dave too seemed to have lost all trust in her abilities. He gave her that look, a look of defeat as though to say, *let it go Eva, you can change nothing.* Did she not measure up to his expectations anymore? Or had the dejection from knowing the board wanted to see him gone contribute to his demoralized state? He'd usually be vocal in a meeting such as this, today however he made an exception. Her uncle stood silent, looking out the bay window, his hands clasped behind his back.

Like she'd vowed the first time she met the board members, she vowed again that she would soon change their opinions about her, about the FBI investigation, and about her uncle's involvement in the company's downfall.

"I vote a no," she announced. Some gasped. Some sighed. Some remained unmoved. She didn't care, because they were wrong in asking her uncle to step down, and she wouldn't take that lightly. "You're giving him no leeway," she went on to say to the board. "He's been loyal to this company from the very beginning until now."

"We're not denying him justice. But if the news about the FBI investigation gets out, this company will be in bad shape," one of the members stated.

"The news will only get out if we let it get out."

That brought a few of them to laughter, but she didn't care. They'd laughed at her before. The mood in the room became increasingly restless, as they shifted in their chairs and chattered among themselves.

"What if the news *does* get out? You need to have a contingency plan."

"Yes, that I agree we should, but asking Mr. Avery to step down is not a contingency plan. It's a cowardly act."

They laughed some more. "Are you calling us cowards?"

"Are you not? You're risk averse. You don't believe in my abilities even today. Even after I've returned the company stock to normal. Even after I've brought us numerous new clients. Even after I've beat the strongest odds of failure that you, collectively, predicted would be S. F. Designs future, when I first started here. If this is not success, what is?"

That had them silenced. *Good*.

"Let's vote," one of the members said.

"Let's, but remember this, the FBI has not found any evidence against Mr. Avery."

They voted, and her uncle…nearly lost.

Her father had picked her for a reason, though she didn't know why, she concluded it had to do with her inability to give up easily. The board had consistently displayed their doubt in her, but their votes conveyed a surprisingly different story, especially when two of the members told to her after the meeting, "We voted yes because of you. Hope we've made the right decision."

Slowly but surely, she gained supporters, and that brought her relief. She now also regained her uncle's support; he'd thanked her after the meeting. Although, from the years she'd known her uncle, today turned out to be a day when a rift had come in their relationship. The FBI investigation had already broken him, but what happened today with the board would loom over him forever.

Needing a break from the day's happenings, at mid-afternoon Eva went to the coffee shop with

Tina. As if her day hadn't gone badly enough, while they sipped their drinks, Eva's nerves jumped once again at the glimpse of someone she recognized. Not Lavato, but Mystique this time. And like it had happened with Lavato, when Eva turned to look for Mystique, she too wasn't there.

Eva's gaze caught with her bodyguard's, who seemed to have appeared all of a sudden. His eyebrows pulled together; he tilted his head to one side, as though waiting for her to tell him what was wrong. How could she explain what had occurred, to him or to anyone else for that matter? What proof did she have that she hadn't imagined Lavato or Mystique?

Maybe Tina had seen Mystique? She turned to Tina, but she hadn't even noticed Eva in all this time. Tina busily flipped through her phone for an image of stilettos she'd been eying to buy.

Eva silently sighed. She placed a finger at her temple and rubbed to massage. *What proof did she have…?*

"Evie, how are you, sugar?"

"Hi, Ma. I'm doing all right. Busy…" She sighed and started to doodle on the notepad in front of her. "Too busy."

"Eva, I know how it is to work for that company. Your father was in meetings all his life. Don't overwork yourself, though, it's not worth it." Her mother's words always soothed.

She set her pen down and leaned back into her office chair making it rock back and forth. "Yeah,

I'm trying not to. But you know I have to, for now, at least…till I get the hang of it."

She hadn't revealed any of S. F. Designs' issues to her mother. She also, especially, hid the matter about her father's death, that the FBI suspected it was a murder and not a hit-and-run incident. Nothing could bring him back. Her mother finding about the danger he'd been in during the days nearing his death could do no good, at least until the FBI's suspicion about his demise had cleared. Her mother had worried for her father for years. Eva would do anything to avoid causing her any further unease.

"Well, I can't tell you how relieved I am that you at least have your uncle to help."

And…about her uncle too, Eva kept to herself. She closed her eyes, her eyes stung. She brought two fingers to the lids, and rubbed to soothe. How much she avoided keeping secrets. When would it all be resolved?

"Anyway, I'm calling because I'll be in the city next Tuesday for a charity event. Want to get me introduced to that boyfriend of yours over dinner?"

"Yes!" The thought of her mother meeting Clive made her heart flutter. Too bad her father wouldn't be there. Neither would her brother, for that matter. A Doctors without Borders Surgeon, maybe right about that time he'd be operating on a wounded kid in some war trodden region.

"Joey's favorite pizza place?" her mother asked.

"Sure."

"Thought since Joey likes it so much, Clive might like it too? We can pick another place if you like."

"No-no, pizza's perfect. What time?"

"Seven?"

"Tuesday, seven p.m." Eva plugged the date into her phone calendar. Yes, she needed one of those now. A calendar to keep track of every event she attended each day, even an event as enjoyable as getting Clive introduced to family. "We'll see you there."

"OK, honey. You take care now. And don't work too hard. Oh, and I almost forgot, love your cover picture."

The cover…

"I still recall your childhood days with Izzy and Allie. You three would raid my closet, wear my sandals and scarfs, and walk around in the backyard as though you were models. And then Joey and Ryan would chase you around with water guns." She laughed. "And look at you now, my little girl all grown up, on the cover of *In Trend*."

"What do you think?" Izzy grinned wide. She held a copy of *In Trend* in her hand, its cover facing forward for Eva to see. "Amazing right? I mean, Kevin really outdid himself this time. He's a genius." She placed the magazine on Eva's desk in front of her.

Eva stared at the picture, unsure how to react to what she saw. In a white bathrobe, purple jumbo curlers in hair, makeup flawless, hot red lips formed into an O, torn dress in hand, Eva simply stared at the camera. To her left stood Mila, eyes wide, mouth partially covered with one hand. She too stared in the same direction. And to Eva's right stood Claire, a half filled coupe cocktail glass stylishly held in one hand, while her other hand rested on her hip, she also looked directly at the camera.

"So?" Izzy probed.

"I...don't know."

"This is a perfect cover, Eva. Who could have imagined that famous dress destroyed? It's so...bold."

"Really? I mean, we aren't posing or anything."

"Exactly, and that's why it's natural, and *very* sexy. I love it." Izzy grinned some more.

Eva shifted her attention back to the cover. *Bold...* "We are not swimsuit models or anything, but...we look unique...effortless."

"Yes..." Izzy almost shouted, but lowered her tone to ask, "Wait, what swimsuit models? You wanted to be photographed in a swimsuit?" She narrowed her eyes.

Not really. Silly as it seemed now, at the time she'd messaged Izzy about being on the cover, subconsciously *or however*, Eva had been competing with Silvia. But now, as she saw herself on the magazine, she couldn't imagine why she'd ever felt threatened by Silvia. She didn't want to be Silvia, not before the photo shoot, most definitely not after.

"Forget I said that." She casually waved. "It looks great, really, it does." She grinned.

"Right? I think so too." Izzy plopped into the chair in front of her. "This will be great for Claire and Mila. And maybe for your business too, no?"

"Well, not sure how it could help my company. But Tina did say I got a few calls this morning from some top brand designers, and now I know why." She smiled. "Thanks for doing this, Izz."

"Thank *you*. We're selling more copies of this issue than any other in the past year." She leaned toward Eva. "More than Silvia's swimsuit issue," she finished in a low voice.

Of course, Izzy didn't miss her slip. Eva ran her lower lip through her teeth. "By how much more?"

Izzy smirked, pulled out her phone and swiped to *In Trend's* latest sales figures.

***

Was it already the day she'd introduce Clive to her mother? Time was flying by fast.

Clive and Eva walked into the pizzeria. The hostess, dressed all in black, ushered them to the table her mother had reserved.

"Joey!" Eva gasped at the sight of her brother. She leapt into his arms and he staggered but regained his balance. They hugged tight. "I should have guessed when Mom picked this place. When did you get back?"

"Yesterday." He grinned the *Joey* grin. "I hardly recognized you without your purple crown, Evie."

Of course, the entire universe had seen her cover photo by then, including her brother.

"Never pictured you to be the *In Trend* kinda guy." She narrowed her eyes.

"You kidding? How else would I know *How to Find That G-spot*?"

191

She rolled her eyes. Well, yeah, so that too had made it to the cover. And many others, from *How to Talk Dirty*, to *25 Ways to Make Him Scream*, to *Jeans for Every Curve*, and *Make Those Lips Pop*.

"Oh stop it, you two. Clive…"

Clive extended his hand, but her mother went straight to hug. Clive was tall, but a little too tall for her mother's reach, she tipped up on her toes, and he still had to bend to hug her.

"It's lovely to finally meet you. Glad you were able to join us tonight."

"Thank you for inviting me." He stepped back.

"Hey man!" Joey extended his hand to Clive. "Last time we met was at that party at your house. Somehow I don't recollect us talking much then."

And why was that? Eva shot Clive a knowing glance. Their evening only got better from then on.

The waiter did a double take when he saw Eva and Clive, as did the host at the entrance and some of the restaurant's guests as they walked past them. For good or bad reasons, they were in the limelight. Sure, people recognized them, but for the most part, they also left them to enjoy their evening.

Her mother's eyes glittered every time Clive talked, or laughed, or gestured. And each time he did any of those, she shot Eva a quick glance of approval.

They ate, drank, laughed, and shared stories. Especially Joey, he had many to tell about his overseas assignments and surprisingly so did Clive from his Special Forces days. Overall, it turned out to be a memorable evening with her family. In no time, Clive became an integral part of the clan that still felt the emptiness from the loss of her father.

"Would have been perfect if..." her mother didn't have to finish the sentence, Eva had already predicted the finish. Her emotions welled every time she thought of her father. Especially when they met as a family, now without him. She brought her hands to her sides, reached for the wooden rim of her seat and gripped onto it tightly.

Just then, something buzzed against her forearm. It took her a second to realize her phone vibrated in her jacket she'd hung from her chair. She ignored it. All the important people in her life were right there with her. Everyone else could wait.

It buzzed again. She ignored it again.

It buzzed a third time, and Joey shot her a glance. She shouldn't have left it on vibrate; she should have set it on silent. And that's what she intended to do now. She dug into her jacket pocket and pulled out her phone. She stared at the message from...

Ryan: *We need to talk.*

Ryan: *It's urgent.*

Ryan: *It's about Clive.*

That last piece made her question reading Ryan's messages at all. Finding about Clive's ex from Ryan and not from Clive was bad enough; she'd made up her mind to never again learn anything more about Clive from anyone else but Clive himself. She messaged exactly that to Ryan. And just when she dropped her phone back into her jacket pocket, it buzzed again. She kicked herself for not having silenced it.

Ryan: *This is bad for your business with Stanford.*

She stared at the message on her screen. Joey said something about watching soccer over the weekend, Clive agreed to join him. Her mom commented on something, and all three of them laughed, but Eva remained distracted by Ryan's message until Clive's warm hand touched her knee. She glanced at him. Her breath halted, while she tried hard not to give away the slightest clue to Clive about how much those last two messages bothered her. But as much as she may hide, and though Clive wouldn't pry, he raised his eyebrows at her and gave her a questioning look. *All's good?*

She forced a smile, *yes*. Because, again, whatever may affect her business with Stanford…

Eva: *I'll wait for Clive to tell me.*

Ryan: *Like he told you why he went to Miami?*

He went to Miami on a business trip, or so she'd assumed since she didn't bother to ask. Why else would he have gone to Miami?

Ryan: *I know you're with your family right now and cannot talk.*

How the hell did he know that? Had he followed her there? This was *so* odd, and *so not* Ryan, and made her *so* jumpy. Ideally, her knee should have begun to bounce and bring her some, if any, relief, but Clive hadn't taken his hand away. In fact, he began to stroke her bare skin with the ball of his thumb. *Damn it!*

Ryan: *Meet me tomorrow, 6:30pm, that bar we meet at on Columbus.*

Eva: *No.*

Ryan: *OK. When you ask him why he went to Miami and he won't tell you, you know when and where to find me tomorrow.*

No way she'd once again let Ryan talk about Clive. Even if Clive wouldn't reveal to her the reason behind his recent travel. But, why wouldn't he tell her about Miami? What did he have to hide? Wait... *is he cheating on me?* She almost gasped.

Clive's thumb continued to caress her skin in slow, deliberate circles. Just like that, a fog of deceptive thoughts lifted off her mind. The wine glass in front of her came back to focus. She'd stared at it until... *how much of that wine did I drink tonight?* She couldn't tell because the overzealous waiter kept refilling without their consent. Not that any of them would have objected. They were all having a really good time. Well, not all of them, because she wasn't, thanks to Ryan's idiot messages.

She pushed her glass toward her brother, who at first, looked at her strangely but almost right away picked up her glass and downed her drink. Typical of Joey to down her drink, or her food...especially her desserts...with Joey around, they never had leftovers.

No matter to what extent Ryan's texts had piqued her interest, now was not the time to think about his messages. Although Clive's thumb stopped moving, he didn't pull his hand away from her knee. From the corner of her eye she sensed his stare...*definitely not the time to think about Ryan's messages.*

She silenced her phone, slipped it into her jacket pocket and returned to her evening with her family.

Unfortunately, her restraint lasted only until they reached his car and she told him, "That was Ryan texting me."

Clive's jaw hardened.

"Why did you go to Miami, Clive?"

The color drained from Clive's face. He stared at her for a long moment.

She folded her arms across her chest. "I will not go with you unless you tell me why you went to Miami." Bratty? Yes. But she needed to show Ryan how wrong he'd been about Clive all along, that Clive did talk to her when she asked, that he would tell her about Olivia someday.

Clive ran his fingers through his hair and brought his hands to rest on his hips. He looked so sexy when he did that. She shook off that last thought.

"Eva..." He cocked his head. "Please, can we not do this now?"

"When then?" She had not planned on talking to him about his past until he chose to speak to her himself. But for whatever reason, especially since he hid things from her even when she asked him, she basically went for it. "Are you ever going to tell me anything about your past? My life is an open book to you. But yours...I want to know all that I missed. From the last time I saw you at that Christmas party, up until we met again a month ago. All I know about you is from Izzy's tabloid stories and my random internet search. You've told me nothing."

"Why do you need to know about those years, Eva?" The depth of agony in his tone was unmistakable. He furrowed his brow. "I love you, and you love me. How does knowing my past change what we have now?"

"It doesn't. But…I'd like to know more about you. From you. Your words. Nobody else's."

"And I'd like you to know too. But not like this. Not today. *Especially* not here."

She sighed. "At least tell me why you went to Miami."

He said nothing. But he averted his gaze.

She pulled out her phone.

"What are you doing?"

"Calling a cab."

He grabbed her phone from her hand.

"Give me back my phone." She tried to take it from him, but he raised it over his head and even her four-inch heels didn't do much good. He grinned at her failed attempt. Not wanting to make him any happier over her distress, she gave up.

"I'm not spending the night with you, unless you tell me why you went to Miami."

Clive sobered. He looked down for a moment but when he looked back up at her, his confidence had returned. He stepped close to her. Their faces neared. Her longing for him awakened. But before she could take her words back about not spending the night with him, he opened the passenger side door.

"You don't have to spend the night with me. But I *will* take you home. And *that's* final."

Chapter 26

Twelve years ago…

Not willing to let Thomas destroy Olivia any longer, Clive headed from the hotel straight to Thomas's apartment. Thomas opened the door. Olivia stood a few steps behind him.

Clive tossed the bag toward her. "Get changed, Olivia. I'm taking you home."

"She's not going anywhere." Thomas's angry gaze locked with Clive's. "Don't touch the bag, Olivia." He squared his shoulders and stepped toward Clive, ready to brawl.

Clive, an eighteen-year-old boy, yet to reach adulthood, stood as tall as he could in opposition to Thomas, a twenty-seven year old man, well-muscled from years of training in the boxing ring. Clive couldn't take him down, but he'd do anything to get Olivia away from her abuser.

"Get changed." Clive gave her a quick glance.

Her face paled. She licked her lips and darted her gaze between him and Thomas. Heavy tears rolled down her cheeks. She shook her head at Clive.

His heart shattered to see her that way. "Please, Olivia"

And before he could bring his attention to Thomas, Thomas had already gone for the hit. He punched Clive in the face. The hard blow caused Clive to stumbled backward. He almost blacked out for a second or two. But before Thomas could return with another, Clive kicked his knee, weakening his defense. Thomas fell. Clive pushed him down. He got on top of his chest, locking him with his legs. He began to punch his face as hard and as fast as he could, not giving Thomas a chance to return his blows.

He went on until Olivia screamed, "Stop it, stop it." She gripped his arms, but as intoxicated as she was, her fingers didn't hold and she ended up scratching Clive's forearm. As she did, she too fell. Clive got off Thomas and pulled her into his arms. They watched Thomas while he lay on the floor, bloodied and bruised, twisting in agony.

Clive panted heavily. "Let's go," he spoke between breaths.

"No." She pushed away from him.

He didn't understand. Had he heard her right? Because, it made no sense that after all that happened to her, Olivia didn't want to go. But, Olivia wouldn't budge.

"You should leave."

No. No. No. "Don't do this." He shook his head. "I cannot let you stay here with him, Olivia."

"I don't want to go with you."

"Fine. Go wherever you want to go. But leave with me, now."

"I don't want to go anywhere. I want to stay here."

Thomas got back on his feet now, looking ready to brawl again.

But Olivia went on to say, "I love him Clive…I love him. Not you…*him*…I love him."

Olivia's words crashed every one of Clive's intentions of ever getting her away from that man. His pulse rattled in his throat, his limbs turned too heavy to move… because Olivia had meant it, because Olivia wouldn't budge.

It was past midnight. Clive paced along his room, unable to sleep. What could he do to get Olivia away from Thomas? Should he tell her family? She'd begged him not to speak to her family. She didn't want them to see her bruises. Should he call the cops? She said she would report Thomas in the morning. But from her last words, he doubted she would speak about her abuser to anybody.

His phone buzzed. It was Olivia. She waited for him outside his house.

He ran to the door to greet her. She'd gotten away from the guy…she'd gotten away from that cradle-robbing-son-of-a-bitch Thomas. But when their gazes met, something shifted in Clive. He no longer saw the Olivia he once knew and loved. He only saw the Olivia who had broken his heart.

She wore the clothes and shoes he'd bought her. Her eyes roamed his face. "I'm sorry for all this, Clive." She tried to touch, him but he grabbed her hand, stopping her.

"Did you leave him?"

She didn't answer. He let go of her hand.

He inhaled deeply. He smelled nothing but her inebriated breath. "Why are you here, Olivia?"

"I just…" She looked away from him. Her lips quivered, then she started to cry.

Was it odd, in all the while he'd known her, that would be the first time he no longer cared about how she felt? She'd brought this upon herself.

She ran her teeth over her lip. "I just wanted to thank you for tonight. For the hotel, for the clothes…"

"But you went back to him anyway. Despite all my attempts to get you out of this mess—"

"I'm over you Clive, and whether you like Thomas or not, I love him. I think you need to move on too."

"How can you love him, Olivia? He hurts you, in so many ways…how can you love him?"

She said nothing.

He shook his head. His anger mounted.

She was drunk. He should offer to let her stay.

She looked too dejected to be left alone. He should ask her to stay.

She didn't want to go home. He should ask her to stay.

She wanted him to ask her to stay. He should ask her to stay. "Please, leave."

"Clive, wake up."

Clive blinked his eyes open, squinting from the harsh light from the bed lamp.

"There are cops at the door, for you." Carter peered at him.

"What?" He rolled off the bed. Cops?

"What happened to your face? And your arms?"

Clive looked at the red lines raised where Olivia's nails had met his skin.

Carter walked to his closet and pulled out a long sleeved shirt. "Put this on."

Carter's phone rang. He answered it. "Yes…yes…he's here." He handed the phone to Clive.

"Clive." It was his father. "Now listen very carefully. We're flying back right away. Until we get home, don't say a word to anyone. Not to your brother, not to your sisters, especially not to the cops. You speak to no one but John. I've chatted with him already. He's on his way. Let him do the talking for you. You understand?"

He didn't understand.

"Clive?"

"Yes."

"Do you understand?"

"Yes." He didn't understand.

"Good. Don't be afraid. We're all here for you. Know that." He exhaled. "We knew this would happen to that girl someday."

Olivia…

Chapter 27

Eva woke up to an all white ceiling, a cold room and an empty bed. She pulled her blanket up to her ears and snuggled. Neither the softness nor the warmth of the fleece rescued her from her depression.

Her phone alarm buzzed. She swiped it off and peered at the screen. Had Clive messaged? He hadn't. That only made her abandon her phone on the bedside table, and sink farther into her bed.

It had been a while since Eva had started her day this way. It bore a close resemblance to that one time she'd had an argument with Clive and she'd woken up in her grandpa's house in Napa.

She closed her eyes and rehashed her exchange with Clive, letting the last few moments of her evening she'd spent with Clive play through her mind in a recurring loop. Although their conversation last night didn't entirely count as an argument, she threw a tantrum and he amicably understood why she felt the need to do so, it still left a searing void in her heart, a hollowness only Clive could undo.

Clive had driven her home after dinner. She'd let him.

He'd held her hand in his through the drive. She'd let him.

He'd kissed her good night, *on* her lips. Though not a wet and luscious full on kiss or anything, but it most certainly was a sweet, warm, *I love you* sort of a kiss. She'd let him.

He'd waited for her to get into her house and lock the door. She'd smiled as she bolted the door to her house. Yes, smiled…because despite it all…she loved him. And yet she'd pushed him away.

That last thought pierced at her. She rolled on to her side and faced the window. Though the curtains were closed, morning light still peered through, shedding further clarity onto the fact that *she* pushed *him* away. She groaned, and yanked the blanket up and over, and covered her head. She needed the darkness.

I'd like you to know too. But not like this. Not today. Especially not here… he'd said. And she agreed. They stood on the sidewalk to a busy street, after all. Also, she didn't know why, but since Clive had hidden his past with Olivia from her all this while, she'd concluded his visit to Miami had to do with Olivia. And if it were related, she'd wait until he was ready to talk.

But just because their night hadn't blown up into huge squabble, didn't mean she'd given up on finding the truth about Clive's past. She hadn't lied when she'd told him she wanted to hear it from him over anyone else. For that reason, she sent Ryan one last text before she'd hit the bed.

Eva: *I'm not going to meet you. Whatever the news, I'll wait for Clive to tell me, whenever he decides to tell me.*

The message indicated that Ryan had read it. He hadn't responded back. *Good.*

Like most mornings, Tom arrived at her door at eight to drive her friends and her to work. She could have declined, but she intended to coerce Clive to talk to her, not anger him. Izzy and Allie chatted through the drive to their office. Other than responding to her friend's questions, Eva remained silent and engrossed in her thoughts. Her day flew by unnoticed. She hadn't taken a break for lunch; neither did she rush home after work like she always did to be with Clive. Her next few days continued the same way. Until one afternoon Tina walked into her office.

"We need to talk."

Eva leaned back into her chair. Her mouth dried when her gaze met with Tina's. Tina's face was expressionless, unsmiling, yet she seemed troubled somehow. "Don't tell me you're quitting."

"Quitting?" Tina winced. "Why? I love it here."

Eva exhaled a breath of relief. "OK, what's wrong then? You look...sad."

"Break?"

Minutes later, Eva collected her tea from the café counter and pushed a lid over to cover the cup.

"I think he's re-thinking this whole marriage thing." Tina sighed long and low.

"How do you know that?" Eva looked around the coffee shop. It had become a routine. Tom and the bodyguard watched out for her wherever she went, and yet, every place she went she scanned each face for anyone who might resemble the creepy-guy or his probable alter ego, Lavato. And of course, she also looked for Mystique.

"Because...he hasn't responded to my texts, or returned any of my calls. We've had no interaction what so ever in over two days." Tina collected her coffee cup from the counter.

"Eva?"

Eva turned to the familiar voice. "Aunty Jamie!" How could she have missed seeing her aunt when she'd looked around for *familiar faces*? She reached over and hugged Uncle Dave's wife, a petite, affable, blonde. "Been a while—"

"It has. The last we met was at your father's funeral, I think."

"Yeah." She sobered, reminded of her father.

Her aunt's gaze darted to Tina.

"Oh, this is Tina, we work together."

They shook hands.

"Do you have to rush back to the office, or do you have a few minutes to chat with your aunty?" She grinned, that red lipped grin. How much Aunty Jamie loved that color. She couldn't forget those summer nights at her grandpa's house. Red lips kissed her brother and her good night, red lips wished them good morning, red lips probably went to bed red.

Tina, a newlywed, should be springing off her feet with happiness. Instead, today she'd pulled her hair into an unkempt bun, her clothes could use ironing and her shoes…first time ever she came to work in flip-flops.

Eva really wanted to talk her friend out of her worries rather than spend time with her aunt. But…"Of course, I have time for you."

They looked at Tina.

"Sorry, I need to rush back." Tina smiled. "Nice to meet you, Mrs. Avery." She gave Eva a quick nod and walked into the building toward the elevator.

Small talk would be no relaxation for Tina today. Besides, they wouldn't have talked about her marriage troubles in front of her aunt, anyway. She'd catch up with Tina when she got back to work.

They found an empty table in the coffee shop and took seats.

"It's lovely to see you again, Eva. How have you been?" Her aunt slapped a packet of brown sugar onto the ball of her palm, tore it open and emptied its contents into her coffee cup.

She'd never been worse. She missed Clive terribly and many times she had the immense urge to forgo waiting for Clive to talk to her about Olivia, and bring their relationship back to normalcy. Just the other day, she'd almost walked up to his office to do the same, to ask him to forget their last conversation, to ask him to return to her.

Mournful emotions welled from the pit of her stomach, to her aching heart. She cleared her throat. "Well…and you? How's retirement?"

"Loving every moment of it." She pulled out a pocket size flask from her purse and emptied its contents into her cup. "I'm drunk by mid-morning, and who'd stop me?" She dunked in a wooden stirrer and mixed the concoction. "Not your uncle, for sure, because he's here, at work. At least for now, that is."

"What do you mean, for now?" Eva took a sip of her drink. *Creamy...sugary...* "He's not planning to leave? Because, I need him here, my company won't function without him."

Her aunt smiled tentatively. What did she want to say? "Your father, too, thought your uncle was important and yet…"

And yet…what? Did this have anything to do with her father not writing the company off to her uncle? Before she could press further on the matter, her aunt continued, "Your uncle is disheartened by everything that's been happening here."

Somehow, it bugged Eva that her aunt knew the slightest of the issues plaguing her company. Because, per Clive, and per the FBI's suggestion, news about the informant had to be kept a secret at any cost. Her uncle knew that, and yet he'd revealed it to her aunt.

But then again, what was he to do? After being interrogated by the FBI, after nearly being voted off by close to half of the board members who, until the FBI's visit, had regarded him with reverence, and after his position jeopardized in the company, of course, he'd reveal it all to his wife of thirty plus years.

"He might be considering leaving."

Eva's breath hitched. She almost choked on her drink. "What?" That made no sense. "Why?" She'd supported him against the entire board. She'd fought for him to stay.

"Maybe you could tell me."

He told her aunt he wanted to leave the company, but he didn't tell her why? Guess he hadn't disclosed all of S. F. Design's recent troubles after all. But what did he leave out?

Unwilling to risk revealing any particulars, Eva steered the conversation to what seemed to be an obvious reason for his decision. "When was the last he took time off from work?"

She laughed. "Coming to work is his vacation, Eva. This is his only relaxation."

Like her father.

"He acts as though it's his company." Her aunt laughed again, with sarcasm and not humor this time. "Which it clearly is not. Your father made sure of that."

Aunty Jamie snapped the wooden stirrer into two. Picked up each of the broken pieces and snapped them down further. She went on until she couldn't break them down any further, she stilled and blinked at the wooden pile in front of her. Almost in slow motion, she brought her gaze back to Eva and pushed her drink away.

What was in that flask?

"I cannot believe I said all that to you. It's this…." She stared at her cup as she tap-tapped her index finger on the table.

Did she know she did that?

"I worry for him, you know? Please, don't tell him we chatted. I'll be mortified if he ever finds out."

"I understand, and my lips are sealed, promise."

Just like that, her demeanor returned to her usual self. She stopped tapping her finger. She pulled her drink back to her...

Should she stop her?

She took a sip. "So, tell me about you. You look good, obviously happy with that hunky new boyfriend of yours."

Hunky. "Yes, I'm happy." Eva grinned wide, as she always did when she spoke about Clive. "He's wonderful." *And yet I pushed him away.*

"Many pictures of you two in the tabloids, in the news..."

"Well, given Clive's fame..." She half-shrugged.

"How would it be for your business if you two broke up though? Seeing how you're tied through that contract."

One evening, alone in her house, Eva lounged on the chaise in her living room. She'd covered herself with a knit throw blanked. Her aunt's visit haunted her. Was her uncle really considering leaving the company? Why hadn't he spoken to her about it? He knew how much his being there for her meant to her.

She flipped through the TV channels. What did she do this time of her evening before Clive? She'd clicked through over a zillion channels, but couldn't find a show she wanted to watch. She settled for world news. A bomb blast had killed scores of people... A train had de-railed... Migrants sank in the sea... Sadness had consumed everyone in the world, including Olivia, including Clive, including her heart... Her eyes began to sting. She closed them to soothe the ache. She kept them closed.

Knock. Knock. "Eva?" Knock. Knock. Knock. "Eva, wake up."

Eva's eyes shot open. Her breath raced. Had she fallen asleep? And... Was someone at the door? Did they call her name?

Maybe she'd been dreaming. She blinked at the TV screen. What time was it? She picked up her phone from the floor and clicked. Eight thirty.

Knock. Knock. Knock.

She flinched. She swung her legs off the couch and stood. Was it Clive? But why would he knock? He had a key to her house.

Knock. Knock. Knock. "Eva?" A familiar, androgynous voice, called. "It's me. Mystique."

Mystique? Here?

Eva's heartbeat picked up pace. Mystique knew where she lived?

Eva rushed to where she'd hung her coat and pulled out the pepper spray from its pocket.

She swiped her phone. Should she call Clive? She stilled. She stalled. She typed 911 and set her thumb ready to dial. Phone in one hand, pepper spray in the other, she began to tiptoe to the front door, but Mystique called at her again.

"Not there, here."

Eva turned and almost yelped. Mystique stood on her patio. She'd been knocking on the glass French door.

"What are you doing here? And how do you know where I live?" Eva shifted on her feet. "I'm calling the cops if you tell me you followed a star or something." She waved her phone at Mystique.

"I followed you."

Followed me... So, she did see her in the coffee shop that day. "Why? And why are you on my patio?"

"Your driver is out in the front."

Tom... She'd forgotten about Tom. Should she alert him about Mystique? She took a step back in the direction of the front door.

"I need to talk to you. It's important. Please, let me in."

Something about Mystique's demeanor confirmed she meant no harm. But then again, *why is she hiding from Tom*?

She shouldn't open the door. She opened the door. She shouldn't invite her in. She let her in.

Mystique folded her hands tight across her chest and trembled. "It's cold out there." Her gaze fell to the pepper spray Eva held. "You won't be needing that. I promise."

Minutes later, Eva poured hot chocolate into two mugs. She pulled out a bottle of Irish cream and tilted a liberal pour into her drink. She looked at Mystique. Mystique nodded. She topped her mug too. They brought their drinks to the living space.

Mystique sipped on her drink. "Umm. Wow. This is really good. Do you always make hot chocolate from scratch?"

"Mostly. Cooking relaxes me." Eva half shrugged and brought her knees to her chest. She held her mug in both hands. Warmth radiated into her palms, soothing her after waking up unsettled by her unexpected visitor. She eyed Mystique from the rim of her cup. Once again she'd worn dark clothing. And that ring...

"What's in that ring?"

"What? Oh this..." Mystique glanced at the ring on her finger in which red liquid moved. "Blood."

Seriously? "Whose...blood?"

"Fluffy. My dog. She died a few years ago." She glanced at her ring again. "This is all that's left of her."

Eva's mouth fell open.

Mystique brought her gaze to Eva. She stared at her for a second, then threw her head back and laughed. Her laughter reverberated in the house, bringing Eva back to that moment when she'd run out of Mystique's parlor. *That voice.*

"You should see your expression right now." She chuckled. "It's so easy with you."

No. It's not.

"No wonder Izzy put you through that prank." She grinned. "This is too much fun."

No. It's not.

Mystique sobered, though a small smile lingered on her features. "Its just some liquid, a chemical maybe." She looked at her ring. Something shifted

213

in her features. "My sister gave it to me for my tenth birthday. I've worn it ever since."

Something happened to her sister. "Are you and your sister close?"

"We are, even now when she's on the other side." Mystique said, deadpan.

Other side? What *other* side? Was she playing her again?

Mystique cleared her throat. "Eva…this man… He came in for a reading a few days after you visited. Something was off about him." Mystique narrowed her eyes.

"Off how?"

She licked her lips. "He asked about you."

A shiver ran down Eva's spine. Was it the creepy guy from the park? Was it Lavato? "What did he ask?"

Mystique remained silent. Why? She wanted to tell Eva something important, she'd said. What was it? Eva needed her to talk. "How did he look? Could you describe him to me? What's his name?"

"He didn't tell me his name. He was middle aged. I didn't think much of him actually, until he spoke. And when he did, I got this feeling…I get that same feeling when I meet those from the other side, especially the bad ones."

Not again! The other side… Should Eva even bother to take anything else Mystique would say? She sighed. "Could you describe how he looked, his features or something you saw that stuck with you."

The person Mystique described resembled neither the creepy guy nor Lavato. Mystique's visitor could have been anybody. Eva leaned back into the couch.

"Oh, but there was this one thing. He had some kind of tattoo or something on his wrist. I couldn't tell what it was. His jacket covered most of it. But, it looked like… ah…"

Eva went to her desk and brought back a pencil and a notepad. "Could you draw what you saw?"

While Mystique drew, Eva texted Trevor.

Eva: *Sorry to bother you at this hour. If you're free, please, could you stop by? I'm at home. The informant might have contacted one more person.*

In less than a few seconds Trevor replied: *Will be there in five.*

Eva: *Thanks. Don't tell Clive.*

Trevor: *Ok. Do I want to know why?*

Eva: *No.*

Eva couldn't make much sense of the shape Mystique traced onto the paper. "What is it?" She squinted at the drawing. "It looks like a tool of some sort."

"Yeah, like the sharp end of a spade."

"Like on a playing card?"

"Yeah, but…that's not what it was. It was more like…" Mystique began to correct the drawing. "Something like this."

Eva looked at the edited sketch. It still didn't look like anything in particular. She continued to stare at it for a moment more when it occurred to her. "Two hooks, facing away from each other…is it…an anchor? The bottom of an anchor?"

"You know what, yeah…" Mystique nodded. "You're right. It was like the bottom of an anchor."

"What did he ask about me?" Eva tried again, hoping she'd get an answer this time.

Once again, Mystique didn't reply. She stared at nothing in particular but she stared. And then, she brought a hand to cover her mouth.

What is she not telling me? "Mystique?"

She brought her hand down slowly and her eyes met Eva's.

"What's wrong?"

"Do you own a boat?"

"Me?" Eva laughed. "No."

Mystique didn't look relieved by her answer, if anything, her expression made Eva's insides twist.

Eva cleared her throat. "I don't own a boat. Why?"

"Do you swim?"

Eva's breath caught at that question. "Yes. But..." She shifted deeper into the cushions on the couch. "I don't. Not anymore." She tucked her hair behind her ear.

Though only slightly, Mystique widened her eyes. It lasted for a fraction of a second, but enough for Eva to conclude something was wrong. Badly wrong. "What did he ask?"

"He asked why you ran out of my parlor."

"And you told him? All of it?"

She exhaled. "I'm sorry. I had to. Like I said, it was that feeling I get when I meet people like him. He is not a nice man. You're in trouble, Eva."

"Why do you think that?"

"He asked me... He asked me if he could be a murderer. I don't really predict such things, you know. That's not what I do. So I told him he is a caring man and wouldn't harm anyone. You know, just in case he was planning to harm you, he might think twice. Then he went on to tell me he speaks to someone over the phone, and this person is tempting him to do things he never imagined he'd do."

"Like committing murder?"

"Yeah. He wanted me to describe that person. Of course, I made up a description. He believed me…I think." She winced. "It's all so odd. Right? I mean, usually people come in to ask me lottery numbers and such."

Eva's stomach rolled. She'd clutched her mug so tight, her knuckles began to throb. She set her mug down onto the table and dragged in a deep breath. She had to focus. She couldn't let fear take over. "Why did you ask if I own a boat or know how to swim?"

"I…" She shook her head and brought a hand to her forehead. "It's just this vision I keep having since I met the man. You are on a boat…"

Eva's breath caught again. *Breathe Evie…breathe.* "And?"

"That's all I see. You are on a boat. Nothing else."

They both flinched at the knock on the front door. Trevor.

Eva walked into the Stanford office for a meeting with Bryan. Once again she held back the urge to walk into Clive's office, to bring him back into her life. Clive's secretary, Trish, greeted her and leaned in to ask, "Is everything OK? I think he's been sleeping in his office the last few nights."

"It's all fine." Eva gave her a wide smile. "He has way too much work to catch up on after that Miami trip."

Trish nodded. "Yeah. He's a very busy man. But he always finds time for you."

That he does.

After her meeting with Bryan, Eva avoided even a side-eyed glance in the direction of Clive's office and hurried straight to the elevators. Were these elevators always this slow? She gave the down arrow button to call the elevator a few extra taps.

She sighed at the sound of the doors opening. She rushed into the lift, hit the thirty-seventh and when she looked up, Clive stood right ahead of her.

She stared in awe at how crazy hot he looked. He wore the same clothes as the last time she saw him, only now his sleeves were pulled up, his shirt crumpled as though he'd slept in it. His stubble had darkened. His hair styled erratic and messier than usual. She was tempted to step off the elevator and run straight into his arms and let him kiss her in that wild sexy way. He most definitely looked like he would like her to do just that. Luckily, he spoke, and what he said returned her to her intended mission.

"About that night...I..." He sighed. "We need to talk, I know. And we will, I promise."

"Are we going to talk now?"

"N—No. Not now. I have to meet Trevor. It's sort of urgent."

"Well then, come find me when you're ready to talk. Till then, don't speak to me," she said simply.

He blinked. He looked too cute when he looked this lost. And she could *so* kiss him right now.

But more than that, she'd never lose an opportunity to tease, so she asked, "Are you OK with that?"

"No." He looked like he needed to be hugged and pampered until he felt loved. He looked like he wanted to say *don't leave me, Eva*.

"Good." Her reply came well timed as the elevator doors closed, leaving Clive behind. *Good*.

Eva returned to her office feeling rejuvenated. He'd *promised* to talk to her. That gave her enough to celebrate.

But just as she reveled, Tina handed her an envelope…from Ryan.

Eva stepped into her office and closed the door behind her, a little harder than usual. Though the envelope came from one of her oldest friends, whom she'd trusted fully, her father's words rang her thoughts…

Trust no one.

She slid a letter opener into the envelope and snapped it open. From within, she pulled out a photograph with a post-it stuck to it. She stared at a picture of Clive and an older woman, seated on the deck of a boat. The woman looked like she might be crying, while Clive peered at her. His expression, stern and dark. Threatening even.

She read the post-it. *If he's not guilty, why is he obstructing an investigation about his involvement in Olivia's death?*

She didn't know what dampened her mood more, her lack of ability to bring change to any of the happenings around her, or the fact that Ryan just wouldn't take no for an answer. She got that he cared for her wellbeing. But that he'd send her such a picture of Clive rubbed her the wrong way.

She had read enough tabloid articles to know the storyline and the embedded photograph almost always didn't portray the truth. Maybe because she loved Clive, maybe because she found it hard to believe he could be at fault in general, maybe because she already knew Clive and Ryan had never gotten along, but to her, the picture and the post it note just didn't fit.

How did Ryan get this photograph anyway? Had he followed Clive? But of course, he had. How else had he known she met her family the other night?

She had to clear things out with Ryan once and for all. She pulled out her phone and sent him a text.

EVA: *See you at 6:30.*

Chapter 28

Olivia's expression is exactly as he saw her that last time. Grim, bruised, broken hearted. She calls to him, as she tilts to fall backward off a cliff. Her hand stretches toward him, but no matter how hard he tries, he is unable to hold on. She begins to fall into the cavern, screaming... Clive... please... help me... please... please...

Panting and shaking from the recurring nightmare that had haunted him for years since Olivia's passing, Clive sprang out of his bed. He rubbed his face with both hands, grateful that despite being life-like, it was once again all in his imagination. The only time he'd not woken up that way was after Eva came into his life.

Eva...

As he did the past few mornings, it took him a moment to orient himself to his surroundings, and soon recent happenings reeled back to his mind.

He couldn't go back to his apartment without Eva. He couldn't sleep in the bed they'd shared many nights, especially knowing he'd wake up alone to emptiness. He'd spent the past few nights in the hidden bedroom attached to his office.

He hadn't brought Eva there yet. He imagined having no memories of her there might lessen the sting of not having her by his side. But that hadn't mattered because thoughts of her consumed his mind no matter where he was.

He'd pushed her away that night, like he had everyone else before when they'd wanted him to talk about Olivia. But, Eva wasn't just everyone. Eva was Eva...*his Eva*. He had wanted to tell her about Olivia from the very beginning. And now he questioned his judgment to have refrained from answering her. Why did he lose all words when she'd asked about Miami? Was it because Ryan had cornered him into it? Had Ryan told her about Olivia?

Thud. Thud. The waitress set down two Pilsners onto the wooden table. "Anything else I can get for you?"

"We're good for now, thanks." Clive smiled at their server. He clinked his glass with Trevor's, took a huge gulp of the frothy, golden drink and set his glass back down on a green paperboard coaster imprinted with the bar's logo. Though the middle of a workday, Clive didn't have the mind for anything else but to contemplate how he should reveal his past to Eva. Trevor didn't want to be at the FBI office, either. More so after McKenzie asked him to take the rest of the day off to *get your shit together*. McKenzie always had a way with words, especially when he cared.

Trevor and Clive sat in their usual go-to bar, the perfect place for a heart-to-heart. Which during Clive's FBI days were far too many. They liked the bar because it was clean, comfortable and low-key, and definitely a place to relax with friends, although neither Trevor nor he were relaxed.

Trevor, too, took a gulp of his beer but set his glass back down with a heavy *thud*. He lowered his head and stared at the honeycomb mug. "I cannot believe I let her die. I was so close."

If anyone in the world would understand Trevor's distress, it had to be Clive. *He'd let Olivia die*.

Trevor had updated him a few times since their first conversation about Lavato. None of Candy's returning visitors turned out to be their guy. Except for the last one.

"Candy texted me about two this morning…" Trevor pulled out his phone and showed Clive Candy's message.

Candy: *Come fast. I think this is your guy*.

"It was strange that she'd text me at that hour. She only worked until midnight and she never brought men home."

Trevor: *At Madam's?*

Candy: *No, home*.

"Right away I knew something wasn't right. Her visitor had to be our guy. And she had no clue how much trouble she was in."

Trevor: *You don't meet them at home, you said. Don't let him in.*

Candy: *I already did. He's paying me double.*

"She put herself in danger, simply to make a few extra bucks." Trevor stared at the table between them for a long moment. "I knew…" He shook his head. "I knew in that moment that I'd never see her again. I knew this would be my last text to her…"

Trevor: *Describe the guy. What's his name? Send me a picture.*

"She didn't text me back. I hoped the guy had kept her busy, trying to get his money's worth." Trevor's expression darkened. He gripped the handle of his beer glass. "I drove to her place; I broke all the traffic rules… He strangled her, man." He shook his head again. "He strangled her." He picked up his glass, took a huge gulp. "By the time I reached her apartment, Jason was already waiting there for me. We lost her."

Clive too took a gulp of his drink. "How do you know it's our guy who did it?"

"We don't." Trevor shrugged. "They traced a few fingerprints. But if it's our guy, we know how careful he is. And we almost knew he'd do this. He warned that he might kill someone."

"Warned? Whom?"

Trevor exhaled. "Eva…"

Clive's heart skipped a beat. His chest grew tight. "He met Eva?" he almost shouted.

"No-No. He…well, at least we think it's the informant, met Mystique."

Every detail Trevor conveyed thereafter about Mystique visiting Eva scorched Clive's heart.

"Clive…"

He tightened his fists hard, resisting the urge to break something…*anything*. He'd left Eva, alone, all this time. And why? Because he couldn't man up and talk to her about Olivia. He hated himself in this moment. When did he turn into such a selfish coward?

"Clive?"

"What about Dave? Is he still a suspect?" He'd gritted his teeth so tight, his jaw hurt when he spoke.

"We showed Candy Dave's picture, but she'd never seen him. We investigated Dave further, by the way. We found nothing. *Nothing*. He's clean…*so* clean that McKenzie doesn't even see him as a suspect anymore. Brother fighting brother over family business is an obvious plot, and Dave's a smart guy, he wouldn't jeopardize his lifelong work and social standing by stooping this low. And what good is a company whose business has already taken a beating?" Trevor grunted. "At least that's what McKenzie thinks."

"What do you think? Do you see Dave as a suspect?"

"I don't know what I think about anything anymore." Trevor said grimly and finished his beer. He signaled the waitress for another one. "Care to tell me what's bugging you?"

"Ryan."

"Oh, did I tell you he knows we know he's snooping around about Olivia?"

"You didn't."

"He knows we know he's snooping around about Olivia."

Clive, too, finished his drink and signaled for another one. "He told Eva I went to Miami."

"That son-of-a-bitch!" Trevor thumped his glass down again after taking a long swig. "Did he tell her why?"

"I don't think so."

"I take it you haven't told her about Olivia yet."

Clive too set his glass down with a thud this time. Somehow, all that glass banging helped them vent.

"What are you waiting for, Clive?"

"I think I'm afraid."

"You? Afraid?" Trevor threw his head back and laughed.

"What if she thinks like I do about it? What if she thinks I should have stopped Olivia that night? What if…what if she thinks I killed Olivia?"

"You are kidding right? Because nobody *but you* thinks you killed Olivia. And because of that you're about to blow what you have with the only true love in your life? Don't let your past confine you."

Don't let your past confine you. Deep, philosophical, and *so* not how Trevor usually talked.

Clive might have ignored his statement, given how grim Trevor felt today, had he ended on that note. But Trevor went on to say, "What you think of yourself is much more than what other people think of you."

Clive mulled over that for a moment. And then a moment longer because... "What? That doesn't even make any sense. If anything, it means I'm right in thinking I killed Olivia."

Trevor sighed. "I don't know what I'm saying anymore, man." His tone sullen, he stared at his glass as though he talked to it. "Nina is making me take this self-help course on the internet. I just say such things now," he shrugged matter-of-factly bringing Clive a smile.

"Since when do you need self-help?"

"Since I met Nina."

Any other day, Clive wouldn't be seen wandering aimlessly in public like he did now. Reporters snooped around him all the time, waiting to snap a picture of him to attach to an untrue story of their imagining. But his last conversation with Eva and the one he'd just had with Trevor had him unsettled.

The FBI had its ways to tackle the issue about the informant, but he had to strategize a plan of his own. There must be something he could do to lure that guy out into the open.

Needing a brisk walk, he left his car where he'd parked and started down the street vibrant with restaurants, bakeries, bars, and bookstores that enticed tourists and locals alike. But his walk came to an abrupt halt when his gaze fixed on the unmistakable face among the horde. Her delicate beauty had lingered in his thoughts since the first time he'd seen her.

Eva appeared to be in a serious conversation with Ryan. She stood with her hands tucked in her coat pockets. Her stance appeared somewhat accusatory. She frowned. She was angry. Why?

Ryan said something.

She gave him a deathly look. Shaking her head, she turned around to walk away. But Ryan caught her by her arm, causing her to spin and face him.

By now, Clive had closed in on them.

"Let go Ryan, you're hurting me."

Clive signaled Tom and Eva's bodyguard not to interfere and became a barrier between Eva and Ryan. Grabbing Ryan's hand off her arm, he shoved him away.

"Keep your hands off her," he scoffed.

"You stay away from her, Clive." Ryan's jaw clenched.

Clive grabbed Ryan by his jacket collar. Ryan too held him with matched aggression.

"Why don't we fix this once and for all, huh, Clive?"

"I won't let you take her away from me again."

"Take whom away from you?" Eva asked.

"She left with me, *willingly*." Ryan tightened his grip. Clive did too.

"Who left with you willingly?" Eva asked again.

When neither of them responded, Eva stormed, "Who, dammit, who?"

"YOU." They replied in unison.

"Me?" She scowled.

Ryan's laugh mocked. "Your boyfriend is still holding on to his grudge from that Christmas party when you walked away with me…*willingly*, after he made you cry."

He should have punched the smug off Ryan's face that very night. Why had he ever waited this long? Heat rushed through Clive's body, his muscles tensed, his temper flared.

228

"What? It wasn't Clive you moron. I was upset that night because my parents were separating, and if anything, Clive was only helping me forg—"

Before she could finish, Clive punched Ryan in the nose. Right about the same time Ryan punched him in his gut.

"What the hell's the matter with you both? Stop it, please." Eva pulled them apart. Her words, not her strength stopped them from returning back to their brawl. Clive breathed heavy, so did Ryan. Clive's hands remained fisted by his sides. His gut ached from the blow, but he couldn't be happier that he knocked that smirk right off Ryan's face.

"He's a murderer, Eva," Ryan shouted.

"What?" Clive snapped. "Must have been *some* blow, because clearly I've knocked your brains out."

"No?" Ryan taunted. "Why haven't you told her about Olivia then? What haven't you told her about the investigation? Isn't that why you went to Miami, to threaten June? Isn't that also why your FBI friends are following me? If you aren't guilty, then what are you trying to hide?"

"What the hell Ryan? I told you I wanted to wait for Clive to tell me about Olivia when he was ready to talk about her."

Clive's insides twisted in horror. She knew…about Olivia. Ryan had told her. How long had she known? Why hadn't she mentioned to him that she knew? Did she blame him for Olivia's death?

"I cannot believe you two," Eva riled. "You're one of my closest friends, Ryan. Sure we kissed that one time…"

What? What?

"But you know as well as I do that we can never, *ever*, be any more or any less than what we already are to each other. And Clive, I love you, *dammit*. That you haven't told me about Olivia, doesn't change that fact, because she's your past and I..." Her eyes softened. "I'm your present."

Clive tried to reach her but she took a quick step back and held up her hand. "I don't want to lose either of you. You've got to figure out how to make that happen."

Before either of them could respond, she turned around and walked away from them.

Clive watched after her as she walked right through a myriad of heart shaped bubbles a street artist had blown.

A child cried, "She broke my heart."

To which Eva snorted, "Get used to it."

The boy's mother pulled him close and glared at Eva.

"Sorry," Eva uttered awkwardly and ducked into a bookstore.

He stared after her for a long moment, and when he turned to look at Ryan, he was gone.

Eva's words touched Clive immensely. That she'd stuck around with him despite knowing whatever that *asshole* Ryan had told her about him gave him relief. No matter how difficult revisiting his past would be, finding that Eva already knew raised his confidence to finally bring himself to talk to her about Olivia.

Chapter 29

Embarrassed by how she'd grunted without realizing she'd responded that way to a child, Eva disappeared into the first store she could find. Only after she'd walked in toward rows of shelves did she orient herself to the small, quaint, locally owned bookstore. She turned around to see if Clive had followed her in. He hadn't. She walked into a random aisle and slumped into a high back chair she found.

Her breath hurried from the startling conversation she'd had with Clive and Ryan. She couldn't believe that all this time, she'd caused their enmity. She took a few deep breaths to suppress the frenzied drumming of her heartbeat. When she inhaled, she breathed the fresh woodsy smell of the books. The memory took her back to her childhood days, when her grandpa read her bedtime stories. She smiled, remembering the hay bed he'd created for her because she'd wanted the exact bed *Heidi* had. Her gaze shifted to find the name of the section she sat in, *Crime and Law*.

It made no sense that Ryan called Clive a murderer. She'd looked at that photograph of Clive and June numerous times since she'd received it, but was never once convinced that Clive had threatened June. It just didn't sound like something Clive would do.

Once she regained her composure, she walked out of the store and halted at the pitiful sight in front of her. Clive bent down awkwardly as he posed for a picture with two teenage girls. He disliked *selfies*, especially with people he didn't know, but he obliged anyone who asked to take a picture with him. He got stopped for pictures all the time. People recognized him from his numerous tabloid appearances. Sadly, he featured in a *lot* of selfies.

He generally avoided being in public, and yet, here he stood, outside the store, on a busy, touristy street, while Eva took all the time she needed to contain her furor. Her otherwise extremely busy billionaire boyfriend, waited patiently, selflessly...*for her*.

His face lit up when their eyes met. He took a step toward her but stopped as though waiting for her consent.

"Want to grab a drink?" he asked.

"But you look like you're having *so* much fun." She smiled. He smiled too. He pulled her to him and hugged her tight.

Upon seeing them together, the teenage girls retuned for another picture. People slowed and stared, making Eva fidgety. How had Clive endured these glances all the while he waited for her outside the store? "Let's go."

"Let's." He circled his arm around her waist and walked toward a black door in a brick wall. He punched a few numbers onto a silver keypad. The door clicked open to dim, soothing light and stylish electronic music. A VIP entrance door to a bar, he told her. He also told her that the owner was his friend. They walked through a corridor that led them directly into one of the many lounges the bar hosted. The maître d' recognized Clive and took them to a secluded section where the music, not too loud, allowed them to be audible to each other without having to shout.

Just as they sat down, a waitress brought them their drinks, two Gin & Tonics, hers with extra lime.

How did she know?

"I ordered ahead as I waited for you by the bookstore." He smiled.

Of course, he did, and she loved him for it. She took a sip of her drink. It was perfect. Setting her glass back on the table, she turned to face him. She rested her elbow on the back cushion and leaned her head into her hand. Angling one leg on the seat and letting the other dangle from the couch, she sat facing Clive.

"I'm not a murderer, Eva."

The uncertainty in his eyes twisted her heart. "I didn't think you were." She hoped her affirmation would bring him relief. But it seemed to have the opposite effect as his gaze dropped to the glass he held in his hand. His melancholy could shatter even the sunniest of days. He sighed, placed the glass back onto the table and sank into the seat.

"I don't know what you've heard about Olivia and me."

She despised how it all had unfolded over a heated conversation between Clive and Ryan. It especially made her furious that, though Ryan knew she'd waited for Clive to share his past with her, he'd talked about Olivia anyway. *What was he thinking?*

It had to be awkward for Clive to have this conversation with her now. He couldn't have expected his day to end this way. Although she'd pushed him to talk to her about his Miami visit, now, more than ever, she no longer cared to know. Because, she couldn't bear to see what remembering Olivia did to Clive. She stared at his sullen expression in silence, letting him gather the memories of his broken past. "I haven't heard anything until I've heard it from you."

He exhaled, still bleak, but his expression relaxed somewhat. The least she could do was assure him that she trusted his word over anyone else's.

"I met Olivia in high school, a few years after that Christmas where I last saw you." He paused, his eyes studying hers. "You know, I wondered if kissing her would be like kissing you. I secretly wished she'd smell of punch, and I don't even like punch." He gave her a small smile. Darkness loomed in his eyes.

She recollected her first kiss with Clive; she'd drank punch that evening. "Were you disappointed when she didn't?"

"Terribly. It was a deal breaker." He laughed a light laugh. "But then she didn't like punch either, so we had *that* in common."

Just as she'd thought he eased, the worry in his features returned, his brow furrowed, his eyes dimmed. If only she knew how to help alleviate his pain…to diminish his grief…

He told her everything, from the first time he'd met Olivia, to the talented gymnast that she was, to how much he loved her before she'd met Thomas, to how much he tried to hold on to her after she'd been long gone with Thomas…to her drug addiction that swallowed her goals, her ambitions, her aspirations…to that night…*that awful night*…

"I'll never forget that night, when the cops came to our house, looking for me. They'd found Olivia's car by the sea. It had run off the road, plummeted off the cliff and crashed on the rocks below. They found her inside her car...*dead*." He remained silent for a moment, then cleared his throat. "My father's lawyer, John Smith, did most of the talking with the authorities." He paused again. "I was the last person she'd met that night," he added softly.

He fell silent again for a few moments.

"Thomas, Olivia and I had bruises on our bodies, and they couldn't figure who hit whom. They found Thomas's DNA on her, so they suspected him. They found my skin under her fingernails, so they suspected me. Her blood report revealed she was heavily intoxicated, but neither Thomas's nor mine showed any traces of alcohol. They had no substantial evidence to implicate either of us. And they never found whoever it was she'd drank with that night. Given her history with drug abuse and that she was driving under the influence, they concluded she had swerved the car a little too much toward the edge when it slipped off the road and dove to the rocks. They cleared us of any charges, called it a teenage DUI death, and closed the case." His expression turned dark, intense and focused.

Her heart sank. He looked as though he'd just relived every moment of the tragedy.

"I'm sorry, Clive." She placed her hand on his. His skin had never felt this cold. She cupped his hand to share her warmth.

Again, he said nothing for a long moment. He picked up his glass and stared at the liquid within. He took a huge gulp and set it back down onto the table. His gaze returned to hers, but something shifted in his expression.

"I'm no saint, Eva, but neither was Olivia. Olivia and I didn't get along from the very start. We fought all the time. I didn't think much of our quarrels, because couples argue all the time. But she'd taken it to a whole other level. She'd go out with other guys from school. Send me pictures. *Revenge porn,* that's what she called it. We broke up a few times, but just as we fought, we also made up. And then she met Thomas." His jaw tightened. "After all the times I'd saved her from ruining herself, she came to see me that night, drunk, telling me she was over me. And that I should move on because she'd found her true love. Imagine that, she was in love, with Thomas, after all the many ways he'd destroyed her…she still loved Thomas. Once I realized that, whether she was happy or not, it no longer mattered.

At least, until the next morning when I heard about her death." His head dropped. "I will never forgive myself for not stopping her from driving that night. I knew she was drunk. I should have forced her to wait until she sobered. I should have taken away her car keys. I should have threatened to call her parents. There was so much I could have done to stop her from dying, and I did nothing. What I did do, was ask her to leave. Ironically, she did."

"You can't blame yourself for her actions, Clive."

"No, I can't be blamed for anything she chose to do. But I most certainly am to blame for not stopping her from driving in the state that she was. How could I not have cared for her? How was I that ruthless?"

That was a lot of guilt for somebody who had done nothing but try to help. "You were eighteen. She'd made your life miserable. Of course, you wanted her gone."

"But not in *that* sense."

"Obviously, not in *that* sense." She shouldn't try to convince him. His guilt was irrevocable, and there was nothing she or anyone else could say or do to change his conviction.

"Her father blamed me for introducing her to drugs. He was right. Her father blamed me for not stopping her from leaving my house that night. He was right."

No, he was not. Why can't you see that? "I'm sorry Clive."

"Please, don't be. Because, frankly, I willingly take the blame. That night, between Olivia and I, I was the sober one. I should have been less selfish. I should have cared."

Neither of them said anything else.

"Is her family asking for a re-investigation?"

"No. They aren't. I talked to them last week." He locked his eyes with hers. "Olivia's parents separated after her death. Her gymnastic fame had helped hold their marriage together. Her success masked all their issues. Her father still lives here but her mother moved to Miami. She lives on a boat. You already know I met her." Looking away, he shook his head. His simmering anger over Ryan's latest gaff evident as his jaw shifted.

"I don't believe that you threatened her." She pulled out the photograph Ryan had given her of Clive and June and handed it over to Clive. "All I see when I look at this picture is a mourning mother and her daughter's ex-boyfriend who'd do anything to take her pain away."

Clive pulled her close and hugged her tight. He kissed the side of her head. "Thank you," his voice trembled. "Thank you."

When they pulled apart, Clive's expression lightened. Did he worry that she wouldn't believe him over Ryan?

She sipped her drink while she gathered her thoughts about Clive and what a huge impact Olivia's death might have had on his life. She couldn't even begin to imagine how troubled he might have been for years…*after Olivia*…"Is that why you didn't have a steady relationship for all these years? Because of what happened with Olivia?"

His pensive mood vanished. His eyes softened. He held her hand in his. Warmth had restored to his skin. "I did not have another girlfriend because of you."

"Me?" For the second time that day he told her she'd influenced his past.

"Yes, *you*. After that last time we met, I thought of you all the time. But as years passed, my memory of you faded. Your features converted to a vague blurry image and, eventually, I rarely thought about you. I hated myself for learning to forget you. But you were gone, Eva, from the school, from the parties, from my life. Yet, through all that time, I think somewhere in my subconscious, I still wanted to be with you. *I missed you*. All those women in my life couldn't make up for what you and I had. Not even Olivia. Never again was it like it was to be with you. Never again was it as simple...until finally...*finally* you came back to me. You're no longer a sweet, wet dream I'd wake up to during my high school years, you're real."

He dreamt of me...like that?

"Yes, many times." He grinned and leaned over and kissed her lips. Heat rushed through her. Her cheeks tingled. Her heart sped. *He dreamt of me...like that.*

They spent the rest of their night and late into the next day in Clive's apartment. When they slept, Clive hugged her tight, as though if he didn't, he'd lose her. When they awoke, he held her hand in his and didn't let go. They talked about Olivia, about

Thomas, about Ryan, about everything else that had occurred before Eva and Clive met again. They talked about Mystique's visit, and also about Ryan's PI work for a reporter, who Clive suspected to possibly also be their informant.

"That's all there is to know about my past. I want you to know that," Clive assured.

"And you now know everything about my past too."

"I have no apprehensions about yours. If you have any about mine you should let me know now."

"I have none." She smiled.

"I will be asking you a question soon, Eva. Really soon."

Her chat with Allie echoed in her mind, *what if Clive proposes to you, today...will you say yes?*

She stared at him, what should she say?

"You should...think about it." He smiled at her mischievously.

He wouldn't heal simply because he spoke to her, he may never heal from his grief for that matter, but his attempt to return to normalcy made her believe that all their troubles would subside in due time.

She cleared her throat. "Could Ryan give you details on who his client is?"

He didn't appear offended that she'd move on from talking about *a certain question* he planned to ask her to a completely unrelated topic. *Good.*

As prearranged, they met Joey at an Irish Pub to watch the soccer match. Izzy and Carter, Allie and

240

Marc, and Trevor and Nina joined their merriment. The highlight of the occasion, Clive had returned to being his usual jovial self. Eva's peace of mind lasted through the rest of the evening…at least until they reached home.

She opened the post box and found a bunch of envelopes, grocery coupons and other assorted advert leaflets. She took them to her couch and began to open the envelopes. The senders were obvious on all but one, which was blank on both sides She shot Clive a quick glance.

"What's wrong?"

She walked to her desk and pulled out a pair of gloves from the wicker basket, then snapped them on and slid the letter opener in to tear open the white cover. She emptied the contents onto her desk. A chill zapped from the nape of her neck to her toes.

This could be you, unless…

Her stomach twisted, *unless what*? She stared at the Polaroid in her trembling gloved hand. The woman in the photo, wearing a tank top and a pair of shorts, lay on disheveled sheets, appeared to be…*dead*.

"Candy."

***

"Why did you kill her?" The voice shouted.

"Those bodyguards were followin' her, that's why." The informant shouted back into the phone's mouthpiece.

"Murder was not in the plan."

"Why not? Besides, practice makes me perfect, don't ya' think." He grinned. Addictive warmth radiated through his body remembering what he'd done to Candy. He'd never believed he could rise above the rest, like his mother had.

I'm not like my father, I'm like you...superior, powerful...

"Practice for what?"

"Killing Eva."

"Have you lost your mind?" The voice roared. "You are *not* killing Eva. That does not work well *at all* with what I have in mind. She is not the rightful owner of the company and we need her to step down. That's all. Not kill her!" The voice huffed. "You know what? You're so stupid, I'm tempted to report you to the cops."

He laughed. "Report me?" He continued to laugh. "You think I won't tell them about you?"

"And, what will you tell them about me? You've never met me. You have no clue who I am..." The voice laughed. "Idiot."

Yes, what would he tell them? He knew nothing about his employer. They'd only talked over the phone through these months. All this while he'd suspected his employer had driven that van and killed Eva's father. But it didn't matter what he thought, because he had no glimpse of his employers face, the driver had a mask on. He also didn't know whether his employer was a man or a woman, because that voice that spoke over the phone...that voice that grunted...that voice that loathed...rough, androgynous...that voice gave him nightmares. All he had was a description from Mystique. But now he doubted her abilities. She'd told him he couldn't harm anyone, yet he'd murdered Candy.

His muscles tensed. His heartbeat raced. Dark thoughts rushed to his mind. He didn't want to be sent to jail, like his mother. He had to avoid being reported by his employer. Maybe he should do a little digging into who his employer was. "You need me, because you have no other choice but to kill her. She's obviously not the fearin' kind." Except for that one time when Eva had visited Mystique. He still wasn't clear about what had scared her then, Mystique's acting or what Mystique had said to her...*Trust no one.* What was so scary about those words?

"And how would you know that?"

He should reveal his meeting Eva at the coffee shop, or how he followed her that bachelor party night, or how he visited her again in the park in New York. He no longer cared about his employer's plan, because why should he when he had a better one of his own? Especially after what he'd done to Candy... He was superior...he was powerful...and he now intended to kill not only Eva, there were many on his hit list and his employer obviously topped them all.

"Well, for one, she's obviously not afraid of threats."

The voice snorted a laugh. "She's not afraid?" The voice laughed some more before turning too eerie even to his liking. "We all have our little fears, and hers...well hers will simply...*sink her.*"

Chapter 30

Trevor struck a golf ball on the indoor golf mat. The ball not only missed the putting hole, it bounced under McKenzie's table. "The only fingerprints they found in Candy's home were Candy's."

Clive had suspected that would happen. The letter Eva received confirmed that the informant and Candy's killer were one and the same person. They hadn't found prints on that letter. Obviously, they hadn't found any in Candy's apartment either.

"What would you do if you were him?" Clive set a golf ball on the mat and attempted to aim as he swung the club back and forth.

"Not send that note, you mean?"

"Yes, because why create a chase? Why attract attention? Unless you think you can get away with it." He struck the ball, and it rolled smoothly into the hole. He gave Trevor a now-that's-how-you-do-that smile and went to pick out the ball.

"He's being cocky?" Trevor gave him a look. As though he'd used the same sentence to point out what he thought about Clive gloating and his golfing skills.

Clive grinned. He loved to ruffle Trevor. "And why not?"

"Yeah, why not. Because it just might work to our benefit." Trevor returned to aiming his hit.

"It might, but only if we force him to be sloppy. Because no matter his level of confidence, the less time he has, the less planned he'll be."

Trevor struck the ball again, and again it rolled off under McKenzie's desk. He sighed. "And the poorer decisions he'll make." Trevor loathed himself for not protecting Candy that night. Regardless of what Clive said about it, he blamed himself for her death. "Any thoughts on how we can get him to mess up?"

"Yes." Not bothering to aim this time, Clive set the golf ball down, struck it and again, it went straight into the putting hole.

"This game is stupid." Trevor threw down his club.

Clive gave him a look. "The *game* is stupid?"

The door swung open. "What the hell are you two doing in my office? Especially *you*." McKenzie pointed to Clive. "You don't work here anymore, remember? Don't you have a nail salon to run?"

"If you mean a five star luxury spa, then yes, I do." Clive gave him a toothy grin. "Eighty seven of them to be precise."

"Still doesn't tell me why you're here. And *you*…" He looked at Trevor. "What happened to finding that poor woman's killer? Any updates from SFPD?"

"Yes, but we have a better lead from Clive."

McKenzie picked up the club Trevor had tossed to the floor, set a golf ball on the mat, aimed, struck the ball, and it rolled smoothly into the hole.

Trevor mumbled a curse and shifted in his chair.

McKenzie glanced at Trevor. "What? Don't tell me you lost again?"

"We weren't counting." Trevor dismissed him.

"Sixteen, zero." Clive grinned.

Ignoring Clive, Trevor handed McKenzie the note Eva had received from the informant, sealed in a see through evidence collection bag.

McKenzie read the note. "*Unless* what? Where's the rest of it?"

"Haven't received it yet."

McKenzie stared at Clive for a long moment before he spoke again, his tone low and teemed with concern, "It might not be easy, but I can try to convince headquarters to get Trevor and Jason to shadow her again."

"I have Eva covered. I've set up security around her house, checked for bugs, and cancelled all my travel plans. I'm with her as much as possible. And when I'm not, I have Tom and an undercover bodyguard looking out for her."

McKenzie gave him a light smile. "You checked for bugs..." He shook his head and shot Trevor a glance. "Imagine that, *Clive* in love. Who'd have thought?"

"He's about to ask her to marry him."

"Is that right?" McKenzie's grin converted to a scowl. "And what if she says *no*?"

What? No, she wouldn't. Why would she? *Would she*?

***

Finding it impossible to forget the woman in the Polaroid, Eva remained distracted all day. Why did Candy have to die? Just so Eva could return to her cushy life? Was Eva's life really worth dying for? Was Candy's life worth that little?

"What's wrong?" Clive asked, as he maneuvered the car out of the Stanford tower in the direction of Eva's home.

She shook her head. Because, where should she begin?

"Is it about Candy?"

She looked at him but couldn't bring herself to say anything at all. Because no matter what she said, no matter how much she questioned all that had consumed her life since her father's passing...*nothing*...*absolutely nothing* would bring Candy back.

"I've thought about Candy all day, and so has Trevor. He blames himself for her death."

"Why? How could he have stopped it from happening?"

"Exactly, he couldn't. And yet he cannot forgive himself."

"Just like I'm unable to forgive myself...am I worth dying for?" She stared out the passenger side window. Everyone they drove past would die someday. What kind of life would they live? Fulfilled? Unlike Candy's?

"You are to me, Eva."

Clive's sweet words liberated her from her shuddering thoughts and brought her to glance at him.

"Look." He took her hand into his, placed it on his lap and continued to hold on to it as he drove. The warmth from their contact comforted her somewhat.

Had Candy had someone to care for her like that?

"I know I should say something amazing to you right about now and get you to stop blaming yourself for Candy, but..." He took his eyes off the road for a moment to meet her gaze. "The best lines usually come to me when I watch you sleep." He kissed her hand and returned to concentrating on driving. "This will all not only be over very soon, but also most definitely forgotten. I promise you that."

"You watch me when I sleep?"

"Every morning."

His playful and contagious grin made her almost forget about Candy. Almost. He parked the car by her house, and her mailbox came into sight. Her thoughts raced right back to that envelope. "What do you think he meant by *unless*?"

At first, Clive looked as though he didn't get her question, but just as quickly, his playfulness vanished. "He'll send us another note, Eva."

Another note. Should she even bother to fear what might be in that note? She couldn't stop it from reaching to her anyhow. Besides, she wanted the informant to finish the sentence. She wanted to know…*unless what*? She laughed a humorless laugh to herself. Who'd have thought there'd come a day when she anticipated a note from the informant?

She inserted the key into the front door, opened it and almost jumped out of her skin as an alarm reverberated through the house.

What the hell? She glared at Clive.

He placed her phone in her hand. When did he take it out of her bag?

"Put your thumb here." He indicated the button on her phone.

She did as instructed, and the ringing stopped.

"That's how that works."

Her heart continued to pound in her chest. She really could have used some warning.

Unaffected, he took her phone from her. "This…" He tapped her screen. "Will show you who's at your doorstep." It did. A video of them standing at the door streamed onto her phone. She looked around the doorframe for cameras, but she didn't see any.

"They're hidden in the frame, see…" he brought his finger to where the cameras supposedly were. They were four tiny black dots on four different locations on the frame, allowing a view of the person standing by the door from various angles. "And there are two more hidden on your mail box so you know if he's holding a weapon or cookies behind him."

He smiled.

She did not, because he really should have warned her. Her heart still pounded hard. "What if the weapon or cookies are hidden in his pocket?"

His face drained of color as though she made him imagine the worst happening to her. Maybe she shouldn't have brought up the possibility of the informant beating them at their game, but Clive deserved this after how he let the alarm scare her to death. To worsen his wound, she smiled.

He did not. "You won't be opening the door for a stranger, Eva. Be it a man, a woman or a child. You won't be opening the door for anyone except me, your family, my family, Izzy, Allie, and Tom. No one else."

"And the new bodyguard."

"And him. Yes. I've also set up lights and cameras around the perimeter of house. If anyone comes within ten feet, the lights go on and a picture of the person is fed directly to Trevor, me and you."

"What if it's a rabbit?"

"The system is smart enough to gauge that."

Her heart continued to pound, but not from the screech of the alarm sounding. All this security meant one thing and one thing only, her life was in danger. *Her life was in danger.*

"Cannot be too careful when it concerns you." He played with her ponytail, twirling it around his finger.

What would she do without Clive? Especially after she'd triggered the ego of a possible mad man, who'd killed Candy and now he threatened to kill her too.

"Thank you." Overburdened by negative thoughts, her body grew heavy. She grabbed the doorframe to keep steady. Had she refused to abide by her father's will, she would have continued to climb that chef ladder, she would have opened her own restaurant. Heck, she would have been on the cover of a food magazine instead of Izzy's *In Trend*…but… would she have met Clive?

"Eva…" Clive grabbed her by her shoulder. "We'll catch the guy. But until we do, we have to outsmart him."

She nodded and walked into the house. She opened a window, and the alarm sounded. She opened her patio door, and the alarm sounded again. She'd become a prisoner in her own home. But what choice did she have?

She could use a drink. "Wine?"

"Sure."

She guided him down to the basement. "Isn't this cute?" She glanced over her shoulder and gave him a small smile as they entered the dimly lit grotto with stone walls. Rustic wooden beams ran across the ceiling. The pebbled floors were meant to provide therapeutic relief to sore feet. And they did just that as she arched her feet back and forth. *Ahhh…* Wall-to-wall wooden racks held numerous wine bottles.

"I designed it myself."

"Really? It's amazing." Clive walked around the small space and scanned her wine collection. He pulled out a few bottles and read the labels.

"It was my grandpa's home office at one time."

"Terrific what you've done with this space, Eva. We should build one in our condo."

Our.

Clive continued to peruse her collection. "How is it that you don't have a single bottle of Stanford?"

251

"No, I don't." Her insides awakened with joy. "Remember that time when we went to…" About a month and half ago, when they'd finally met again, and what a ride it had been so far.

"Santa Barbara." He grinned and pulled her to him. They kissed for a long moment…or two…or three. Who was counting?

Because, when in the grotto, the outside world didn't matter. Exactly why she'd built it in the first place. "This is my place of escape when life becomes a bit much."

Before he could respond, she said it herself, "I know you'll take care of it all for me…and that everything will be fine…soon." She tried to smile, but overshadowed by gloom, she sighed. "Let's forget about it all for a while."

He nodded and took a seat on one of the benches adjacent to the small wooden table in the middle of the room.

"So, no, I don't have a single bottle of Stanford wine, which totally sucks now that I think of it, because that wine we had in Santa Barbara was so good, right?"

"It was. I'm glad my brother bought that winery."

"Me too."

"I'm happy that you're happy for Carter." Clive smiled that mischievous smile again, reminding her with just one look that he'd ask her *that* question.

Shit.

She should have prepared. What would she answer if he asked her now? Was this *that* moment? Is this how she should feel in *that* moment? *Damn*

252

it! She should have poured that wine sooner; she really needed to have downed a glass…or two.

Something in her expression might have given away her dilemma because he said, "Not here. You already have memories here, I'd hate to replace them."

Phew!

But if she really did feel like she'd dodged that one, why was she disappointed that he hadn't asked?

Her face heated. He continued to grin *that* grin. She should look away. So she did. "I might have something similar to the Stanford we had." She pulled out a dusty bottle and wiped it down with a cloth.

Clive brought two glasses to the table he'd found in a cabinet shaped like a wine barrel.

Eva opened the bottle, pulled out the cork and poured the burgundy liquid into one of the glasses for Clive to try.

"What do you think?"

He took a long sip, twirled the liquid around his mouth, and gulped. "It's wine."

She laughed. "You have zero wine tasting skills."

"Hold on, now. That's not entirely true. I can tell you if it tastes good or bad." He grinned.

"And that's pretty much all you need to know."

"Good…and it tastes good. Not Stanford good. But good."

She filled his glass and hers too, and took a sip. Yes, not a Stanford, but still a very good wine. "You know what would go great with this? Cheesy wild mushrooms on Tuscan style bread. Want?"

He laughed. "You should see yourself. Your face glows when you talk about food, you know that?"

"I bet it does." She picked up her glass to take another sip when Clive's phone buzzed. She gave him a look. "No phones allowed in here."

"I figured, but you'll like what I'm about to show you." He waited until she nodded a one-time exception to her rule.

He pulled his phone out of his pocket, tapped it a few times and showed her the screen. "Specially handpicked by the owner himself, to be delivered to your doorstep, tomorrow at six p.m." The picture showed a box of Stanford wines Carter had put together for her.

Clive always, *always* looked out for her. "Thank you." And if he was still wondering what her answer would be to that question he had planned to ask her some day…her heart fluttered at that thought.

They'd downed a glass, or two… again, who was counting? After which, they headed back up to the kitchen for Eva to put together that mushroom bruschetta she'd waited to make.

Clive sat on one of the bar stools, sipping his wine, as he studied her in her element. "Trevor's right, I can learn a lot by simply watching you cook."

"Yeah? What did you learn?" She leaned against the counter, knife in one hand and a slice of bread she'd just cut in the other.

"That you most definitely have the cutest ass I've ever seen."

She gasped and threw the slice of bread at him. Of course, he caught her weapon and ate it, too.

She went back to cutting the bread.

"And you also have the best tits I've ever seen."

She cocked her head slightly and withheld a grin.

"Wait, aren't you going to toss me another slice? I'm starving here."

"More like going to toss the knife."

They brought their food to the breakfast nook. They drank, they ate, they laughed… It was lovely to forget it all for a while. Clive forced her to stay glued to her chair as he put away the dishes. She brought their wine to the living room while he kindled the fire in the fireplace. She lay down on the carpet close to the heat, and he joined her. She turned her head to look at him, he was already looking at her. His hand reached her face, his thumb brushed her jaw, their faces neared, and their lips met.

Chapter 31

"I know my talking with you about this case breaks all investigator-client confidentiality laws, but I didn't like how we left off that evening." Ryan referred to their recent altercation when he'd called Clive a murderer.

Clive did a double take when he received a message from Ryan that morning asking him to meet him at a nearby restaurant for lunch. He prepared for another brawl. But upon seeing Clive, Ryan extended his hand to greet him. "Sorry about the other day."

"Me too." Clive took a seat in front of Ryan.

The waiter took their orders. They both ordered the same lunch burger special, and they both ordered ice-tea. They both wore a white shirt and they both had rolled up their sleeves. The only difference, and a huge one at that, though they both loved Eva and would care for her till their deaths, only one of them got to call Eva his girlfriend. Call it a man thing, call it territorial, call it caveman behavior, Eva was Clive's, and between Ryan and him, Clive had won. He tried hard to contain his grin.

Ryan narrowed his eyes.

He contained his grin.

Minutes later, Trevor also arrived. "What's this about, Ryan?"

"I was hoping you'd tell me."

They'd all worked together in the past on several FBI cases, and they most definitely trusted each other as far as investigative work was concerned. Neither Clive nor Trevor minded Ryan's questioning them about the recent happenings with regards to Olivia or Eva, for that matter.

"I noticed Eva now has a bodyguard in addition to Tom. I don't know what's going on, but if it has anything to do with my client..." He darted his gaze between Trevor and Clive.

"It has everything to with your client." Clive went on to bring Ryan up to speed about the issue with the informant.

"I'll do anything for Eva."

Clive picked up his glass to drink but stopped half way at Ryan's words.

"I mean...Eva is one of my closest friends, and I'll do whatever it takes to help her."

"What can you tell us about your client?" Trevor asked, just as the waiter brought his food.

"Again," Ryan wiped his mouth with a napkin, "I'm breaching some serious conflict of interest clauses here. If I get caught, I'm taking the FBI down with me."

"There won't be a need for that. We'll bail you out before any of this gets out." Trevor took a huge bite of his burger.

"Does McKenzie know you're meeting me?"

Trevor almost choked. He set his food back onto the plate and took a sip of his soda. "Not yet, but once he knows why we met, he should be cool." He picked up his food again.

Ryan threw a crumpled napkin on the empty plate in front of him. "*Should* and *is* have totally different meanings, Trevor." He leaned back in his seat and folded his arms across his chest.

"I'll talk to him right now. Would that help?"

"Yes."

"I'll send him a text."

"I'd like a copy of his response."

"Jeez. What crawled up your ass?" Once again, Trevor returned his food to the plate.

"You did, and so did your partner. Why are you following me?"

"Because you have our guy."

"What guy? I haven't met any guy. In fact, I'm not sure if it's a guy at all. The person definitely used a modulator. So, *this guy* you are looking for might as well be a gal. I couldn't trace the call, which makes me wary. Although, I've met all kinds of loonies in this line of work."

Trevor, too, threw a crumpled napkin onto the table. He pulled out his phone and texted McKenzie. He set it on the table and got back to his food.

"What does your client want?" Clive picked up his drink and sipped through the straw.

"To find out why your father made sure none of the details about Olivia's death reached the media." Ryan, too, began to sip his drink.

"He had a business to run, he stayed away from bad press as much as possible."

"That could be one reason…"

Trevor's phone buzzed with an incoming reply from McKenzie. They peered in to read.

McKenzie: You are doing WHAT???

Ryan set his drink down with a thud. "OK, I'm not talking until McKenzie gives me what I need."

"Ryan man, relax." Trevor picked up his phone. "I'll call him right now."

Other than his father attempting to deflate bad publicity, the possibility of any other reasoning behind keeping Olivia's death from the media hadn't occurred to Clive in all these years. And now, if any other reasons were brought out to the public, it would mean trouble for Stanford.

That might have been the informant's intention all along. If he couldn't get Eva's company to break down, he'd try to break the company that held Eva's company up. But Stanford wasn't just *any* company, and with Clive as the owner, especially considering his reach in the FBI…the informant had just messed with the wrong guy.

"What's your client's name?" Trevor tilted his chin up, still on the line with McKenzie. "Mac wants to know."

Ryan didn't reply.

"C'mon, after all that you've already told us? You do want the FBI to bail you out, right?"

"If my business fails because this blows up, I'm taking both you idiots down with me. And McKenzie too." He waved his pointer finger between Trevor and Clive.

They nodded and shrugged a *sure, whatever*.

"Adam Lavato."

"*Shit*, that's our guy." Trevor talked with McKenzie for a few more seconds and then disconnected his call. "Mac says your protection is guaranteed. He'll send you a transcript of our call as proof. And by the way, your clients name is *not* Lavato."

Ryan laughed. "I know. I checked him out. Lavato is a reporter at the Local Chronicle. But that's the name my client's going with, and now you've told me about the stolen badge. How long have you been investigating this again?"

Trevor exhaled. "Since before Mr. Avery's passing."

"How can you not already have found the guy? Tell me you at least have a plan to lure him out, especially after Candy's death."

Yes, Clive had a plan. A really good one at that. He glanced at Trevor.

Trevor grinned.

Trevor liked his plan.

Ryan darted his gaze between Clive and Trevor. "What's the plan?"

Chapter 32

"Loving these new spa designs your team has put together, Eva. Really liking where we're going with the environmentally friendly approach."

Bryan Austin, the Director of Design at Stanford, had changed for the better since that contract termination incident. He had been difficult to work with during that time when Stanford withdrew their long-standing contract with Eva's company. But when Clive reverted Stanford's decision, her relationship with Bryan took a positive turn.

Slowly but surely, her interactions with Bryan became cordial. Today, he actually threw his head back and laughed out aloud, surprising not only her, but the Stanford team, too.

"Great. When do you think we can get started?"

"The construction of our spas in Prague and Saint-Tropez are near completion. We can get started on the interiors right away."

Eva wanted to scream from the rooftop in celebration. Less than a month and half ago, S. F. Designs had neared losing their biggest client, Stanford. And today, Eva and her team readied to proceed with implementing the designs for not just one but all of Stanford's spas.

With a special spring to her step, Eva walked toward Clive's office to share her happiness but…*Silvia*…

From her vantage point, Eva couldn't tell if Clive sat behind his desk. But she could tell Silvia's hatred for her.

Silvia held her stare, and on any other day, Eva might have indulged. She puffed out a deep breath. The way her day went, nothing could spoil this moment, not even Silvia.

So, she smiled, at Silvia. Who'd have thought?

And Silvia? At first gave Eva a strange look. Then blinking, she averted her gaze.

Dodging Silvia's animosity, Eva walked to the elevators. She'd come back for Clive later. Besides, after Clive shared his past with her, neither Silvia nor any other woman's existence around him threatened Eva anymore.

He'd wanted Eva before, he wanted her now, and he most definitely wanted her forever…

The elevator doors opened to Clive…the same Clive, *the tabloid hottie, clothed in a dark gray suit, a crisp, white shirt with the top few buttons undone, hair ruffled, and looking straight at her from inside the elevator car.*

"Took me right back to that day I saw you for the first time again, Eva."

Like that day, today too she'd vouch; she'd never get tired of looking at this man.

Clive stepped out and gave her a tight kiss. That kiss, too, would never get old. She tingled from it every time.

"Went well with Bryan?"

She nodded, biting down her grin. "We're ready to start in Europe."

"That's terrific. When are we going?"

We…"You'll go with me?"

"Of course, I will. I thought we decided already, that the last time I travelled to Miami was the last time I was going anywhere without you. Isn't it the same for you?"

Could her day get any happier? "Yes, it is."

"Good." He kissed her cheek. "Trish will handle all the bookings, just let her know the dates." His gaze drifted beyond her toward his office.

She glanced over her shoulder. Silvia had walked out to talk to Trish. *Whatever.* She turned back to Clive.

He gave Eva his full attention. "She's here to talk to Trevor about the sex tapes. Join us?"

"Nah! You go ahead." She half shrugged. Though it didn't matter to Eva if Silvia liked her or not, Eva cared enough to spare Silvia additional embarrassment by being there when they talked about the tapes.

He smiled. "I love you." He kissed her cheek, sending heated sparks all over her body. "We're invited for lunch."

"Oh, by whom?"

"John Smith. Ryan will be joining as well."

She blinked. Did she hear that right? "Ryan? As in…Ryan Cohen? The same Ryan we both know…that Ryan?"

Clive grinned. "Yes, that Ryan. We talked."

"Talked? As in…talked for real? And not glowered or brawled?"

Clive laughed. "Yes, we talked for real. Trevor was there too. It's a serious problem to rat out his client but…he'll do anything to help a friend."

Wow…who'd have thought…Clive and Ryan actually getting along?

"His client wants to know why my father hid details about Olivia's death from the media."

"So…Ryan's client is someone who dislikes your father?"

He pulled her close, warning her in advance about what he'd say next.

"Ryan's client is the informant."

A shiver ran through her. The informant had influenced Silvia to cause a media riot. Now he went after damaging Clive's reputation. And if he'd succeed, it would be far bigger and far more challenging to wade out of than a mere tabloid incident.

"So…they've caught the informant then, right? Since Ryan knows him… Right?"

Chapter 33

Eva recognized John Smith right away. Clive had left her with Silvia to talk to the same man that Mct Gala night.

The elderly, burly Mr. Smith seemed more affable than she'd somehow imagined a well-known lawyer would be.

"And she's the reason why you didn't stick around to chat with us that Christmas party night, I take it." John's cheek's dimpled.

Surprising, after all these years, that he'd still remember.

"She was the one…still is, the *only one*." Clive gave her *that* look which told her how thankful he was to have her in his life.

Ryan smiled a light smile. Did he…look happy? For them?

Mrs. Smith leaned in. "It's incredible how you found each other again."

Clive had forewarned her about Mrs. Smith's interest in the tabloids. Somehow, though her many questions should have made Eva want to escape, soothing warmth radiated through her when she talked about her life with Clive.

But she stayed burdened by the reason for their visit to the lawyer's home. Clive's future loomed her mind. After all, she'd dragged him deep into danger. Why hadn't her father left her details about what had troubled him nearing his death?

After lunch, Mrs. Smith left them to talk business. They sat in John's home library, which was also his office. Their conversation narrowed to Clive's past and Olivia's death.

John cupped the bottom of the cognac glass in his hand, swirling it as he spoke. "There is enough evidence that supports the cause of Olivia's death. There is no point in re-opening the investigation. What's concerning is that it's being rehashed through a wrong channel." He looked to Ryan. "No offense."

Ryan shook his head.

She didn't understand. "Why would it be concerning when Clive's innocent?"

"We can no longer control what's released to the media. If someone wants to defame Clive, they will. Of course, if that leads to opening the case again, we will win again." He turned to Ryan again. "Like we've already discussed, there's no evidence that would point to Clive being in the wrong. I did enough leg work back then, I should know."

Eva sagged into her chair.

Clive and Ryan exchanged glances. Why?

"Sure, I can help you with the case if it re-opens." John went on. "Yours might be the last case I work on before I retire." He went back to twirling and sniffing his drink. "Although, I don't know how much I can help you avoid the media this time, Clive."

Ryan shifted in his chair. "What my client choses to do is one thing, but my company won't disclose any of the details no matter who asks. I've already told it that to my client."

Ryan and Clive exchanged *that* glance again. *Why*?

Eva clutched the fabric of her skirt tight; it remained her only resort to restrain her anxiety. She gave in. "What is it that you're not telling me?" She darted her gaze between Clive and Ryan.

Ryan remained silent. He looked at Clive.

"Olivia's father received a note, *an anonymous note.*" Clive paused.

Her heart sank. *The informant.*

"The note claims there's additional information about what happened that night, right before Olivia's death, that could somehow implicate me."

Her mouth went dry. But John had assured them. There weren't any loose ends. There weren't any wrong doings. What in fresh hell was this then? "And what's the additional information?"

"We don't know."

"It could be a hoax." She licked her lips. Surely they agree. She darted her gaze to each of them. Well, did they agree? They remained silent. *Damn it.*

Ryan cleared his throat. "Maybe it is, but we have to plan for if it's not."

"Who else knew about the case?" Clive asked John.

"Well, obviously, your immediate family and I knew." John paused. He tilted his chin at Eva. "Your father knew. He was, after all, Clive's father's closest friend."

Eva's blood ran cold. Her uncle...did her uncle know?

Shit.

Just when the FBI had begun to declare him free of suspicion...

"How about my uncle?"

She held her breath in anticipation of John's answer.

"Dave?" His eyebrows shot up. "No." He shook his head. "Your father was tight lipped, especially so when it concerned the Stanford family. He never told anyone about this case, I'm very certain of that. Besides, aside from the people I've already mentioned, the only others who knew were the judiciary, the cops investigating the case and Olivia's immediate family."

Her heart leapt that her uncle had dodged one more implication, but her concern for Clive elevated. The informant bothered about Clive's past only because of her. He'd surfaced at all because she took over her father's company. He'd tried to reach her clients first...then he moved on to destroying her relationship with Clive and now...he tried to bring down Stanford. Had she not taken over the company after her father, there wouldn't have been an informant in any of their lives. What did the informant want from her? Why was he so determined to bring her company down?

Clive stopped the car by a steep curve on the shoreline highway at the bend in the road where Olivia's car had skidded off and fallen onto the rocks below.

"Her family used to leave her fresh flowers here every week." As years passed, everyone moved on from the tragedy, everyone except Clive. "I bring her a rose for her birthday... A pink one... She liked pink."

Eva stared at the looming black sea as it transformed into fierce white foamy waves and crashed onto the rocks below. Tears rolled down her cheeks, but just as quickly, gusty, howling wind lifted them away, drying her face before Clive took notice of how emotional she'd become for the troubled Olivia, for that teenage Clive, who even today suffered from the dark memory of Olivia's death.

They remained quiet for the rest of their drive back to San Francisco. Thick fog had settled in. Only the bright orange towers of the Golden Gate Bridge that peeked from within directed them into the city. As they neared the toll plaza, Clive's phone rang into the cars audio. It was Trevor.

"We need to talk. Are you home?"

"Should be there in about twenty minutes."

"OK, I'll see you there."

Trevor arrived right when they did. They sat in Clive's living room. Opaque fog had casted a veil of gray beyond the windows of Clive's condo.

"Got a call from Lavato. The real Lavato. He sounded frightened, nervous, that his wife would find out about him and Candy."

"How would she?"

"The informant contacted him. Not over the phone, not via a letter, they met…in person."

"What?"

"Yes, but get this," Trevor started to laugh, "He was dressed as Lavato."

Clive winced. "Lavato met Lavato?"

"Yeah, imagine that. Anyway, since the real Lavato is a crime reporter and not a celebrity news hoarder like our fake Lavato was portraying him to be, our crook asked him to find whatever he could about Stanford Enterprises that should be in the news but is hushed down because of Stanford influence. Not suggesting that's what you do, Clive, just quoting what Lavato told me about his conversation with this guy."

Clive nodded. "Go on."

"This guy really got Lavato worked up. He threatened not only to tell his wife about Candy, but also showed him pictures from the night of the murder as proof. He dressed as Lavato when he killed Candy."

"Son-of-a—" Clive shot Eva a glance and cut short his words.

"Yeah, a total bitch!" she finished, startling both Clive and Trevor.

Trevor cocked his head slightly. "Wow, I somehow never thought you swore. Well, makes it that much easier for us from now on to talk around you." He looked at Clive, nodding as though he'd agree.

Clive gave him a deadpan, "Continue."

"So imagine the coincidence. Of all the newspapers, the one that Lavato worked for was the one that actually did suppress news about Stanford. When Lavato had first joined the Chronicle, a fellow reporter had written an article about rich kids who got away with murder. It was about you and Olivia, but that article never made it to print."

"Got away?" Eva almost shouted. "Clive's innocent."

"That he is. Oh and by the way, the article listed a few other names."

"What other names?"

"Don't know yet. Of course Lavato is now using that as his protection, he wants the informant off his back."

"Get the informant off his back?" Eva shook her head, laughing. "Did you tell him to get in line?" Once again, Clive and Trevor stared at her. "What? We're all thinking it."

That got Clive to smile for the first time since they'd left John's home.

"Lavato is willing to hand over that unprinted article to us."

Chapter 34

"Hey, Mom!"

"Why am I the only one who hasn't met *your* Eva yet? Even Mila has met her, but *I* haven't met her? Is it my new hairdo? You're embarrassed by it, aren't you?"

Of course, she'd throw that in. "Mom, you look lovely no matter what you do to your hair. Even when you got that perm that one time. Everyone hated it, but *I* loved it. Remember?"

"Then why haven't you introduced her to me, Clive?"

His office door opened and Eva walked in. She leaned in for a quick kiss and sat on his desk. He switched the phone to speaker.

"I've been too busy, that's all. I'd love for you to meet her." His gaze caught with Eva's as he spoke.

Eva mouthed, *mother?*

He nodded.

"Good. What are your plans for the weekend?"

"No plans yet." He raised his eyebrows at Eva to confirm. She half shrugged a *yes, no plans yet*.

"OK, you're coming home this Saturday then. Your father's firing up the grill, so bring your appetite, and bring that pretty girlfriend of yours to meet your mother, will you?"

Eva smiled and nodded a *yes*.

"I will."

Of course, his mother continued, "You know, since you haven't bothered to introduce us yet, I have half a mind to go to her office and meet her myself."

"But you met her, years ago—"

"So I've heard. See how terrible that sounds? *I've heard*, not from you, but from Carter and Claire and your father and Mila, basically everyone *but you*."

"We'll be there Saturday, I promise."

"Good." Not bothering to hide her obvious delight, she went on, "I'm *so* excited to finally meet her, Clive."

"Hello, Mrs. Stanford," Eva added sweetly.

His mother gasped. "Eva?"

"Yes." She laughed.

"Not *Mrs. Stanford*, please, call me Diane. And, you'll visit us this Saturday, yes?"

"Yes, we'll be there."

"Excellent. Can't wait to meet you, Eva. You know, just the other day I was looking through old albums, especially the New Year's one, since *Carter said* I might find you in there, and guess what, among all those pictures, not one was of you and

Clive. How odd is that? Anyway, very happy that we're finally meeting, *again*."

"I wish it was Saturday already."

"Me too! I love that you said that…Oh Clive, I love her already!"

Clive shook his head. "Got to go, Mom."

"Yes, OK. Your father will be delighted to know you're coming over." Her excitement brimmed in her tone. "See you both Saturday!"

Clive pulled Eva into his lap. "What's up?"

"I miss you."

They kissed a nice long kiss. He missed her too.

Chapter 35

"Wow, this view... and you can see Stanford Towers too." Eva stared at the San Francisco skyline from Clive's childhood bedroom window. "I wondered how it'd look from here in daylight."

He moved her hair to one side and kissed her neck. "The many times I imagined you standing here again." It had taken forever for this moment to return.

She turned around to face him, and before she knew it, he captured her mouth to his. Seconds later, he took her to his bed and he hovered on top of her. Her body warmed to his touch. She felt tender and soft when he held her this way.

The moment intensified to more than how lovely she felt in his arms. After all these years he'd waited for her, she'd returned to him, to this room where they'd first kissed.

Since that first time he'd seen her, the way she'd looked at him then, the way she looked at him every day now…she completed him. Eva became his happiness. Eva became his life. It was as though this day had been meant to come. They had to be together. He'd leave the world behind for Eva.

"You love her, yes?" Carter had asked. "What are you waiting for then?"

Yes, what am I waiting for?

If Clive had ever wished for anything, he'd only wished to be with Eva again. She was all he'd ever wanted. But, had Eva always wanted him too? His insides did a tumble at that thought. His heart picked up pace. His breath hitched.

"Eva." He breathed against her flushed cheek.

The depth of desire in her hazel brown eyes heated.

"God, Eva," he sounded hoarse even to himself. "You're…" All breath left him.

"What?"

"We'll do this again later, I promise."

She blinked. Of course, she did, because he didn't make much sense, at least, not yet. He needed to get to what he tried to say before she lost interest.

"But, I need to know…now…"

"What do you need to know?"

He held her face in both hands, and their gazes remained connected. The moment had come…and he went for it. "Will you…marry me?"

He stilled. He waited for her response. And her response…her response…she stared. She didn't blink. She didn't move. And…she didn't answer.

She didn't answer.

Was it a…*no*?

Shit.

He shouldn't have asked her like this, unexpectedly, here…in his room…while they were like this…him on top of her.

Shit, shit, shit!

Why did he *ever* think it a remotely good idea to propose to her *in his bed*? Actually, he never imagined he'd propose to her this way. That he did now came as a surprise to him too. But the moment seemed right. Or, at least, it did before she hadn't answered. And now, everything was wrong.

This was *so* bad…*so, so, so* bad…

"Eva?" He surprised himself when her name tumbled off his lips, because after what just happened…what was still happening…it would seem best that he never spoke again.

"Yes." She blinked. Her eyes widened.

OK, she spoke and she also blinked…*which was good, right*? They progressed. *Did they progress*?

Yes as in yes she'd marry him, or yes as in…what did she mean by that *yes*?

"Oh, God." She blinked again.

Oh, God.

"Yes." She nodded. "YES." She started to laugh.

He closed his eyes. He exhaled a sharp breath he didn't even know he'd held. He buried his face against her neck and almost shook as he began to breathe again. He breathed deep, breathed her in.

Her neck smelled of something floral and fresh. He liked how she smelled.

And…she said yes…*Eva said yes*. He placed a few quick kisses along her neck to her lips, and just to be certain, he asked, "Are you sure?"

"Yes, I will marry you!" Her face lit up.

He grinned too. "A second more of that silence, and I'd have dropped dead."

"Sorry…I was…my past…you know…and then my parents…and…well…yes, yes, yes!"

He placed another quick kiss to her lips and pulled out a ring from under the pillow.

She gasped. "Grandma's ring."

He knew she'd like it. "I met your mother today."

"My mother? You drove to her house?"

"She gave me the go ahead." Had he ever grinned this much?

"Aw…you asked her for me?" She tightened her arms around his shoulders and pulled him close.

"I talked to your brother too."

They kissed and kissed and kissed.

He brought the ring to her finger and slid it on. She splayed her fingers and stared at her hand. "My grandma's engagement ring is now *my* engagement ring. I love it. I love you, Clive."

They returned to kissing with a renewed fervor. Within seconds they were both naked. He touched her everywhere, and the more he touched her, the harder he gripped her. And she gripped at him too. Their intimacy turned assertive, their lust turned raw.

His kiss bruised her lips.

Her nails clawed his back.

He dove into her, and she moaned a soft, sexy moan.

She moved her hips in a purposeful way. He took her with a dominant drive.

Her breath turned ragged.

So did his.

Their aggression became exceptional. Their togetherness grew primal. Their hunger for each other amplified…

His ears rang.

Her body convulsed.

His heart practically jumped out of his chest as her orgasm propelled his, his filling her. They lay in each other's arms for a long time, spent and sated.

He hugged her tight and rolled her over to lay on top of him.

"I'm sorry." He kissed where he'd bruised her lip. "That was rough, I know, but I had to. I needed to."

"I needed it too."

She smiled, *that smile*. And his insides leapt with happiness when it occurred to him, *Eva said yes*. "I can't wait to introduce you to the whole world as my fiancé. The future Mrs. Stanford." His jaw ached from all that grinning, but he couldn't stop grinning.

She widened her eyes. "Your mother is *Mrs. Stanford*."

She had a point. "How about Eva Stanford Avery?"

"Middle name…nice…I like…but, I already have my grandma's name as my middle name."

"But you also already have her ring."

She splayed her fingers on his chest and smiled, at the ring. "OK, middle name it is."

They lay in his bed until they heard dogs bark. The metal gate to the backyard opened with a squeak like it always did. His parents had returned from walking the retrievers.

Clive and Eva freshened up.

Had he ever felt happier? Had she ever looked happier? Something changed between them, forever, for the better. He gave her one more kiss, interlaced his fingers with hers, and walked her out of his room to show her off to his family.

"Clive," his mother yelped as they descended the stairs. "And, oh my, look who we have here, *Eva*." She grabbed Eva close and hugged her in a long tight hug.

His mother pulled back and studied Eva. "You're beautiful in pictures, but in person..." She shook her head.

He loved when Eva blushed. Her gaze dropped, her face flushed. Well, it was already flushed, but it flushed even more.

His father hugged Eva. "Please call me Francis."

"Let me see it." His mother grabbed Eva's hand.

Eva widened her eyes at him. Yes, he'd told everyone.

"So, how did he propose?"

Shit.

"Um…" Eva licked her lips. "We were in his room…" She shot Clive a quick glance.

"Where in his room? By the window? In the bed?"

"Mother!"

"Di!"

Chapter 36

"You're wondering why he left you the company?" Francis tossed the last of the steak fillets onto the hot outdoor grill. Tall, but shorter than Clive, muscular but less built than Carter, his hair thick and grey, Francis had the same charming smile as Clive and the same caring eyes too. She'd met him last at her father's funeral. He'd stayed the longest of all of her father's friends.

"You're his daughter, that's why. It's as simple as that. He had no other hidden intentions, and if he did, I'd have known. He was my closest friend." Something shifted in Francis's expression when he said that. He took a swig of his beer.

Given her father's busy schedule, he'd had no time to keep up relationships. He had few friends, and if he ever talked about them at all, he spoke of only one of them. "He thought very highly of you."

"It's very difficult to make friends in this business. You might come to find that yourself soon enough. Our friendship mattered a lot to both of us."

Since Francis knew him that well, had he known about her father being followed? Did her father talk to him about the informant? Did he tell him about FBI's involvement? Should she ask? But what if he knew none of that?

He flipped over one of the fillets, and the meat sizzled. The sweet aroma of barbecue sauce wafted through the air. "Don't look for a reason why the company ended up in your hands."

"Why not?"

"What if you never find a reason?"

"Maybe my father has left me a letter explaining it all. Maybe Simon would hand it over to me some day." That was one way to find out whether Francis knew about the issues that persisted her father until death.

Something shifted in his expression again. "Maybe."

He knows…about the letter. What else does he know? Should she tell Clive?

"Were you surprised that he picked me to lead the company?"

"Not at all." He smiled and got to flipping over another fillet. "Your father had a lot of stories to share about you. And I had many about Claire and Carly. We loved talking about our daughters, but not so much about our sons." He laughed. "I thought you were an interesting choice. Different from him, but just as mentally strong as he was."

Her uncle had said that to her too. "How would you know that?"

His gaze locked with hers. "I'm retired, but I still follow my favorite company's market standings. Old habits." He half-shrugged. His smile conveyed satisfaction, as though proud. *Of her*? "And it's not easy to deal with that board of yours." He flipped another fillet.

Tell me about it.

"Your father would have been pleased to see the way you've handled them and the company after him. And I'm not just saying that because you're my future daughter in law."

Her face heated, and not because of her proximity to the grill.

"I read about your successes. Your father's choice, as usual, is impeccable."

She had no words. Francis thought of her that way? "I fail as often, or even more often, than I succeed."

"We all do, Eva. That's the nature of this business. But the important thing is, are you enjoying the job that you do? You win some, you lose some, but you should enjoy it all."

"Something my father would say."

His gaze drifted past her, possibly not looking at anything specific, possibly remembering her father. "Yes, that's something Robin would say."

He knew her father too well. He had to know her father's troubles. She cut to the chase and went for it. "The issues with my company, they think it's because of my uncle."

283

"The FBI can think whatever they want. It's not Dave."

He knows...about the FBI...he knows everything...

He met her gaze. "It's anyone *but* Dave." His voice was low, assertive.

"You two look so serious."

She flinched when Clive's hand circled around her waist.

Clive's expression sobered. "Jeez, are you OK?"

She smiled. *Yes, more than OK.* Especially after finding the one person who could possibly reveal more about her father's last day's than the FBI, than her uncle or than Simon could ever tell her.

"Swap that water for a beer?" Clive indicated the glass in her hand.

"Or some Stanford wine if you're interested." Carter approached. "Welcome to the family, Eva." He kissed her cheek. "Guess you both were meant to be together all along, congratulations."

"Thank you." She grinned. "That New Year's night...who'd have thought we'd be engaged one day?" The image of fifteen-year-old Clive standing by the punch table, watching her, desiring her, flashed her mind.

"Oh, Clive knew. Believe me, I was there." Cater went on as he poured her a glass of the burgundy wine. "When he saw you with Ryan, I thought he'd cry."

"He didn't think that." Clive shook his head.

Ignoring Clive, Carter continued, "It was hilarious. He was a nervous wreck. He didn't want to talk to you."

"I was *not* a nervous wreck. Don't listen to him, he tried to mess it up for us right away. He made me offer you punch."

"Please, you stared at her long enough to know whether or not she already had a glass in her hand. If you didn't, then what the heck were you looking at?"

"Eva!" Claire rushed to her so fast, Eva almost lost her balance when they hugged. "*Finally*, he asked you." She partially covered her mouth, hiding her words from everyone else but Eva when she asked, "Do I want to know how he did it?"

Eva shot Clive a quick glance. "In his room, where we'd spent most of that New Year's Eve."

His face brightened. She imagined him say, *excellent answer*.

"And that's why there aren't any pictures of you two in that album." Diane set a huge bowl of salad onto the patio table. "Childhood sweethearts, how romantic!" She gushed. Diane reminded her of Claire, fun, ebullient and giggly.

"Uncle Clive, Uncle Clive!" Among the many people Clive's three-year-old niece, Emma, could have run to, she first went to Clive. He had mentioned Carly would bring her today. Dressed in a pink jumpsuit, light brown hair tied into a topknot, Emma rubbed her face with her dimpled hand after Clive's stubble brushed her cheek for a kiss. "Pokey."

"Eva, hey!" Carly reached for a hug. "I saw you in Santa Barbara that one time, too bad we didn't get a chance to talk then."

Though Claire and Carly weren't identical twins, like Claire, Carly had blond hair and seemed to be of the same height too. "Congratulations!" Carly grinned.

Had Clive left anyone out from foretelling about the engagement?

"Where is she?" Emma whispered, delightful in her uncle's arms.

"Who?"

"Eva," she whispered again.

"Right here."

Emma turned to look at Eva and popped a few fingers into her mouth.

"Hi Emma."

Clive pulled down her hand, making her fingers slide out. "Con-gratu-lations, Eva." She went back to hugging her uncle.

Apparently, he'd told her too.

Chapter 37

"Show me, show me, show me." Allie hurried Eva to show her the ring. "Oh, it's beautiful! I cannot believe you're engaged."

"Wow, it *is* gorgeous." Izzy stared at the emerald shaped, uncut diamond, a surprisingly contemporary ring for an antique. "Great choice picking out her grandma's ring, Clive."

"Thanks." Clive cut Izzy a quick look from the rearview mirror.

Despite the recent threat to Eva's life and her company, Clive ensured her daily routine hadn't changed much except for a few minor adjustments, like they no longer took the subway because either Tom or Clive drove them to work. Izzy and Allie didn't mind the shift. The nights Eva stayed at Clive's, her friends took the train anyway.

"I love it." Eva gazed at the ring. Her jaw still ached from all the grinning she'd done over the weekend. First, at Clive's parents' house, and the next day at her mother's. She never imagined being engaged would bring her so much joy. She liked being engaged to Clive.

"We need a girl's night to talk about all the details." Izzy said. "Sorry, Clive, no boys allowed."

"No problem. Just tell me when to disappear."

No problem? Really? He would leave her for the night? Unsupervised? It had become a habit for him to methodically check all the rooms and closets and every nook and cranny before he let her into her house, or even his. The only place he let her walk around without his prior inspection? The Stanford Tower. Though, she suspected he checked the building's security feeds all the time.

"Tonight?" Izzy asked.

"Works for me," Allie said.

Eva shot Clive a glance. *Are you really OK with this*? Izzy and Allie knew nothing about the recent threats to her life. Had the time come for her to reveal it all to her friends? As though Clive sensed her concern, he pulled her hand into his and held it in his lap.

"How about my place?" Izzy suggested.

Clive squeezed and shook her hand, *no, not at Izzy's*.

"How about mine? I have a way better wine collection." Eva suggested.

"You *totally* do."

"OK, your place then."

Eva gave Clive a side-eyed peep. He pulled her hand to his lips and kissed.

After his routine inspection of her house, Clive stayed until Izzy and Allie arrived.

Allie placed a hand on her chest. "Aww…he's really *so* in love with you."

"Right? You're perfect for each other, Eva."

"We are." Eva grinned. Thinking of Clive melted all else away. Whether or not the issue with the informant existed, Clive would have stayed with her until her friends arrived. That's just how much she meant to him. He comforted, he cared, he endeared. Everything about him was his love for her.

Eva sat with her friends in her wine cellar. She poured them each a glass of Stanford. She told them the story about how Clive made Carter ship the bottles to her at the highest priority.

Izzy took a sip of her drink. "Wow! This wine is out of this world." She brought the glass back to her lips and took a big gulp. "When Carter talked about his Santa Barbara winery, I didn't realize their wine was this delicious. He invited us to visit by the way."

"Let's get away one of these weekends then? Wine tasting and spa?"

"Let's. I'll check with Carter when he'll be available to give us a tour."

They looked at Allie.

She played with the cork Eva had pulled out of the wine bottle, rolling it back and forth on the table with her index finger. "I want to be loved like that."

"Like what?"

"Like Eva and Clive."

"You do have a love like that, Allie." How could she be this oblivious to how much she meant to Marc?

"What's up with you and Marc anyway? Is he still in new York?" Izzy probed.

Allie told Izzy about her turning down Marc's proposal.

"Why would you do that? The poor guy has been in love with you since we've known him, which is what, since high school?"

"I know." Allie rested her face in both her hands. "How did you decide on a *yes*, Eva?"

"I didn't."

"You didn't?"

"I didn't until the moment he asked. And even in that moment, I froze and didn't answer right away."

They stilled.

"Of course, I felt terrible that it took me a while to reply to him. I almost drained the life out of him."

"He waited for you to think it through?"

"He did." Eva laughed. He'd always been so patient with her. "Can you imagine that? I made him wait…scratch that…I made *Clive Stanford* wait on a question like that. I mean, sure I know him from way back when, but he isn't just simply *anybody*."

They nodded hurriedly. "And then?"

Eva refilled their glasses.

"Anyway, my mind raced, anxious, until I asked myself, who else would I want to spend the rest of my life with, if not Clive?"

"Right." Izzy and Allie spoke in unison, their faces intensely focused, as though watching the ending of a chick-flick where the girl is about to give the guy another chance.

"So…who came to your mind?" Allie asked.

"Huh?"

"Who is it, if not Clive?"

Was she serious?

"Clive," Izzy gave Allie a stare and started to take her glass away. "*Clive* came to her mind."

"Hey…stop." Allie slapped Izzy's hand.

"You're beginning to…you know…drift a little," Izzy clarified.

"*No,* I'm not." Allie pulled her glass back. "I was just making certain Eva didn't have anyone else in mind, that's all."

"Anyone else like who?" Now more than ever she really needed to know, who else could Allie have thought she'd want to spend the rest of her life with if not Clive?

"Ryan."

"What?" Now Eva and Izzy spoke in unison.

Izzy shook her head. "No more wine for her."

"What's wrong with that alternative? She did have the hots for him, at some point."

"Ryan is not an alternative to Clive. No one is." Eva swallowed a huge gulp of her drink, emptying her glass.

Silence ensued. *Ryan.* Yes, Ryan had come to her mind. But not in the way Allie implied. His expression of happiness, in John's house, when he watched Clive and her together, that's the Ryan that came to her mind.

"You know, by the time that tabloid incident happened, I was already sure there'd be no one else I would ever love as much as I love Clive." Again, her words drifted away into silence. She stared at her empty glass, remembering her past, her parents past…

"Well, get on with it already, you're killing us."
Izzy winced.

Allie chewed the tip of her fingernail.

"So yes, I thought whatever our future may hold, we'll figure out…when things need figuring out. And with that realization, my apprehensions ended. And I said *yes*." She grinned wide and her friends did too.

But just as they did…"Can I help you?" Clive's voice, unusually loud, startled them all.

Eva almost jumped out of her skin. Only her eyes darted to look at her friends. They reacted the same.

"What was that?" Allie asked.

"Was that Clive? I thought he left." Izzy said.

The security system that Clive had set in place had kicked in. Someone stood at the door, and a video had streamed into Clive's, Trevor's and her phone, alerting them of the visitor. An alert she'd obviously missed, since she'd left her phone upstairs. Now, more than ever, she kicked herself for her *no cell phones in the wine cellar* rule.

"Shhh…" Eva sat still, trying to hear if the visitor would respond.

"What? Why? What's going on?"

"It's a security thing Clive set up."

"Since when do you need security?"

"Shhh…not now."

Izzy and Allie complied.

Clive would be there in less than ten minutes, since that's how long it should take to drive from his building to hers at that hour. He'd measured.

In the meantime, Eva rushed to the cellar door and closed it. Not that it would do them any good, because the door wasn't much of a door but an ornate iron grill. She switched off the light, although the light from the stairway continued to gleam inside the cellar. She moved to a corner, less obvious for anyone to take notice of unless they neared the iron grill. Izzy and Allie cowered close to her.

"Eva, I'm scared," Allie whispered.

"Me too," Izzy added.

If they were already that scared, how would they react if they knew who might be out there? She looked at her friends. Even in the dim light their faces glowed pale.

The front door opened, and her heart practically stopped beating. Her mouth ran dry. She crossed her fingers and squeezed her eyes shut tight.

"Eva?"

Had she ever been so relieved to hear Clive's voice? She drew in a deep breath. *Wait, how did he get here this fast?*

"We're here in the cellar," Izzy shouted.

"Stay there." *Trevor?* And how did *he* get there that fast? He lived across the Bay. It should have taken him at least twenty minutes, even if he'd driven with the siren on his car. Yes, Clive and Trevor had timed that too.

After a few lengthy minutes of waiting, the words she'd imagined she'd never hear came to her rescue. "You can come up now," Trevor announced.

Eva ran up the stairs straight into Clive's arms. He held her tight. A cold tremble shot to her toes. Her skin raised into bumps. Clive rubbed her arms to soothe. "He's gone." He tilted her face up to look at him.

Trevor's laugh reverberated in the silence. "Look at him run." He laughed more. "He didn't know you had a security system." Trevor played the video recording on his phone. They peeked in to watch a man.

"Lavato," Izzy and Allie called out in unison.

"Nope."

"Who then?" Izzy grimaced.

But before Clive could answer, Allie pointed to Trevor. "You." She narrowed her eyes. "You're not Eva's client like you told us that night at *Bourbon and Branch*." She studied him. "What are you, a cop or something?"

"Or something," Trevor stated simply and proceeded to summarize the recent happenings.

Izzy and Allie stood with their hands plastered to their mouths as Trevor recited it all.

"We knew you were having trouble with your company, Eva, but it never occurred to us that your life was in danger." They neared and hugged her.

"What can we do to help?"

"Yes, anything at all we can do?"

Weren't her friends the best? And Clive had laughed when she told him about Izzy's Taser.

"Wish my one and only friend was this nice," Trevor said to Clive.

Ignoring Trevor, Clive went on, "Thank you." He smiled at her friends. "But we've got it covered. What you can do, though, is stay vigilant. The guy definitely has seen you with Eva."

Allie gasped.

"I'm not saying you're in danger, but it doesn't hurt to be cautious and also, relax, we've got it covered." He grinned that sweet grin of his.

Whether he had the same effect on her friends or not, Eva did swoon some when Clive grinned like that. But first things first. "Were you outside all this time? Guarding us?"

Clive rubbed the back of his neck. "Not exactly outside. We were down the street, at *Harry's*."

"And you were planning on staying there all night?"

"Yep." Clive shoved his hands in his pockets. He shifted on his feet.

"He misses those all-nighters from his FBI days. So, we thought, why not, the girls are having fun, we should too."

"How is staying at the bar all night without drinking any fun?" Izzy probed.

"Well, we'd play darts and then move on to pool, and when the night wound down, the owner would join us for poker. You know, *guy fun*."

Once again Clive had gone ahead and inconvenienced himself just to care that much extra for her. How did she get so lucky to have this adorable man for a boyfri... *fiancé*...her thumb involuntarily reached over to feel the ring on her finger. But just as fast, her comfort lifted when her gaze drifted and caught a glimpse of a white envelope on the coffee table. "Is that...?"

"Yes." Trevor exhaled. "We found it by your door. He probably meant to put it in your mailbox, but when the lights turned on and he heard Clive speak, he dropped it and ran."

Her attention narrowed to the envelope. Clive asked her something, but she didn't know what, because her ears started to ring, her throat felt crushed, her every sense intently focused on that envelope and the envelope alone.

She flinched when Clive picked it up with gloved hands.

"If you don't want to know what's inside—"

"I want to know." Her jaw hurt as she uttered those words. Had she clenched that hard?

Her stomach curdled. Her breath raced as Clive brought a letter opener to the envelope, tore it open, pulled out the note and stared at it unblinking.

"W-What does it say?"

He placed the note on the table, and once again, they all peeked in to read.

*Unless you break **all** ties with Stanford...*

"What does it mean?" She knew what it meant, but she didn't want to believe it and dearly hoped someone corrected her dreary thoughts because no way she'd break *any ties* with Stanford.

"It means he's walked into his own trap," Trevor said. "He thinks you'll do what he says. But…"

"But he just provoked his worst enemy. He messed up, big time." Clive added.

They exchanged glances and smiled, but she didn't understand why. "I'm not breaking up with you, Clive." She shook as the words left her mouth. Her right hand cupped her left, and she held on tight to her ring finger. "Not now, not ever." *Never.* Emotions welled. She choked, ready to cry.

Before she knew it, Clive pulled her to him and cocooned her in his arms. "We are *not* breaking up, *ever*," he whispered by the side of her head.

She pressed closer against him. Their togetherness and his words consoled her. Her ragged breath began to slowly straighten. They held each other in long silence.

"I love Marc."

Eva and Clive flinched at Allie's announcement.

Stumped, they stared at Allie.

"Yes...my answer is YES!" She grabbed the sides of her face, her grin seemingly uncontainable.

Was it really the wine? Or was it seeing Clive and her together this way?

They continued to stare at her, speechless, until Eva cleared her throat. "Well...that's...very romantic, Allie." She added a quick smile. "Marc will be relieved, no doubt." She looked to Clive. "But..." She cleared her throat again. "What should we do now?"

"Oh, I think we should call him," Allie continued. "Wait...what time is it in—"

"She meant *the letter*." Izzy glared at Allie.

"Right...of course."

Chapter 38

Just when she thought he couldn't look any hotter, he'd gone and worn an elegant, steel grey, three-piece suit, silver tie and a crisp white shirt underneath. She suppressed the urge to rip off his clothes and make out in whatever room hid behind the door she eyed from where she stood watching Clive preparing for a press release.

"I know what you're thinking, Eva, but, wrong place, wrong time." He adjusted his cuffs.

"Right place and the perfect time." She pointed to the door.

"Coat closet?"

She nodded.

He adjusted his suit jacket, like those male models do in men's wear ads, only much...*much hotter*.

"Stop it, Eva. I cannot go out there in front of all those cameras with a raging hard-on."

Raging, he said? "Well, there's one way to get rid of all that *rage*." She slid her hands along his chest, ripped despite all those layers of clothing. Ripped *without* all those layers of clothing.

Her senses heightened…her core clenched from imagining his fingers, his tongue, his breath, his mouth…*there*.

He shook his head, holding her hands, halting them. "Later, *most definitely*." He grinned looking mischievous.

"There?" She signaled to the door again.

"Wherever." The smooth darkness in his words alone could bring her to climax.

"Can't wait."

"Me neither." He cupped her face in his hands and pulled her to him. He placed a tight kiss to her lips. "Let's do it."

Her heart leapt, but he'd meant the press release.

"What this means is, Stanford Enterprises and S. F. Designs are one and the same company. It's not a takeover. It's a joint alliance. S. F. Designs will continue to perform on its own. However, Stanford will provide all the resources it needs to thrive in this industry. Be it financially, be it…"

She remained in awe at the confidence and brilliance in Clive's speech. She scanned the room, studying people's reactions to Clive. He made them listen, he made them laugh, he made them respect… *Her* Clive was quite the orator.

And quite the charmer too as his gaze darted to her. It was special how he looked at her. A slight glint in his eyes conveyed to her that she belonged to him, he belonged to her, and no threat from the informant or anyone else, for that matter, could change that.

They asked him all sorts of questions. *Why make this change now? Aren't you worried about Stanford's market standing should S. F. Designs not perform well? How can you have no stake in S. F. Design's profits?* Their queries rolled on, but the one question he most definitely seemed happy to respond to, *are you and Miss Avery engaged?* Clive's face brightened when he talked about her, *about them*.

Clive walked her away from the reporters and photographers. *Not now*, he'd said to Trish who looked crestfallen to be unable to deliver what appeared to be an immensely important update for Clive. He left them all staring as he walked Eva into the room they'd waited in before the press conference and closed the door behind them. He walked her to the walk-in coat closet, and the lights auto turned on. He closed the door after them.

"Clive, there are so many people out there who still want to talk to you. What if they come in here looking for you?"

"I own this building, Eva," he said hoarsely. "If I choose to make out with my fiancé in the coat closet, who will dare to stop me?"

Her breath hitched at his words. She licked her lips.

He stepped toward her until her back met the wall. He placed his hands on the wall behind her, locking her between his arms. Their position reminded her of the time he'd closed off the space between them that same way in her kitchen. He grinned that slow charming grin. "You lure me in here, and now you blush? This *is* what you wanted, isn't it?"

Yes, oh God. "Yes." Her voice, barely audible, as she became acutely aware of the possibilities of their nearness.

"What?" he whispered back.

She opened her mouth to say it again, but her word melted to a gasp when his mouth crashed against hers. Her hands gripped his hair, pulling him closer, kissing him deeper. He groaned, a sexy, needy groan, and tore away from their kiss.

"It's a yes then."

She glared at his boldness.

She pushed at his suit jacket and within seconds his coat, his vest, his shirt, and her dress, met the floor. Lights went off, and other than the harsh gleam from the space between the door and its frame, they were mostly in darkness.

His hands roamed all over her, pulling down the cups of her bra. She moaned when his warm palms met her aching breasts with a restless need she'd become accustomed to. She undid the button and zipper of his trousers and pushed down his briefs and pants.

His hand moved past her hips, and with one tough tug, her thong snapped. His fingers met her moist folds, flicking her fast to the brink of an orgasm. Consumed by the excitement he unleashed, her knees trembled. With strong hands, he gripped her behind and raised her off her feet. She wrapped her legs around his waist, letting him pin her to the wall.

"Eva, this will be rough." His mouth at her ear, his warm breath, sent tingles all over her body.

Feeling him hot and hard between her legs got her wetter, wilder. "I want it."

His one hand went behind her head, as though to protect her from the wall, his gesture, sweet and thoughtful, especially in the midst of his sexy seduction.

She smiled.

"What?"

Was it strange, even in complete darkness, he knew she'd smiled?

"I love you."

In one thrust he pushed into her, and she exhaled.

Muffled footsteps and chatter as people walked through the room beyond further amplified the erotic pleasure from being sexed like that. She gripped his biceps, and her core clenched around him as he pushed and pulled in strong, pleasurable lunges.

Rough, yes, deliciously so when his every dive met her deep, hitting that sweet spot only Clive had proved existed. She loved her body in that moment. How much it was capable of making her feel.

Clive's exquisite skills rolled her off the edge into a blissful trance. She clenched against him and shuddered from her release. He held her tight and slowed his moving, letting her revel in the extended orgasm. She held on to him until her legs gave out and she brought one to the floor. She let the other remain circled around his hip.

"Wow." She panted.

He too breathed hard.

He tugged her leg around his hip, latching tight, and started to push into her again. She moved rhythmically with his thrusts. He picked up pace right away. His movements were raw, powerful and delightfully dirty.

Her desire renewed. Slick from all the sensations he'd awakened, her hot molten moisture rushed onto him. "God, Eva..." His hand tangled and gripped her hair, pulling her head back slightly as he sucked on the side of her neck. His bite, hard enough for her to moan from distinctive gratifying pain, and yet soft enough not to leave a mark.

He drove into her strong a few more times, until he too came with a hoarse grunt. His body pressed into hers tightly, and he jolted to his finish. He pushed her slightly to lean against the wall and let her other leg slip back down to the floor. Kissing her a few times on her lips, on her cheek, he held her head to his until they caught their breath.

"Yes, wow." He laughed.

Chapter 39

"Aren't you a little over dressed for a take out lunch?" Eva asked Izzy as they stepped out of the elevator into Stanford Towers entrance lobby.

"Are you kidding? You're engaged."

She didn't understand. "What has that got to do with your wearing a fur coat?"

"First of all, faux fur, and second of all, it has got *everything* to do with your being engaged. I'm going to be all over the news, all the time. And you better stop and talk to those reporters, Eva."

Eva huffed a laugh. "Or else what?"

Izzy halted. "C'mon, I dressed for this."

Eva rolled her eyes. "Fine, but only if I like the questions they ask."

Izzy didn't look happy with her response, but she'd live. Eva would do anything to avoid the reporters from getting under her skin.

"What the heck, Izzy? You should have reminded me to dress up too. Of all the days, today I had go and wear a boring pant-suit."

"You know, I don't think I've ever seen you wear anything but a pant suit to work."

Actually, yeah.

"Well, I'd have worn the white one." Allie peeked into one of the mirrored walls, shoved her fingers into her hair to scrunch and add volume.

They stepped out of the entrance door toward Tom. Eva stopped in her tracks, blocked from the public by Tom, Izzy and Allie on three sides. Her only escape was to turn around and walk right back into the Stanford building. She waited, allowing Tom to do his security thing. He looked to his left. Izzy and Allie followed his gaze. He looked to his right. They followed his gaze again.

"What are you both doing?"

"Keeping you safe, Eva."

"Staying vigilant, like Clive asked us to do."

She exhaled and at the first chance of an opening in their barrier she began to walk in the direction of the Chinese take-out cafe. Clicks…flashes…and just like that they were surrounded by a bunch of reporters. Eva's bodyguard lurked around somewhere close, while Tom stayed by Eva's side, ensuring the press stayed back at least an arm's length from her.

Have you set a date yet? Are you changing your name? Where are you getting married? Will Silvia be there?

Eva immediately regretted this walk. She should have sent Tina to bring back their lunch. She picked up her pace, her gaze stuck to the pavement. She wished to be anywhere but here. The more they questioned, the faster she walked until Izzy tugged at her arm, slowing her.

Izzy flashed her a well-practiced toothy grin.

"Don't like," she said to Izzy.

Will your two friends be your bridesmaids?

Finally, a good one, Eva halted and gave Izzy a quick glance. Izzy smiled, seemingly thrilled. Eva deliberately angled so Izzy and Allie could pose along. Well, more like so Izzy could pose, because like Eva, Allie appeared awkward in her own skin. And, when did Allie put on bug-eye sunglasses?

"Yes." Eva grinned.

Flash. Flash. Click. Click. Click.

How is Silvia doing, is she OK?

And they were back to talking Silvia...Eva turned and walked into the Chinese restaurant, leaving the cavalcade behind.

Izzy looked happy. "This is so much fun!"

Oddly, it was fun when she posed for the cameras with her friends. But had it been only her, she would have rushed away from the commotion.

"I mean, imagine your life, Eva. You can vacation whenever you want, wherever you want. You can drink in the middle of the day…"

"Wait, why can't she drink in the middle of the day now?"

Izzy made a face at Allie, but went on, "The point is, you should live a little and…" She grinned. "Let me live with you too."

"Don't you have Carter for that?"

306

"I do. But the more publicity for my magazine, the better."

When she put it that way...

They picked up their food and walked back to their office. Of course the reporters followed them back. They'd asked several questions about Silvia and Clive's past, until they once again brought the conversation back to her friends.

What are your friend's names?

And for some godforsaken reason, Eva decided to respond, so she halted, but Izzy spoke for her, "You don't know who I am?"

"Not really," one of the reporters said.

"Editor of *In Trend*, right?" another one asked.

"There you go."

And who's your other friend?

Eva didn't care to answer, knowing Allie wouldn't care either. Just as they were about to step into the Stanford Tower... *Do you believe in fate, Eva? Is that what brought you both back together? Will you love Clive forever?*

Those last questions sent a delightful jolt to Eva's nerves. She turned the ring on her ring finger with her thumb. It had become a happy habit now.

Fate. Eva believed in science—the existence of fate remained to be proven.

And yet... Had her father not signed that contract with Stanford, Francis wouldn't have invited them for that New Year's party. Eva might not have met Clive. Though she may have taken over her father's company, there might not have been a reason for her to meet Clive again, at least not the way she had. Every happening in her life seemed to have occurred just so she could eventually be led to Clive. If it wasn't fate…

Eva turned to look over her shoulder and grinned. "Yes. Forever."

Clive and Eva's story concludes in Book 3:
Killing Eva

If you enjoyed Loving Eva please write me a review
(even a one-liner will do, it's the stars that matter)
on

Amazon
Bookbub
Barnes & Noble
iBooks
Kobo
and/or *Goodreads*

HUGE thanks in advance!
Much Love,
Camellia

***

BONUS
Killing Eva: Chapters 1 & 2

Chapter 1

"Nine-one-one, what's your emergency?"

"Yes, hi. Ahh…this lady…she's bleeding. She might have been shot."

"Could you provide your location, sir?"

"I'm on the 101 to Pacifica."

"Thank you. Is she conscious?"

"N-no. She's…ahh…let me check. Oh! Oh God, she's not breathing. There's no pulse. She's dead. She's dead!"

"Sir, please, calm down. I'm sending you help. Now, are you related to the woman?"

"What? No! I don't know her. I found her…on the side of the freeway. It's raining, and when I saw this car, with lights on, but no one inside—look, I'm only trying to help."

"I appreciate you calling us, sir. Help is on the way. Please, could you stay in your car until they arrive?"

Chapter 2

"Wow!" Eva skated a few feet away from the ski lift chair toward the beginning of the trail but came to an abrupt halt at the first sight of Lake Tahoe's sapphire blue water glistening against the pristine, snow filled slope that sprawled ahead of her.

"Yes, wow." Clive placed a soft kiss on her cheek.

The way he looked at her, it wasn't the lake he complimented. Even in the icy cold of the high elevation, Eva's face heated to Clive's adoration. How much she loved this man. His kiss reminded her of their first kiss, in his bedroom on that New Year's Eve, in his parents' home in Sausalito. How much her life had changed since then. Her parents' divorce had led her away from Clive for a long fifteen years, only for her to meet him again in the very building her father's office, S. F. Designs, had been in all the while. Clive had told her once, had she not taken the helicopter ride with him to Santa Barbara, he would have pursued her however long it would take to make her go out with him. Such was Clive. An intense, powerful, persistent man who'd get what he desired, by will or might, and in her case, by love. Nothing could tear them apart. She wouldn't allow it. He wouldn't allow it.

"Ready?" Carter angled the ski poles he'd pierced into the snow, preparing for a forward push.

They gave Clive's brother a nod and turned to their friends to confirm.

"Not yet." Allie screeched and bit into her lower lip.

Eva couldn't tell why her best friend would take up a challenge knowing she'd fail. Like that time Allie prepared to jump off the dock into the lake, of course, her feet slipped on the edge. Of course, she fell on her behind and bounced into the water. Or like that time she'd prepared to trim her waist-length red hair, of course, the stylist sneezed just as she had been about to make that first snip. Of course, Allie cried for months about her short bob. And then that time she prepared to chug a full glass of beer...

Allie didn't look one bit confident in the challenges she'd set herself up for then, nor did she now. Why the sudden need to impress Marc? He loved Allie years before Allie found out that he loved her. Before he could muster the courage to ask her to prom, she went with someone else. Before he could ask her to go out with him, she'd already started to date someone else. And when he did go out with her, before he could ask her to marry him, she'd already decided to refuse. But Allie did agree to marry Marc in the end. Had that been why she attempted this feat? To make up for all those times Marc had been a step ahead of her?

Marc crouched in front of Allie and tugged the strings on her snowboard boots. "How's that?" He looked up at her, his smile filled with adoration for Allie.

"Much better." She grinned.

Not a real grin. Izzy stared at Eva and shook her head. The numerous times Izzy, Eva's other best friend, looked at her that way after something Allie did. When Allie bounced into the water, when Allie cried about her haircut, when Allie chugged that beer.

Marc placed a quick kiss on Allie's leg and moved on to fixing the other boot.

Izzy pushed her skis and slid to Eva. Eva cut a quick look at Allie, hoping Allie hadn't witnessed Izzy's disapproval. She hadn't.

Izzy leaned in as though for only Eva to hear. "She snowboards now?" Her voice, though a conspiratorial whisper, still seemed a bit loud, and Eva cut Allie yet another glance. "I mean, after the many times she talked me out of taking snowboarding lessons, claiming I'll cause her emotional distress."

"What?" Clive's brows shot together.

"Shh. Come closer." Izzy waved her gloved hand.

And he did.

Eva tilted her head to Izzy, giving her a what-are-you-doing glare.

"You know I deserve to feel this way, Eva."

"You should have taken that lesson anyway."

"Well…" She shot Allie a hesitant glance. "I did."

"And?"

"And, Allie's right. But that's not the point."

Clive leaned into their conversation, exposing a level of curiosity, that until now, Eva hadn't known existed—apparently her tall, sexy lover liked gossip—he looked unfazed.

Izzy rolled her eyes. "She claims I'll just sit there, in her way, obstructing her skiing experience." She leaned farther in toward Eva and Clive. "But now that Marc snowboards, she snowboards?"

"Okay. We're ready now." Allie gave them another one of her halfhearted grins. But then she moved and, in slow motion, Allie tilted forward and fell flat on her face.

Eva held back a chuckle, but Izzy threw her head back and laughed aloud. A few birds bolted into the sky from a nearby pine, away from them, away from Izzy.

"I'm definitely recording this." Izzy tugged at the Velcro closure on her coat pocket to pull out her phone but stopped halfway at Allie glaring at her as though ready to shatter the phone to pieces.

"Why don't we get started and do a few runs, while"—Clive gave Allie his signature megawatt grin—"Marc turns you into a pro snowboarder?"

That got Allie to smile. A genuine smile.

Because who could resist Clive's charm? The same charm that reeled Eva closer and closer to him every second she spent with him. The same charm that made her want to pinch herself to ensure it hadn't all been a dream. That he had asked her to marry him. That she had agreed.

She pushed the fingers of her left hand deeper into the glove and the metal of her engagement ring rubbed against her skin.

Real.

Her longing for him, her love for him was all so real, her eyes stung from the emotions that tightened her chest, warming her, soothing her, exciting her about all that the future would hold for her and Clive.

Something in Clive's expression confirmed similar thoughts raced his mind. He pulled her near for another kiss. She tilted her head, angling her cheek, but he reached for her lips.

"Can't wait to do it."

At the exaggerated seriousness in his voice, laced with mischief in his expression, his innuendo unmistakable, she exhaled a light laugh. Of course, he also meant he couldn't wait to ski with her for the very first time.

"Ready?" He grinned and pulled down his goggles. As though a punishment for her relentless gawking the sensual visual of his greenish-blue irises were replaced by an opaque iridescent lens that displayed her reflection. Her heart crumbled. She could never have enough of this guy.

She gave him a light nod, and then they started to ski down the groomed slope.

Freezing wind blasted at her as she sped. But the bright sun provided the right amount of warmth to cut through the cold. The crisp fragrance of lush pine trees tickled her nostrils, awakened her senses, and brought back sweet memories from all the times she'd been on this slope. Many times with her family, a few times with her friends. Each time her skis cut the crusty snow, excitement and joy filled her. And to think she'd share this all with the love of her life. Clive met her speed and crisscrossed the trail she'd left behind. She let her smile linger on her face, because really, she couldn't have wished for a better day.

They reached the end of the slope, and seconds after Izzy and Carter followed. Knowing Allie and Marc would be nowhere close to them, they queued at the end of a long line to get on the chairlift that would take them back to the top of the trail.

"Too many people here today," Carter grumbled as he shuffled ahead.

"I was thinking the same. We should try the Nevada side," Clive suggested.

"Let's." Izzy, too, shuffled ahead.

"Maybe we do a few more runs here so Allie and Marc can catch up?" As Eva said that, the chair arrived, and they got on. Clive held her gloved hand in his through the entire ride up the mountain. A thing they did now all the time, and yet, their togetherness sent waves of happiness through her. She tightened her grip and he pulled her hand into his lap.

They skied down the slope a couple more times.

The first time Eva passed Allie, she waved at her friend.

Allie attempted to wave back but fell flat on her face.

That definitely hurt.

The second time Eva passed the run, she met Marc. "Where's Allie?"

He pointed with a gloved finger.

She shot her gaze in that direction and found Allie lying in the snow, again, face down.

And the last time Eva passed Allie, she caught her hiking down the slope. Allie stomped into the rental shop and disappeared, while they gathered near the ski lift and waited for her. Minutes later, Allie returned. Snowboard gone, she threw a pair of skis down on the snow. "Well, at least I tried." She pushed one boot into the groove and snapped on the ski. Repeated the same with the other.

"Guess I can take those snowboarding lessons now." Izzy said to Allie.

"Thought you already did. And, I was right, you totally sucked."

Per Clive's plan, they got onto the chairlift to traverse from California to the Nevada side of the mountain.

Clive pulled down the protective bar and read the attached trail map.

"This is where we want to go." He pointed the location with his finger. "One thing, though, see how this forks into two? You want to go this way." He swiped his finger along the trail he'd intended them to stay on. "And not down here, which is through the trees and off the trail. It's beautiful, but they rarely groom this piece. It's a steep drop at the beginning, and if you aren't careful you'll tumble right down. So, let's avoid that and go this way, to the left. Okay?"

Yep.

"Where are Trevor and Tina? Weren't they supposed to join us?"

"Yeah, let me call him." Clive pulled one hand out of the glove and brought his phone out from his jacket pocket. He dialed his friend Trevor.

"Hey man, where are you? … Okay. We're heading to Nevada. … Okay. See you there. … What? Oh yeah, tell Tom to join us there."

Eva stepped out of the ski lift and slid a few meters down the slope to an overlook. Clive had it right; there were fewer people on this slope. Other than them, a couple of teenagers, and a family of four, the starting point of the trail was deserted. Eva glanced at the lift. A few empty chairs rolled by, then one carrying a man dressed in all black approached.

The man began to ski off the lift on to the mountain when Carter asked, "Let's go?"

Eva swiveled around to face the slope. "Let's."

"Stay to the left." Clive reminded.

Just as they began to descend, a feminine voice caught Eva's attention. "Excuse me."

Eva jerked to a halt and looked over her shoulder.

The woman had called out to Clive. "Please, could you take a picture for us?"

"Sure." Clive took a pocket-size camera from the woman and cut Eva a quick glance. "Go ahead. I'll catch you."

Eva gave him a nod but continued to gaze at the family of four gathering for the group photo. She'd posed like that many times with her family, with her mother, her brother, and her father—in that exact spot where this family stood.

Clive shot her one more look, and right away brought down the camera as though the family wasn't waiting for him to take their picture, his expression readable.

Before he could ask what was wrong, she nodded again, drew in a deep breath to stabilize her thoughts as she faced the trail, and began skiing down the slope, following her friends.

Eva and her father were avid skiers. Her mother skied only to please her father, and her brother skied only for the hot chocolate. Because it wasn't just any hot chocolate; when her mother wasn't looking, her father would pull out a tiny flask and pour a shot of alcohol into Joey's mug. She smiled as that visual passed her mind. Those were happy days. And these days were too, with Clive and her friends. They should take a group photo from that overlook when they went back up for their next run.

Oh shit.

She had passed the section of the trail that forked in two directions and absentmindedly drifted toward the wrong run. The only way to recover would be a sharp turn to the left. She maneuvered her skis to do just that, when from the corner of her eye, she glimpsed a shadow of someone, or something. Bears did roam these slopes. She flinched and before she could recover from her shock, that someone or something shoved. Hard. Aggressive. She lost her balance. She fell. Off the cliff, down the trail Clive had warned her to stay away from. She dove sideways a few meters off the sharp drop, till she hit the powdery snow, and tumbled farther along the steep slope. One of her skis dislodged and stayed behind while the other remained stuck to her boot and twisted her knee. An excruciating pain darted through her leg each time she rolled and skidded down the trail. She cringed in agony each time her knee met the ground and deepened the twist in an awkward angle.

Though it seemed like she'd been falling for eternity, it also happened so fast, when she came to a stop, everything around her turned dark. She panted. She gasped. And when she tasted snow, it occurred to her that she lay face down. Like Allie. A light laugh escaped her.

But humor disappeared when she pressed her gloved palm flat on the snow and pushed the ground to turn over. A difficult maneuver, given all energy had been sucked out of her from the fall. The rollover corrected the position of the one ski that remained stuck to her boot. She lay still. Blinked at the sky, tinted pink through her goggles. She drew in a deep breath. And held it there. Pain emerging from the pit of her stomach radiated and consumed every inch of her body. Her kneecap throbbed. She rubbed the area to soothe, but it did nothing.

What just happened? Who the hell was that? A bear? Shoving her like that? Maybe not. Clive? No. Can't be. He'd always been gentle with her. He would never nudge her for fun, let alone shove her down the slope he'd insisted she avoid. Maybe he lost his balance and bumped into her? Or it must have been Allie. She lost control, again, thanks to her idiot snowboarding obsession. No. Allie had switched to skis. So, not Clive. Not Allie. Someone else. Someone else… Her insides did a quick tumble at that thought. She shot up to a seated position. Unintentional? Deliberate? But who?

Two black skis skidded to a harsh halt ahead of her.

She tilted her head back, and her gaze met with the man dressed in all black she'd spotted earlier on the chairlift.

Deliberate. "What the hell is wrong with you?" she screamed.

"Me?" He chuckled. "Nothin'. You on the other hand, missy, are gonna get yourself killed if you don't listen very carefully to what I'm 'bout to say next."

The accent… That accent. Her gut tightened. The informant. The nerve of this guy. Wasn't it enough that he'd threatened her father until his death, and once Eva took over S. F. Designs, sent her threatening letters? He'd watched her when she went for a run in the park. He'd met her outside the coffee shop, posed as a reporter. One night, when she'd had girlfriends over, he came to her home, dropped off a note blackmailing her to break all ties with Clive.

She'd expected him to meet her, especially after Clive had announced Stanford Enterprises' continued partnership with S. F. Designs, effectively challenging the informant's latest threat. But, that he would make a move with all her friends and Clive around, seemed reckless even for this guy.

Feminine laughter echoed through the rustling trees. Startled but grateful, she turned her head sideways and glanced behind her. On the steep slope that would forever appear in her nightmares, she found no one. The voices must have come from above the ridge, the trail she was supposed to be on.

"Help!" she shouted the loudest she'd ever shouted. The word scorched her throat as it left her. "Hel—"

"Don't."

Something clicked, and her insides collapsed. Because that sound could mean only one thing.

She should scream. She couldn't. She should breathe. She couldn't. Her mouth dried out. Every inch of her body tightened. She sat frozen, not from the biting cold of the crusty ice she sat on, nor from the winter wind that gusted past her, but from the unexpected fear that had consumed her when she stared at the muzzle of the handgun pointed at her.

The warmth from the sun vanished. A sharp chill sprinted along her spine, and she trembled in her fleece insulated clothing.

"Clive will come looking for me," she mumbled her only hope as loud as she could, barely over a whisper.

He chuckled again. "I'll be long gone before he'll find you here. Besides, he's too busy playin' a photographer. The one time he should be protectin' his fiancée."

She hated his guts. But what could she do?

"And where's that bodyguard? Tom? Big man. Guess he's afraid to ski. Which means it's just you and me for now."

Though a balaclava, dark goggles, and a helmet masked his face, the laughter hidden in his tone gave away his arrogance. She riled. She wouldn't let him belittle Clive, or Tom for that matter. She wouldn't let him threaten her and get away. Not this time.

Because he feared too. He feared getting caught. Like that time when he'd met her by the coffee shop. Alarmed by Clive's call, he'd run away from her. When she'd chased after him in Central Park, again, he'd run away from her. When he'd come to her home to leave that threat letter, hearing Clive's voice on the intercom, he'd run away once more.

Her gaze drifted back to the handgun. He wouldn't shoot her. He said she'd get killed if she didn't listen. "What do you want?" she spoke through gritted teeth as her fight for survival strengthened.

The informant had it right. Clive would not get to her as fast as she hoped. Unless he'd seen her be pushed, in which case he should have already been here. Otherwise, he'd find her missing only after meeting with the rest of their friends. The soonest way to get to her would either be via the chairlift, and skiing down the steep cliff, or hitch a snowmobile ride with a ski patrol. Whichever method, he'd be with her in about seven to ten minutes. Too long. She had to fight this guy by herself.

With the slightest pressure of her thumbs she pressed the top of the ski poles she held in her hands and unhooked them from her gloves. She gripped the handles tight, readying for the opportune moment when she'd lunge up and swing them at him.

"Leave the company," he said. "You have…eh…one week."

Had he just made up the threat? Her newfound strength won over her otherwise rational, practical, sane mind. "Not gonna happen." Her heart jumped as the words left her lips. What am I doing?

He took a quick step forward, making the gun point that much closer to her. "Don't push me, Eva."

Yes, don't push him, you moron. "One week is too soon."

"Okay, how about one month?"

"And who's to take over after me?"

"You'll get one of them letters."

She tried hard not to seem bothered by the humor in his tone. "Why can't you tell me that now?"

He didn't answer.

"Why do you want me to leave the company?"

No answer.

"Is someone paying you to do this? I'll pay you double if you tell me who that is."

He took another quick step toward her and just as fast she jerked backward. She tightened her grip on her ski poles. Should she swing at him now?

His silence, his demeanor, not to mention that gun, shook her. Her nervousness took over, her palms grew sweaty inside her gloves. "Why are you following me? Did you follow my father too? Did you kill him?"

"I didn't kill your father," he snarled.

"Then who did?"

He didn't answer.

"I can get both of us out of this. Just tell me who it is."

"Don't. Push. Me."

The way he steadied his gun this time, he'd do it, he'd pull the trigger.

All words left her. She stared in disbelief. She wanted to be with Clive more than she'd ever wanted to be with him. Had she known that last kiss would be their last kiss… Her chest grew heavy with rising anguish. No. This is not how her life should end. No! Not here. Not today. Not like this. She wouldn't let it. She tightened her grip on her ski poles.

"One month. You can make all of this go away, just like that."

She stared at him, unmoving, ensuring he didn't sense what she was about to do.

He kept the gun pointed at her for a moment more and then moved his finger off the trigger.

Just as he did that, she sprang up, and in one hurried motion held both her poles together and swung them at him as hard as she could. As quick as she was, he lurched to one side and dodged her blow. She struck the gun instead and it slipped from his gloved fingers. The gun landed nearer to her than to him and sank into the powdery snow. She leaped for it and picked it up, but before she got to aim it at him, he'd already turned around and skied fast away.

Her chest hurt at how heavily she panted, but she continued to clutch the gun in her shaking hands, pointing it in the direction he'd gone. Not like he would hike back up the slope, but it did take an eerie screech from a large bird somewhere among the trees to alert her that he wouldn't return, and to think about what she should do next.

She set the gun next to her, on the ice, zipped open her jacket and pulled out her phone from the inside pocket.

Should she call Clive? Her finger hovered on speed dial. But he'd still be skiing down the slope unaware that she tried to reach him.

She dialed the next best person to handle the situation. "Tom." Still winded, she spoke slightly over a whisper, "Where are you?"

"Parking. What's wro—"

"Man. All black clothing. Black skis and helmet." She paused, only to draw in a much-needed breath. "Should be getting off the slope any minute now. He's the informant."

"I'll track him down."

Good, but… "He knows you."

"I see." Tom sounded grim. "Does he know Mike?"

The informant had spoken of her bodyguard, but in singular. Maybe he hadn't yet spotted the undercover security guy Clive had set up for her. "I don't think so. He named only you."

"Okay. We'll send Mike after him." He paused. "Eva, please tell me he didn't hurt you."

Rare for Tom to call her Eva. But he did on occasions when he worried for her the most. "I'm fine. He separated me from the rest of the group and, as always, he got lucky."

"Never again. I'll make sure of that." The fury in Tom's voice gave her the courage to move on from the incident, at least until she reconnected with Clive and her friends.

As Eva ended her call with Tom, her phone flashed with an incoming call from Clive.

"Where are you?"

And just like that, all the strength she'd gathered drained. Her emotions welled from hearing Clive's voice, from the worry in his tone, of his fear of losing her, of how much he loved her over everything and everyone else.

Her vision blurred from the tears that filled and stung her eyes. She shut them tight. Heavy warm drops trickled down her face and settled on the inside rim of her ski goggles. She tugged at the frame, stretched the elastic, and rested them over her helmet. The cold wind that brushed past her brought a sense of relief that, though only for this moment, her obstacle had abated. Her gaze fell to the gun next to her. She picked it up with a shaky hand.

"Eva, what happened?"

Dread in Clive's voice begged her to say something, anything, but where should she begin? How much should she say? And over the phone? Because even the slightest hint of her strained mental condition would shatter Clive further. He'd blame himself for it all.

She'd recount every detail of the incident to him, but in person, in a few minutes when she saw him again. She swallowed her sadness and brought control to her scattering thoughts.

"Took the wrong run. Heading down now. See you by the lift."

She tapped the End Call button before Clive could probe. He knew she hadn't told him everything. She'd terrified him. But that her phone didn't buzz meant he'd wait for when she would be ready to talk. Typical Clive. Doing it her way, even when it hurt him the most. Even in high stress he treated her with such patience and love. But her calm should give him hope that she was not in as much a terrible situation as he may have imagined.

Eva hiked up the steep mountain and collected her ski. She slid her shoes between the bindings. Ignoring the throbbing knee, she started down the slope.

Preoccupied from her dreary thoughts she remained unmindful of the difficulty of the terrain she maneuvered. She relived the encounter in her mind. Her insides rattled. Her heart bled. The reality of what had happened began to set in. She'd come face to face with death. The informant, his arrogant tone, the gun, the threat to her company, the one-month deadline, the entire horrific experience played like a movie in front of her eyes.

She descended down the path that connected her to the initial trail Clive had wanted her to take. Her awareness returned when she made a final turn toward the lift, and her gaze fell on Clive and her friends, gathered for her.

Clive pulled his phone away from his ear and slid it into his pants pocket, his hardened expression easy to read. He'd spoken to Tom. *He knows.*

She abandoned her skis, the poles, her helmet, and ran into his arms. He squeezed her tight against his chest. His heart pounded against her ear. Deprived of his familiar warmth since the moment she'd left him on top of the mountain, she breathed relieved and wilted into his protective embrace.

"I'm so sorry, Eva," he exhaled her name in a whisper filled with too much unwarranted regret.

She moved in closer and pressed deeper against his chest.

He nuzzled his face into her hair. "I shouldn't have asked you to go without me. I should have let you wait. I-I'm so, *so sorry.*"

***

He inserted a small shiny microchip into his cell phone and dialed his employer's number. "It's done. I want my money now."

His employer's familiar rough grunt no longer affected him.

"It's done when I say it's done."

Usual for his employer to sound grouchy. Usual for him to wish he'd never taken this job. But he no longer wanted to play this game. "It. Is. Done." He mimicked his employers tone. That should get his message across.

But it didn't. Because silence.

"You said we were only threatenin' her. Which I've done plenty. What else do you need me for?"

Silence.

He cupped his hand over his jaw and covered one side of his mouth. "I kept my part of the deal. Now pay me, dammit," he whispered as loud as he could. In reality, he wanted to shout. And, though he sat away from the rest of the passengers, on the last seat of the skier commuter bus riding to the parking lot where he'd left his car, he couldn't risk any of them overhearing him. Given how well his plan to intimidate Eva had gone, he would be stupid to draw attention now. Maybe he should have waited until he'd gotten into his car to make this phone call. But he'd endured far too much from his employer. He needed to get paid...he needed to put an end to this job.

"I'll pay you."

His employers switch to a casual tone caught him off guard. There had to be a catch. "When?"

"When she leaves the company."

"No. You pay—"

"Tell me exactly how it went."

From the start, he'd hated every second of every conversation he had with his employer. It only seemed fair to plan revenge. That day, when they'd finally meet, that day, when he'd finally get paid, that day would be a terrible day for one of them. He smiled, imagining the last moments of his employer's life—moments the ingrate would spend begging him for forgiveness.

He narrated what had occurred between him and Eva. "Who is to take over after her?"

"That's none of your business."

"I told her she'd get another one of those notes. Am I delivering that?"

"Like I said, it's none of your business."

"Good. I'm done workin' for you anyway. All I want now is to get paid."

"And all I want now is for you to continue telling me exactly how it went."

He gritted his teeth at that bristling tone. Without thinking, he slipped and mentioned leaving the gun behind. Anticipating his employer's reaction, he winced even as the words left his mouth.

"You colossal idiot. How difficult would it have been to snatch it right back from her? Is it registered to you?"

He let that slide. Because, sure, he could explain every detail of his encounter with Eva, but more than anything else, he wanted to get paid. And something told him his employer had never intended to compensate him. "I want my money."

"Are you being followed?"

He knew it. She was never going to pay. *She?* Why did he think his employer was a woman? And being followed? "No!"

"Are you sure?"

He spun around and peeked outside the back window. "I don' think so."

"Son of a—" his employer shouted.

"What are you so worked up for? So what if someone's followin' me? I didn't do anything they can prove. Was just Eva and me. Nobody saw us."

His employer exhaled sharply.

He pulled the phone away from his ear.

"Do you have a place to stay, *other* than your damn boat?" his employer asked.

Not his damn boat. It belonged to his grandpa. Actually, it belonged to whomever his grandpa stole it from. A secret his grandpa shared only with him. It had become his hiding place all those times he'd run away from home. His mother's home, his childhood home, he hated that home. So, no, he didn't have a place to stay other than that damn boat.

"Why?" he asked.

"They are following you, *you idiot*."

He swiveled around in his seat once again and peeped through the rear window. A few cars trailed the bus, but none of the drivers resembled Eva's bodyguard, or her fiancé. Imagining either of them following him made an anxious fear dart down his spine. Maybe he shouldn't have mocked them to Eva? He scanned once more, slower this time, and examined the passengers inside the approaching cars. "I'm s-sure, I'm not being followed."

And silence.

"Hello? Are you there?"

"If you go to your boat before Eva leaves the company—you hear me? Before she leaves, if you go to your boat, I will not pay you. Ever."

"Where am I supposed to go then?" Not to Mama's house for sure. Besides, he never could stay there for more than a couple of hours.

Memories from his horrid childhood colored his mind dark. His father's drinking, his mother's shouting, their fighting, the blood that pooled under his father as he laid dead, his mother's regretless expression after she shot a bullet right through his father's chest.

His heartbeat rose to a painful pace. He pressed his palm flat against his chest to suppress the agony that welled from his reminiscence.

No. He couldn't stay at his mother's. Maybe a motel. But short on money, he'd waited for this gig to fill his pockets. "Pay me half now, and the remainder later."

"No."

"Listen, I need the money, okay?" His jaw hurt from how tight he clenched.

"You'll figure something out."

"No. I won't. You better pay me, bitch."

"What?" his employer barked. "What did you call me?"

"Asshole. Whatever. I don' know who you are, an' I don' really care. Give me my money, and I'm gone. I'm not waitin' a whole damn month."

And silence. Again.

He'd worked hard on this job. Eva had it right. He had followed her father. He didn't dislike the man. He seemed like a nice guy. And Eva too, he liked Eva. He liked her friends. He liked her life. His encounter today with Eva began to settle in. His heart shattered from the guilt of what he'd done. He would never do it again. He'd never threaten Eva again. He'd never follow her again. He hated that all this time she blamed him for her father's death. Good he'd cleared that up.

He'd better end his suffering once and for all. "I'm—" He cleared his throat, as though that could subside the rising guilt that had prepared to choke him dead. He exhaled in defeat. "I'll stay at my mama's house."

"Good. And I'll signal you when I have the money."

"Before the end of the month?"

"Yes."

"How?"

"You'll know when you see it." That usually irritable voice sounded eerily calm. He much preferred his employer angry.

"Guess I'll finally be meetin' you." How he waited for that moment.

"Don't call me again."

"What? Why not? You'd better pay me, you hear?" Silence. "Hey? You there?"

He tried to redial the number, but the call didn't go through. "What the—" he muttered, and tried, and retried to reach his employer.

"Fuck. Fuck!" He hit his phone against the back of the seat ahead of him.

A few passengers turned and looked his way. Among them all, his gaze settled on the man seated nearest to him, and he gave him his best deathly stare. But the guy did not flinch. He stared him down with matched vigor.

If only he still had that gun.

"Asshole," he mouthed from his balaclava-covered face without making a sound.

The guy turned back around.

Good. He smiled at his little victory.

He pulled out the microchip from his phone and snapped it in two. His anger lightened from the swift crack of the thin plastic, as though he'd snapped his employer's neck. Wrinkly neck? Not like that would matter. *She'd better pay me. She? Could be a he.*

He rehearsed in his mind his plan for when he'd meet his employer. Would his employer plead for mercy? To spare his life—his life, her life? It killed him that he hadn't found his employer's identity yet.

If only he knew who it was. Heat flushed through his body.

If only he knew, because he'd then have leverage to blackmail back. His muscles tightened to the point of pain.

If only he knew. He pulled his hands into fists and punched the back of the seat ahead of him. A light crack appeared where his fist had made contact.

That guy turned to look at him again, and this time he stood from his seat.

The fury he carried in this moment for his employer encouraged him to brawl with this guy. He pulled out his gloves, stretched his fingers back and forth, readying for a knockout punch.

But the bus came to a halt, and just like that, the guy stomped away in his ski boots and exited the bus.

He stared after the guy. His chest heaved. He took off his helmet and peeled back his balaclava. Chilled air crept from the open door and rushed to his face. The sweat that had begun to trickle from his hairline began to cool.

He dragged in a deep breath.

He would have killed the guy.

What's wrong with me?

ACKNOWLEDGMENTS

Huge thanks to my editors, Nancy, and one other secret magician, at The Red Pen Coach. It's only because of you that I'm a better writer today than I've ever been before.

To my lovely sister-in-law, Pallavi, and my dear friend, Maya, the best beta readers in the world. Can never thank you enough for making Loving Eva a smooth read.

To my husband, for…everything. I love you more than words can say.

And to the dearest and sweetest people I will ever know, my readers. You motivate and inspire me every day. Thank you!

ABOUT THE AUTHOR

Camellia Hart, a techie turned author of romance, lives in California with her husband, the love of her life. Other than writing her next romance novel, her hobbies include traveling, lazing on a beach with a good read, watching movies with happy endings while gorging on endless buckets of popcorn, red wine, and chocolate truffles.

Visit her website…

www.CamelliaHart.com

Follow her on…

Instagram: www.instagram.com/camellia_hart

Bookbub: https://www.bookbub.com/authors/camellia-hart

Goodreads: www.goodreads.com/CamelliaHartBooks

Facebook: www.facebook.com/CamelliaHartBooks

Twitter: www.twitter.com/HartCamellia

www.ingramcontent.com/pod-product-compliance
Lightning Source LLC
Chambersburg PA
CBHW051331250626
47155CB00007B/2543